Inca Kings

(Matt Drake #15)

By

David Leadbeater

Copyright 2016 by David Leadbeater
ISBN: 978-1540607072

All rights reserved.
No part of this publication may be reproduced, distributed, or transmitted in any form or by any means, including photocopying, recording, or other electronic or mechanical methods, without the prior written permission of the publisher/author except in the case of brief quotations embodied in critical reviews and certain other non-commercial uses permitted by copyright law.
All characters in this book are fictitious, and any resemblance to actual persons living or dead is purely coincidental.

Thriller, adventure, action, mystery, suspense, archaeological, military, historical

Other Books by David Leadbeater:

The Matt Drake Series
The Bones of Odin (Matt Drake #1)
The Blood King Conspiracy (Matt Drake #2)
The Gates of hell (Matt Drake 3)
The Tomb of the Gods (Matt Drake #4)
Brothers in Arms (Matt Drake #5)
The Swords of Babylon (Matt Drake #6)
Blood Vengeance (Matt Drake #7)
Last Man Standing (Matt Drake #8)
The Plagues of Pandora (Matt Drake #9)
The Lost Kingdom (Matt Drake #10)
The Ghost Ships of Arizona (Matt Drake #11)
The Last Bazaar (Matt Drake #12)
The Edge of Armageddon (Matt Drake #13)
The Treasures of Saint Germain (Matt Drake #14)

The Alicia Myles Series
Aztec Gold (Alicia Myles #1)
Crusader's Gold (Alicia Myles #2)
Caribbean Gold (Alicia Myles #3)

The Torsten Dahl Thriller Series
Stand Your Ground (Dahl Thriller #1)

The Disavowed Series:
The Razor's Edge (Disavowed #1)
In Harm's Way (Disavowed #2)
Threat Level: Red (Disavowed #3)

The Chosen Few Series
Chosen (The Chosen Trilogy #1)
Guardians (The Chosen Tribology #2)

Short Stories
Walking with Ghosts (A short story)
A Whispering of Ghosts (A short story)

Connect with the author on Twitter: @dleadbeater2011
Visit the author's website: www.davidleadbeater.com

All helpful, genuine comments are welcome. I would love to hear from you.
davidleadbeater2011@hotmail.co.uk

Inca Kings

CHAPTER ONE

Kenzie sat as demure and coyly as she was able, practically having to sit on her right hand which had begun twitching about ten minutes ago—just two minutes after she'd walked into this auction house—as it craved for the welcome weight of the hefty katana she preferred to be sheathed over her left shoulder. It wasn't just an idle craving.

Some of these assholes, they needed to see the glint of that blade, to blink in terror as the razor edge gleamed, to experience that touch of dread as the perfect steel rose before them.

Kenzie managed to hold in an unladylike snort. *Pretentious, wealthy assholes.*

It could be said that Kenzie harbored more than a single grudge against those in authority and those that had the power and affluence to sway them. But the katana would cut through all that, right here, right now—and put her in prison forever.

Somehow, she calmed herself.

The auction house sat right in the middle of Paris, along the magnificent Champs Élysées, inside a nineteenth century hotel built by one of France's richest families. Kenzie saw glitz everywhere; from the gilded chandeliers to the ornate doors and paneling, and the glowing wall sconces. A soft hue illuminated the large room and the noise of conversation drowned out all other noise.

The occupants were seated in rows, apart from those that stood at the back, their well-tended behinds parked on sumptuous leather, their jackets and ties clearly a step too far as the room began to warm up. Even the ladies looked uncomfortable in their tight sequined dresses. Kenzie saw more than one bead of sweat popping out of a distinguished brow and hoped the gathered array of Paris's most expensive perfumes was up to the test.

As for her, this morning she had purchased a little black dress, and tonight she'd slapped on some of Dahl's aftershave. A quick comb and she was as glammed up as she was ever going to be. But no mind. Kenzie was no stranger to lavish auctions.

The fossil beside her, squinting even through black-rimmed goggles, placed his hand dangerously close to her knee as he leaned across. "First time, lovey?"

"Ah, no." She tried to affect an English accent. "You?"

The old man looked affronted. "Me? No, of course not."

He pulled away. Kenzie smiled to herself and took in the room, tuning out the hubbub. *Once a trained Mossad agent, then a fierce fugitive, now a . . .* she paused in her thoughts.

What am I right now? Or rather—what am I doing with this struggling band of misfits that somehow still manage to come together to form one of the most effective Special Forces teams in the world?

You're lost.

The answer was as clear as the decanters and glasses in use all around her. Life had taken her on a nightmare rollercoaster ride, and right now the latest pause on the latest loop was right here in Paris. If she knew what to look for she might stand a chance.

But not today.

Evening had fallen across the Champs, and the well-to-do packed inside the auction house were finally starting to settle. Kenzie half-turned in her seat and passed a glance across those who accompanied her—Torsten Dahl and Mai Kitano—and thought about those who didn't, primarily Mano Kinimaka who roamed the outside. *Misfits among misfits,* she mused. Some lost almost as deeply as she.

Several weeks had passed since their last mission ended; complex developments had taken place. But Kenzie was waist deep in danger here, and being the only archaeological relic hunter in the team, the one best placed in the very eye of this frantic storm.

The clock ticked.

Kenzie watched the patrons; seated as she was toward the back she could see 75 percent of the assemblage, although none looked familiar. She took a moment to consult the small booklet she'd been given on entry. They were interested in Lot 59, so time to spare yet. She breathed a little easier. The main worry they had was that one of Kenzie's old "acquaintances" might be here and recognize her, thus destroying their undercover operation.

Because—the trouble was—they had no idea who they were looking for.

Kenzie considered the developing mystery that still surrounded the Incas and their lost treasures. Her fellow trio of misfits watched from the back and outside. At the front of the room half-a-dozen suited men appeared and mounted a stage. One approached a microphone.

He started speaking in French, introducing the auction. Kenzie spoke the language well and listened as her eyes drifted. Directly behind him hung an electronic monitor upon which would be shown the current object up for auction and the value it attained in ongoing bids in euros, pounds, dollars and other currencies. To the man's left a space existed for the actual object. Kenzie watched men wearing white gloves bring out Lot 1, a gaudy painting, and place it carefully upon a ledge for all to consider.

Bids began to be fired out over the hushed chatter and the auctioneer pointed, nodded and shouted out each bid. The white-headed hammer clutched in his right hand indicated the current highest bidder during lulls in the bidding and then hovered for a moment. Kenzie saw that sometimes he was having to work hard to draw out another bid from men and women leafing through their booklets, maybe checking ahead to see what else they might buy. In the end though, the hammer came down with pomp and a flourish and they moved quickly on to Lot 2.

Kenzie watched closely, noting the main players and those that left; newcomers and those that skulked in corners, cellphones to their ears. These were the most likely, and the ones the rest of her team would be focused on. But Kenzie found it hard to trust them completely, no matter their proven skills.

She flashed across several noteworthy individuals and stored their faces in her memory for later. Again her fingers gave an involuntary twitch as the woman to her left flicked away an imaginary speck of dust, fingers and wrist jangling with high-priced ice.

"Lot 22."

And the auction went on. Earlier they had reviewed the physical security and found it strangely lacking. Didn't anyone ever rob auction houses? You would think not. In contrast, there were surveillance cameras everywhere. Kenzie grimaced. If the cameras were monitored by Interpol she might find herself in serious trouble.

Still, the lots were tumbling nicely. Dahl stayed on the back wall and Mai, finely attired, glided to left and right, moving confidently among the stylish and the grand, whilst Kinimaka had stayed purposely outside, watching as many entries and exits as he could manage. No comms systems today. They were relying on plain, old-fashioned instinct.

"Lot 50."

Kenzie took another look at the relevant page in the booklet. A dull golden cup stared back quite literally—the dour face that adorned one side of it glaring at her with uncaring, empty eyes. Just a golden cup then, and cleverly disguised by the seller, its true identity known only to a chosen few. Called here The Blind Man's Cup, it could not be officially declared as hailing from Peru. The Peruvian authorities claimed everything of archaeological value from the region. The auctioneer would not know. The auction house may well have been fed expensive, forged documents as to its origin, but the sellers wanted its sale to be public—for unknown reasons—so here they were.

Waiting for the bids on one single piece of one of the greatest and most notorious unfound treasures of all time.

The eighth piece in the last decade.

Kenzie looked up as Lot 58 was announced, studied the crowd one last time and then gave the auctioneer her full attention. Two minutes passed and then the hammer came down. The woman beside her squawked with pleasure, having obtained a near-naked Roman statue. Kenzie sat hard on her hand.

The auctioneer took an inconspicuous sip from a bottle of water, then watched as the next item was brought out from the back.

"Lot 59," he said.

Kenzie watched as the modest little item was brought into the room. The same man with the pristine white gloves handled it, placing it gently atop a gleaming pedestal, then arranged it so the light caught it just right.

"Blind Man's Cup," the auctioneer said in French. "From the collection of Balzac and Baudier, recently made available after a fifty-year wait. I will start the bidding at one million euros."

Kenzie knew it was all a veil, something made up to conceal the real truth. The auction house wouldn't dig too deeply. The well-heeled wouldn't look too closely. Everyone's a winner. She picked out the various players as the bid rose to two million.

Behind and around her she knew, the team would be making ready. Having attended several auctions before, Kenzie knew hot items such as this moved very quickly once purchased. The trouble was, it was the seller they were after, not the buyer.

As the price went north of two-point-five, the bids began to thin out. This was when the serious buyers usually came out of the shadows—or rather from the further corners of the room. Kenzie heard a new voice now and slowly drifted her eyes in that direction.

He stood leaning against a shiny white pillar, partially concealed by the tall man at his side, but Kenzie recognized him in a heartbeat.

Tremayne.

The only name she knew him by, but a noteworthy one nonetheless. Tremayne was a relic hunter, just as she used to be, and was known to be just as ruthless. It was a rare day when Tremayne didn't come out on top, and wasn't protected by at least three expert guards. She frowned, and looked away. The gentle hubbub surrounded her but she distinctly caught Tremayne's tones now that she knew he was there and knew where to look.

"Three million."

A hush. People were surprised and took another long look at the unassuming artifact, perhaps re-evaluating. What did this bidder know that they didn't? Kenzie had seen it before and knew that most wouldn't take a risk. She fixed her eyes ahead, wishing the woman's perfume drifting in from the left was a little less toxic and that they had employed a communications device after all.

Tremayne was big trouble.

Still, she waited. Moving would only attract attention. The animations of the auctioneer became more intense as the bid approached three-point-five, and they all took another look at the cup. Lights shone, gasps rang out, and excitement filled the air. Another bid flew and then another. Finally, Tremayne held up a hand and announced:

"Four million euros."

The hammer was raised, the cup offered once and then twice. With no challenges the hammer finally came down and the auctioneer moved smartly on to the next lot. Kenzie watched Tremayne and noticed Mai hovering around the blind side of the pillar. The Japanese woman was too close, but Kenzie respected her skills.

With difficulty, she stayed put and watched.

Tremayne closed his booklet, laid it down on a table, and nodded to the tall man at his side. No awareness was drawn as the pair made a slow, circuitous route around the back of the room and toward the holding area. Clearly, they were here for one thing and now in a hurry to claim it.

And then vanish. Kenzie knew the routine.

As Tremayne and his guard negotiated the packed wall at the room's far side, she rose gracefully out of her chair, cinched the little black dress, and forced herself not to tread on the whiffy woman's toes. Once in the aisle she made eye contact with her team and headed toward the back.

Dahl was already there. "You know him?" His voice was barely a whisper.

"Too well, I'm afraid. He's the male version of me."

Dahl blinked. "That bad?"

"That good. He'll be on this like a cold-blooded divorce lawyer." She paused. "Whoops. Didn't mean that to sound so harsh."

"Of course you didn't. Let's go before we lose them."

Mai had already drifted past and now Kinimaka, having just entered, pushed through a crowd at the front of the room to catch up. Kenzie winced. Never one for subtlety, the big Hawaiian, he'd been even worse lately since Hayden took a million pins to his emotional cushion and decided to jab them all in at the same time.

A chair toppled, with its occupant holding on. Kinimaka picked them both up, apologizing quietly, and accidentally shoulder barged the man with the white gloves. Luckily, he wasn't carrying a priceless artifact at the time. Kenzie motioned to Dahl and the two meandered their way toward the holding area, which was at the back of the room behind a set of rich, crimson-colored curtains.

Tremayne and his guard had pushed through twenty seconds ago. Mai held up a hand to her face, a subtle signal to wait. Then she proceeded to step through, sweet smile already being produced to help disarm the men and women she might meet.

Kenzie leaned in to Dahl, feeling her head touch his broad shoulders. "Risky."

"Mai can handle it. She's a total pro."

"I know. But so is Tremayne."

Dahl looked like he might agree. "Wait, here's Mano."

She nodded at the approaching mountain, then looked behind him. "You know, you trampled a pink poodle on your way past."

"I did?" Mano looked stricken, then caught up. "Oh, funny. Are we waiting for Mai?"

Kenzie was mission leader and made the snap decision. "No. We follow. We can't lose Tremayne tonight, because I guarantee you if we do, we'll never find him afterward."

Dahl stopped her. "But you could?"

"Maybe. But the danger would be off the scale. As fraught as any Mossad mission. This is still our best chance."

They approached the curtain, still drifting, making a play of watching the latest lot. Kenzie knew it would be best to push straight through with confidence, but if Tremayne waited on the other side she had no doubt it would all end in blood and bullets.

"You go," she told Dahl. "Don't be long."

Mai slipped through the gap in the curtain at that moment, almost colliding with Kenzie and ending up in her arms.

"We must move," Mai said sharply. "They wasted no time back there, but did not suspect me."

Kenzie started walking fast. "They're already leaving? Damn."

Mai nodded as she pushed the gathered wealth out of her path. "Totally unceremonious. A wire transfer exchange and then the cup was wrapped and placed in the smaller guy's back pack."

"And they're headed out the back," Kenzie finished.

"Isn't that what you would do?"

"Well, yes, but . . ." She paused, giving herself a mental kick. The rigors of running with a new team and playing within the law were taking a toll on her focus. "I assumed wrongly that they'd leave by the front door."

"Don't worry," Mai said a little infuriatingly. "It's your first mission in charge. You're allowed a mistake."

"So long as you don't get us killed." Dahl pushed ahead, determined not to lose their one lead. Kenzie clenched her teeth together. The team left the auction room and followed an opulently furnished corridor into the main lobby. Even here, the tone was hushed, the patrons all standing and walking around with an air of sophistication. Kenzie made sure she led as they exited the hotel and walked down some steps onto the Champs Élysées.

"At least we came prepared," Kinimaka said.

Kenzie cringed a little as she approached her battered scooter. It had been decided that the best way to carve through the nightmarish Parisian traffic and keep their quarry in sight was to hire four old scooters and cut through the flow. The locals did it all the time, barging through the traffic jams using inside and outside lanes indiscriminately at rarely less than thirty miles an hour. Amazingly, not many died.

Embracing the local rationale, the team jumped aboard and fired up their low-powered scooters. Kenzie felt the engine ping to life, and looked around. Mai sat demurely aboard her cycle, looking ridiculous but determined, her dress all gathered around her waist. Dahl grimaced, clearly unhappy but willing to accept Kenzie's recommendations. She gave him the raised brows.

"Well one thing's for certain. They won't expect a special attack team looking like we do."

Then she noticed Kinimaka. Oh, if they only had time to take a cellphone pic she could blackmail him forever. If there was a straining scooter under the Hawaiian's bulk it was barely in evidence. In another way though, Kinimaka looked ultra-cool—appearing to sit and glide above the concrete.

They sped around the side of the building, Dahl taking the lead and heading straight for the underground parking garage. Sure enough, the high, wide metal door was just opening, raising outward. Headlights showed below—a car waiting to climb the steep ramp up to the street above. Dahl manhandled his scooter and told them all to back off.

Soon, the car—a black Jaguar F-Pace—powered up the ramp and bounced onto the street. Dahl sat astride his scooter, taking a look at the occupants. As the vehicle passed he nodded to the others.

Game on.

Kenzie had made several risky but educated assumptions for tonight's mission. She assumed she would know the middleman. She assumed he would take the artifact. And she assumed he would stay in Paris—hence the scooters. If Tremayne now peeled off on the motorways toward Lyon or further afield they would be left floundering. Now, the mission's entire success counted on her best guess.

Kenzie was rarely less than confident and felt the same now. Tremayne—or rather his bodyguard—took the F-Pace to the bottom of the street and pulled up to the curb. Kenzie saw three black-suited men climb in—more guards. Now they faced five, including the relic dealer and, in Kenzie's experience, they would be no mere mercenary pushovers.

The team did have a stash of weapons close by, but no time to reach it now. In single file they followed Tremayne, staying at a good distance, especially as the car turned back toward the Champs and entered the slow flow of traffic. Establishments closed for the night lit both sides with soft, golden glows beside restaurants and clubs, their facades alight. She saw a pub—Comptoir De L'Arc—where, a long time ago, she'd passed a happy night with friends. Long gone. Long past. An entirely different world now.

Kenzie came up alongside Dahl, her ears filled with the straining wail of a youth's scooter. "Now we wait. See where he ends up."

"My guess, somewhere quiet," Dahl shouted back. "He'll be calling the buyer and seller from the car."

They both turned as Kinimaka's scooter let out a strange tortured shriek. The Hawaiian gave them a staunch wave, clearly ignoring his machine's pain. Mai flicked in and out of traffic carefully as she kept the Jaguar in sight. Headlight beams shone all around, catching their clothes and fake jewels with sparkling light. Cars moved aside as they undertook. The streetlamps illuminated the way ahead as their target vehicle crawled along.

"Bollocks, it's that bloody roundabout."

Kenzie watched as one of France's most notorious roundabouts came up near the Arc De Triomphe, along the Champs Élysées, the only place she knew where insurance companies refused to pay out 100 percent for an accident.

The scooters proved easier than the cars though, and they soon had to back off as they approached a little too close to Tremayne. Kenzie found herself sat at the curb for half a minute, alongside Dahl.

"How bad is this guy?" the Swede asked seriously.

Kenzie let out a pent-up breath. "As bad as they come."

The F-Pace passed and they prepared to follow.

"My kinda mission then," Dahl growled. "I'm going to enjoy this."

CHAPTER TWO

Kenzie tucked her scooter in behind traffic, weaving steadily in the same way as the locals. Dahl came alongside her for a while, then shot down the white lines in pursuit of a youth, blending in. The Jaguar crawled ahead, unhappy in the Parisian gridlock and making slow progress.

After thirty minutes they peeled off the main road and headed down a tree-lined thoroughfare where hotels and restaurants made up the bulk of the buildings. Kenzie saw mostly young people sauntering about, students and shoestring tourists. Ahead, the road narrowed and she backed off, allowing Mai to take point and trail Tremayne.

The journey continued for another twenty minutes and then Tremayne's driver crossed a road bridge. Kenzie paused for a moment to get her bearings and realized they were approaching a more industrialized part of the city. As she had expected. In her experience a lock-up or private container increased anonymity, and was always useful if you had to leave town for a while. The F-Pace motored downhill, away from the busier roads, and entered an area comprised of warehouses, fast-food places and small offices. The team backed off fully here, watching the car's progress by its taillights, then approaching the point where they last saw it.

Eventually, it pulled into an empty parking area in front of an unlit building. Kenzie threw her scooter to the floor and took shelter behind a padlocked burger van. The F-Pace idled. The building's stark, empty windows reflected the lights. The other members of her team drifted a little closer, hiding behind a landscaped hill that bordered the building. Kenzie took a moment to join them.

"What's happening?" Dahl deferred to her mission status, though probably not happily.

Kenzie shrugged. "Could be a number of things. Still on a call. Or maybe they're getting ready to stash the artifact."

"In an office building?" Kinimaka frowned.

"Just because it looks like an office doesn't mean it's a functioning one. To be fair, it's a good front. They use a small team to man it during the day, make it look genuine, and then conduct a shadier business after hours. It's what I would do." She coughed. "Would have done."

Dahl shot her a speculative look. "But would you return to it?"

Kenzie didn't look away. "Ask me in a few more weeks. We're all in flux right now."

It was honest and direct and the best he was going to get, though she knew he wanted more. The Swede was vouching for her among his esteemed friends. He saw the good in her—a good she barely believed in herself. All that was good and cheerful and optimistic in her had been wrenched out long ago.

Mai crawled to the top of the small slope. "Car is switching off." She looked around. "It's now or never to catch them off guard."

Kenzie knew it too and nodded. The team crept over the slope and moved among some bushes until they could make out Tremayne's features and those of his bodyguards. The blanket of darkness helped them. One of the guards leaned into the car's back seat as Tremayne wandered over to the office.

Kenzie broke cover, streaking toward the car, Dahl at her side. Mai and Kinimaka came a step behind. The first the guards knew of them were the black flashes approaching their peripherals.

Kenzie hit her target with a flying knee, striking the ribs. He fell backward, but not down, hitting the car and grabbing hold. She struck again, a blow to the face. His head snapped left but still he did not go down nor make a sound. His face came around now, eyes narrow and furious.

Immediately, she knew she'd chosen a deadly opponent.

She barged him again, ensuring his spine hit the car. He rebounded and twisted away, grimacing, but gaining space. She saw a gun under his jacket, holstered, and a knife at his waist, pinned to his belt. But he reached for neither. He came at her with fast hands, first hitting her cheekbone, then her temple. The rest she caught on her wrists and elbows, dishing out some agony of her own. But she backed away.

He circled.

She grabbed a quick glimpse of how the rest of the team were doing. Kinimaka was absorbing blows like a punch bag, but not just taking them. Like a boxer he would accept his opponent's best punch just to get inside their defenses. The man he fought staggered even as Kenzie looked away. Dahl traded clobberings with the tall guard, both refusing to give an inch. Mai skipped around her adversary and for a moment it seemed they were dancing, her dress now torn to facilitate the kicks, and her knuckles bloodied where they had struck his nose. The fourth guard was zeroing in on the Japanese woman too, and Tremayne was fumbling for keys, still holding onto the backpack that contained the cup.

Kenzie dropped as her guard leapt. His trailing leg caught her forehead, making her see stars, but she delivered a much more telling punch to his abdomen. His gasp filled her ears with gladness and he fell to one knee. Kenzie was about to whirl, then saw the arsenal of weapons in the car's trunk space.

Shit. There's enough hardware here to turn the streets into a war zone. She counted a dozen semi-autos and a boxful of handguns and other items. By that time her guard was standing again, regarding her.

"I thought this was just about the relics," she breathed.

A shrug. "It's about everything. Always is."

She hissed, not accepting it, then feinted but he didn't fall for it. A smirk was her only reward.

"You can't hope to best me."

Kenzie caught a glimpse of Mai twirling around two opponents, their necks and heads snapping to and fro. "Maybe not, but she will."

The guard stared aghast as his colleagues fell to the floor. Kenzie lunged, hitting straight at the most vulnerable areas she knew. The guard took two blows and then tried to roll away, legs buckling. Kenzie was after him and never let up, kicking, striking, finally landing on his belly with the full force of her body, knees first. His groan told her she'd broken something.

Dahl retreated from his opponent at last, but only to give himself chance to approach the side of the F-Pace. A quick maneuver and the man went head first through the side window, glass shattering, and then the Swede wrapped him up in the seatbelt, securing it to the steering wheel.

Stood back and watched the feet kick ineffectively. "That'll do. Who's next?"

Kinimaka stood toe-to-toe with a guard, neither man retreating but neither gaining the upper hand. As Kenzie rose and Dahl approached, the Hawaiian clearly decided he didn't want to be the only one needing help. He rushed hard and fast, hit the man's midriff and lifted him off his feet.

Then came down hard on top of him.

Game over.

Kenzie directed Dahl to guard the car and its stash of weapons, then reached down to pick up her comatose opponent's handgun. Tremayne stood calmly by the now unlocked door, black pistol in hand and pointed at the floor.

Kenzie assumed he had some kind of plan. "Drop the gun."

"Damn it, girl, what the hell are you doing? Ain't we on the same side?"

Her reputation ruined. "Of the law? Maybe. Of a prison wall? Nah."

"They'll never take me down. I ain't done yet and you know it."

In truth, she knew Tremayne only by reputation. Their paths had crossed only twice and then only briefly. By what she'd heard, though . . . he was telling the truth.

"Took your best guards down. Why not you?"

Tremayne smiled, but said nothing. No bravado. No challenge. And that was worse.

"We want the backpack, Tremayne, and we want to know who the seller is."

A faint flicker of confusion. "The seller?"

"Ideally we want everything." Dahl spoke from his position near the back of the Jag. "If you wouldn't mind."

"I still have a gun," The barrel of the pistol lifted an inch.

"We have about a hundred." Dahl nodded at the cache they'd found.

"Good point there." Tremayne shrugged at Kenzie. "So what do you want, girl? The seller, you say? That's possible, but you can't take the relic. If I don't deliver this, I die."

Kenzie returned his gesture. "Live by the sword..."

He grinned. "Such a perfect axiom for you, but I see they've stripped you of yours."

"I saw no real need for it here." But Kenzie's tones were dulled.

"We'll get it out of him," Mai said.

Kinimaka looked doubtful. "How?"

"Any way we have to." Mai raised the weapon she'd taken from one of the dead guards and sighted on Tremayne's gut.

"Wait," Tremayne said. "I can only tell you what I know, and I meant it when I said that if I don't deliver, I die. Even I don't mess with my buyers. Not these guys."

"The buyers don't matter," Kenzie said a little too fast. "We want the seller."

"But why? It doesn't make sense."

Mai moved so fast even Kenzie barely saw her move. Tremayne was standing one minute, then groaning on his knees the next, disarmed but managing to cling to the backpack. Mai was beside him, regarding the clutching hand as if she might happily break the fingers.

"Whoa. That was fast," Kenzie said, impressed. "Did you see that, Tremayne? Probably not."

"Wait... wait..."

Struggling up, Tremayne cast a glance behind toward the office. Mai correctly guessed that the entrance held some kind of secure door and frame, and stepped around, pushing him further out into the night. In the end he spread both hands.

"Look, girl, I don't know who the fucking seller is, all right? I don't freakin' know. I'm a third party, facilitating the sale through the auction house. You know how this works. A phone call, a collection, and then a wire transfer into some obscure, untraceable bank. Happens every day. They know me. That's their security. I don't know them. That's mine."

"How many times has it happened this way?"

"With them? Maybe five. Twice a year."

Kenzie made a face at Dahl. Clearly, Tremayne wasn't the only outlet for the masquerading relics.

"He's hopeless," Mai said. "We should rid the world of one more plague and have done with this business."

"No, we should take him in," Kinimaka said. "Justice will decide."

Kenzie regarded Tremayne. "You are useless to us without your seller. We'll take the cup and leave you at the mercy of your buyer."

She approached the backpack.

"No. there is something else. Something I could help you with."

Kenzie jerked the strap from his hands, heard him gasp. "Fuck off, Tremayne."

"No, no, girl. Listen. The same seller is moving a different item next week. Assured me the same quality and provenance as this one. If you let me finish with my buyer I can take the next relic from the seller, maybe dig deeper."

Kenzie thought about it. As far as she could tell, Tremayne was on the level, but the logistics of sticking with the man and making sure he delivered were tricky to say the least. Only one person in the SPEAR team was qualified to go undercover as part of a relic smuggling team.

"Shit."

She would be at Tremayne's mercy.

"Shit and bollocks."

Dahl came up and laid a large hand on her shoulder. "I know what you're thinking, and it's not going to happen. Too risky."

"You're joking, right?" Kenzie whirled on him. "We're stuck hard in one of the craziest, deepest and most dangerous missions your team has ever encountered and now, finally we have a lead. No way am I backing off. No fucking way."

"You will," Dahl growled. "If—"

And Mai now laid a small hand on his wrist. "I say let her decide. Don't you?"

Dahl drew away, a little embarrassed it seemed. "Well, yes. I guess. The danger though . . ." He shook his head.

Kenzie flashed a seething glare at Tremayne. "Take me with you, boss."

CHAPTER THREE

The man in the white, tight-fitting Gucci T-shirt and jogging bottoms moved stealthily across the office, the odd, inconsistent chain around his neck clicking. The T-shirt—because he enjoyed expensive clothes for being expensive. The jogging bottoms—for freedom of movement. The chain—a lifestyle requirement.

With liquid grace he sank into a leather chair and sighed. All was well on the mountain today. His people were content, satiated and loyal. Today could be counted on as a good day.

Not quite yet.

No, the call hadn't come in. The man was not worried though. His connection always came through.

With time to spare and the dawn yet early, he ignored the few notes that had been placed upon his leather-bound desk and looked into the small, round bowl of delicacies perched at the very edge. Immediately he spied something he enjoyed and began to nibble, rising and drifting over to the ceiling-length picture window.

A deep valley stretched below, and then a sharp rise to the next mountain. High peaks stood sentry to left and right, their majesty immense, their summits lost in haze and drifting cloud. Narrow passes could be picked out meandering here and there, a route through the maze but not without natural perils and their own, more human set of watchmen. Solitude and peace held sway over all, and the man himself was content.

The food was delicious, done just right. He scribbled a quick note to reward his head chef. They were a strong-knit community here, a family that thrived on togetherness and devotion. If one strand of their kinship became strained then it added tension to all the others. Wellbeing and happiness in one's self was all he asked for, all he preached.

And he was lord and master over all. The only lord and master.

He was a solitary man, a loner it might be said. And this commune, this spectacular chateau perched on the side of a mountain, this growing family that practiced a most sacred and ancient ritual; every aspect was his brainchild.

Of course, that which was buried below. That was happenstance.

That which was buried below gave them all life. It gave them subsistence. It gave them security. But it also presented their greatest danger.

The man finished his food and drank water, still devouring the grand view. He was the king of all he could see. He smiled after a fashion, not meaningfully or even happily. Just a smile untouched by emotion. He hoped the sentiment reached all the way down through the floor of his office at the highest point of his house, past the lower two floors and into the caves below where most of his people lived.

Time sped on. The man saw a rigid working day ahead. As he turned back toward his desk, chest swelling with satisfaction, the single black cellphone atop the gleaming leather started to vibrate.

Communications devices were few in his house, as were computers. And all detached from the Internet unless necessity dictated otherwise. This phone though, it might be plastic, but it was sheer gold.

"Yes. This is Dantanion."

"Sir, this is Tremayne. All went as expected last night and the item has been delivered, the auction and supplementary monies exchanged as usual. No issues and I am ready for the next."

Dantanion picked a soft piece of tissue from between his teeth. "Good news. And the acceleration of our transactions, will that cause problems?" He was a soft spoken man and always to the point. No point saying three words when two would do.

"It's not a problem, sir."

"I rely on you, Tremayne." A cold lie.

"Thank you, sir."

Dantanion thought of the trio of middlemen he had moving the artifacts. He doubted they would ever cross paths, but better to be safe.

"I rely on others too."

A pause. "Understood then."

"Lyon next week?"

"Yes, sir. That's the next auction we can reasonably make. In reference to your earlier comment though—I should say something."

Dantanion paused. This was new. "Really?"

"Only that the more frequently these . . . items . . . are floated, the more attention they will receive. Until recently the frequency was about right."

Dantanion accepted the slight warning. After all, the man was correct. "I do understand what you are saying, but Lyon has to go ahead."

Tremayne didn't falter. "It will, sir. All is in place."

Dantanion killed the call and destroyed the burner, then replaced it with another. Any call from Tremayne would be rerouted half a dozen times before it clicked onto the new number; Dantanion's main compromise to modern life. The next artifact would be lucrative, and imperatively so.

Tending for, watering, and bringing up over one hundred followers took a toll on a single man, and on that man's finances. In truth, Dantanion saw that which was buried below as a gift from some kind of god, a ritualistic idol that valued his offerings and the frequency in which he received them.

Sumptuous offerings.

Opulent, deliciously extravagant offerings that squirmed and cried and bled just right even as they were slowly being devoured.

Dantanion reached back to the bowl of delicacies, this time choosing an item that had been cooked slowly, over days, marinated often, and then snipped free of the still-living, still-watching body. He remembered it well.

Savored the taste.

Wiped his lips as a string of drool spiraled down, then laughed, this time a full-on belly laugh. Tonight, he would send the monsters out again.

Tonight would be good.

He started to work slowly, methodically, sorting through the piles and the priorities. The cops in Cusco needed their cut. The captains both in Cusco and Lima needed more. The authorities that governed Peru took some small slices here and there, but remained almost oblivious.

The legend of the Cannibal King was local legend only, not even old enough to be passed down from mother to daughter, father to son. But the locals believed it. They had plenty of reason to do so.

Dantanion took his time finishing up and then rose. It was time to pay a visit to the caves, take in the thick ambiance, the stench, the sweat and the exultance, and bask deep in the heart of it all. It was time to pat the backs of his followers and join them in ritual. It was time to plan for tonight and give them purpose.

And it was time to tread beyond the caves, delve deeper down, into the great vaults of the mountain where the greatest lost treasure of all time had been found. Extremely unsafe to say the least, Dantanion nevertheless ventured there alone.

As in all things.

With one more genuine smile he left the office and headed for the elevator that would take him down . . . down toward the bowels of the earth and the monsters that dwelled there.

CHAPTER FOUR

Matt Drake flinched as Torsten Dahl's face filled the video-screen set up on the desk before him. "Whoa, pal, they say the camera adds a few pounds but how many frogs' legs have you been eating?"

Dahl took the jibe stoically. "You're saying I look fat?"

"Well, not exactly. Fatter."

Alicia joined him. "And here's me thinking you'd be slimmer since you're all alone with Kenzie now."

"What does that mean?" Dahl demanded.

"You want me to spell it out? Or act it out?"

"No, no." The Swede drew back quickly, then gave them a somewhat pained smile. "I am still married, guys."

Drake squeezed Alicia's wrist as she opened her mouth to say something flippant like "not for long" and felt proud of her when she shut it with an audible click. He checked the office to see who else had drifted in.

Hayden and Yorgi stood behind them, both seeming alone despite standing side by side. Drake nodded. A moment passed and in walked Kinimaka and Mai, freshly returned from their European escapades. More quiet nods. The only people missing were Smyth and Lauren.

"We'd best get this done," Dahl said, his voice distorted. "Kenzie's due back any minute."

"How's the trust between you two?" Hayden asked.

"She's doing well so far. Seems straight up. Honestly, I can't fault her. She's becoming more and more a vital asset."

Hayden coughed. "I meant between Kenzie and Tremayne."

"Ah, well, obviously he's aware of who she is and who we are. He knows who backs us. He knows our Interpol contacts. He might be slippery and he might be tough but the man knows when he's in a lose-lose. He'll come through and she'll ensure it."

"High confidence."

"Well, don't forget I'm here too."

Dahl backed away as they all heard a knock at the door. Presently, Kenzie's frame appeared in screen and then she approached. "Everyone okay? Still fighting?"

Drake assumed she meant in a general way, but ignored it just to be sure. "What's the latest out there?"

"Tremayne is all go. Made contact today with our target whom he only knows as sir, apparently. They arranged for the next artifact to be sold in Lyon."

"And Tremayne's going to dig a little deeper into his client this time?" Hayden asked.

"Yeah, that's the idea. We're working on the details."

"Did you hear this man speak?" Kinimaka asked.

"I did. Sounded reserved, used short sentences, educated. No accent that I could read."

"We're sending you a gift," Hayden said. "CIA's finest. You get this guy on the phone again, attach this baby, and it'll trace anything pretty damn close in a minute no matter the safeguards they got in place."

"All right. I don't wanna spook him though. Everything has to appear authentic. I'll talk to Tremayne."

"Well, if the auction's soon we might as well wait for their next communication," Dahl said, out of picture. "The item has to be dropped off, exchanges arranged. Might be tomorrow or the next day."

"Sounds good." Hayden walked over to pour herself a coffee. "Anything else?"

"No, but we're fully committed with this. Don't worry."

Dahl signed off. Drake watched as his friend's face disappeared abruptly, trying to force down a wave of gloom. The recent divorce filing from Johanna—Dahl's wife—had left the Swede melancholy and his future uncertain. Would Johanna stay put in America? Would she take the children or make access difficult? These were the thoughts at the forefront of Dahl's mind right now and the sole reason he immersed himself in hard work.

Or at least, Drake assumed that was it. The Swede had been

first to volunteer for the Europe mission after they all agreed Kenzie should take lead. He stared around the room.

"Where the hell are Smyth and Lauren?"

Rain pelted sideways at them as they stood frozen in place.

Smyth glared as water ran down his face, the droplets lit by an array of bright lights that fronted the office building. Not the Pentagon anymore, but an obscure frontage deep in the commercial district, it was far from the top-notch secret base they had been hoping for. It angered Smyth, but then everything usually did.

"Nothing has changed," he said shortly. "Nothing."

"This isn't the place to discuss it," Lauren said, her dark hair soaked and plastered to her shoulders. "Or haven't you noticed?"

"I know damn well that you're avoiding all this. So let me lay it out for you right here, right now."

Thunder cracked overhead.

Lauren narrowed her eyes, the New Yorker attitude taking over. "Oh, go ahead. You lay it all out for me."

"Stop visiting Nicholas Bell. I know there's something between you. He's a fucking prisoner. A terrorist."

"This is your ultimatum?"

"Yeah, that's it."

"Nobody tells me what to do. Even when I was a hooker they didn't tell me what to do. I told them. Now go on into the office, Smyth. And tonight? Get yourself a hotel room."

"This is a mistake." He wiped water away. "Why can't you talk about it?"

"Because you don't understand. You won't. You can't. He's no monster; he was manipulated, dragged in deep, and you refuse to see it."

Smyth held up his hands. "Stop visiting the man. Move on. In truth he should die in prison."

Now Lauren blinked in shock. "You want him to die there? No proper trial? No reward for his help so far?"

"Help?" Smyth reached out in despair. "The man's looking for a deal. An easier life. A way out, God forbid. He's desperate and so fucking dangerous, Lauren."

"I know him." She backed away, looking to the car. "Y'know. I just can't do this anymore. The missions. The chasing. The battles. This is where it all ends, Smyth, right here. I'm officially out."

He stared. "What? You can't do that. Remember Jonathan. Remember . . . everyone. You can't quit."

Lauren's face streamed with tears, drowned with rain. "I remember them all and quitting does not taint their memories, or their actions. I'm done, Smyth. Just get the hell outta my life."

The ex-soldier glowered, almost marched off in anger, but something stopped him. "Just promise me you won't see him again."

Lauren shook her head. "Goodbye, Smyth."

Drake stared as Smyth came in, soaked from his head to his toes, face streaming and red. Alicia let out a playful guffaw.

"You walk here, dickhead? Car break down?"

"Something like that." Smyth shook his body like a drenched dog and then glared at everyone.

"Where's Lauren?" Alicia went on. "Fixing the engine?"

"Just get the fuck on with it. I don't have a lot of time."

"Oh well, excuse the nation and its needs. Best press on, Drakey, before Smyth implodes."

Drake saw something in the man's face, but didn't want to push or pry. The whole team had their secrets, some more so lately, and some destined to be revealed now that Tyler Webb had made such a bold statement. The man—now dead—clearly had a nasty little stash of information somewhere and had wanted it revealed.

"Dozens of agencies and powerful individuals all around the world are watching this," Hayden spoke up. "For good and bad, I'm sure. For wealth. For their passion. For reputation, retribution and respect. No, we don't know all the details yet but there's no doubt that the marketing of these artifacts will have far-reaching consequences."

"I still don't see how you come to such a dramatic conclusion," Mai said. "Relics are bought and sold on the black market every day."

Hayden frowned. "You're right, to a degree. Like I said we don't have all the details surrounding these relics yet, but I will paint you the same picture I painted Drake and Alicia recently from the latest information. Somehow the most valuable of all Inca treasures came to be in the same place at the same time. Somehow, they got lost to history. Now, almost as incredibly, these relics begin drip-feeding onto the market, starting over a decade ago. One a year. Then two. No real provenance. Disguised from the masses but revealed to just a few. Whoever sold them preferred even his middlemen not to be mired in shady, backstreet deals where a thousand things could go wrong. He wanted it all in plain sight, and with less risk. Less chance of the relic being stolen by thieves even worse than himself. Perhaps then, he isn't a career criminal, a dyed-in-the-wool gangster. Perhaps he has other vices. In any case, the regularity with which the Incan relics appeared increased until now we have one every two months. And today, one a week, it seems. The money could be running out. The sheer size of the treasure hoard might be an issue. Or maybe he just can't hold his wad anymore. Either way, we have to track every single treasure that has been sold and we have to find the man behind the sales. We have to shut this down."

"Agreed," Mai said, being minimalist on her reply to prove a point. "But why SPEAR?"

"What's up, Sprite? Scared they're gonna try and sell little old you as a relic?" Alicia grinned.

"I may be little." Mai scowled. "But you'll feel me any minute."

"Funny," Alicia reflected. "I used to have a boyfriend who said that."

"Why SPEAR?" Hayden interjected quickly. "It's a good question. I'll answer with a few of my own. What would happen to a country, any country, if a billion-dollar treasure was dumped among its criminal elements? What would happen if it was gifted to its bankers? Its politicians? Its agents. Believe me when I say—everyone is watching this."

"Global impact," Drake said. "Hence—SPEAR."

"Ah, now I see."

"Funny. But there is something else too. It's believed that this lost Inca treasure contained an item of such importance, such value, that it all but dwarfed the rest of the pieces combined. The impact and importance of finding it can't be overestimated."

Drake turned back to the empty screen. "And it's all in the hands of the Mad Swede and a sword-wielding bird on the run from Interpol." He paused. "What could go wrong?"

Alicia grimaced. Smyth glared daggers. Even Hayden blinked rapid-fire as she avoided a look from Mano.

"Way to go," Alicia muttered. "Ya just jinxed it all again."

CHAPTER FIVE

Kenzie watched Tremayne as the illicit relic hunter watched her. In another time and place they might have been partners. In another—lovers. In still another—enemies trying desperately to kill each other.

"You thinking what I'm thinking?" Tremayne asked with a smirk.

"I doubt it. Unless you're wondering how you'd look with a katana in your neck."

"Oh, I could probably pull it off." He grinned. "How is it that we never met?"

Kenzie looked away, distracted as one of the new guards Tremayne had hired strolled past. It was a ridiculous question and he knew it. They were thieves; they valued little more than the dark, their own company and a great heist plan. "Why would I ever want to meet you?"

"I have my uses."

She shook her head, wanting this to be over. She'd been watching Tremayne closely for days, watching his bodyguards, ensuring the path to the next deal and the next phone call remained free of obstacles. They had fail-safes in place. Tremayne knew they could make him pay if he failed to come through, but they sure as hell couldn't watch him forever.

"Any news?"

"Not yet. But the Lyon auction is tomorrow and the deadline for lot entry is tonight. It will happen soon."

"How will the artifact arrive in time?"

"My guess is it's already here. Maybe among others, maybe not. No, scratch that," Tremayne dismissed himself. "This guy is as careful and painstaking as they get. But he never fails. And neither do I."

Kenzie considered reminding him about what had happened

during the last job, but let it go. Another guard wandered by, looking aimless. Kenzie chuckled as Tremayne almost whimpered. The last set of guards had been good—challenging even Dahl—but this new set were so far below par they might as well be ushers. She diverted her thoughts, mulling over Dahl and all that was happening in his life. The Swede was distracted, yes, but handling it well. Kenzie could only imagine the distress a person might feel if forced to move away from their children, no matter the distance.

Once a Mossad rising star, Kenzie had been considered among the best of the best. When the government she worked for failed to protect her family, and then lied to her about it all, she descended toward anarchy. Moreover, when they tried to cover it up she found and fostered a deep hatred for authority and for the power-hungry figures that invariably ended up at the helm.

But was there still some good in her?

Dahl thought so. He'd noticed without even trying. She still wasn't trying but seemed to have found a new lease in life. A way to escape the endless degenerations; the descent into depravity that, eventually, grabbed hold and never let you escape.

Tremayne clicked on his laptop, no doubt organizing shady deals all across France. On request, he showed Kenzie an image galley of the Lyon auction house and a blueprint of the area. Google maps helped with the roads and alleys to either side, the faster routes, the dead ends. When she looked around it was after midnight.

"Time to go," she said and fixed Tremayne with a glare. "You've been a good boy so far. Tomorrow's the big one. Don't fuck it up."

He saluted smartly, eyes hidden beneath dark clouds. She left the place wondering what was to come, because where Tremayne was involved you never could really tell.

Dahl let her into his hotel room, the T-shirt and jeans ensemble making her double-take.

"Shit, you look normal."

"I am normal. It's all the rest who are crazy."

She perched on the arm of the sofa. "Did it arrive?"

Dahl poured her a shot of brandy, her favorite tipple. "No, and that's a problem. When is Tremayne confirming collection and drop-off with our mystery seller?"

"In the morning." Kenzie threw the Napoleon back in one and then spread her arms. "That's all he said."

"We have to narrow that down. Better still, delay it. If the CIA device doesn't arrive in time this is all for nothing."

"I doubt Tremayne has a choice, but I will try."

Dahl leaned against the side of the mini-bar, facing her. "You think he'll run?"

"I don't. Not now. Truth be told, his job isn't that hard."

"How about after the job?"

"We never spoke about that. Does he have a deal?"

"Not if I can help it," Dahl grunted. "Man's a dangerous criminal and should be treated as such."

Kenzie waved her glass for a top up. "So was I. And yet here I am."

Dahl almost choked. "You're suggesting we bring Tremayne on the team?"

"No, no, of course not. I just wondered why I was the chosen one." She reached out for the glass and held it, touching his hand. Her eyes twinkled.

Dahl backed away quickly. "I thought we covered that."

"I only worry that I'm going to prove you wrong. Your friends . . . most of them think I'll mess it all up."

"Did they tell you that?"

"No . . . no they didn't."

Dahl looked hard at her. "I understand what happened to you. Hell, if the same thing happened to me I'd lose my mind." He swallowed involuntarily. "It almost did. Different circumstances perhaps, but I couldn't speak for my actions if I survived that night and my family didn't."

"I imagine most people think that way, but few would implement it."

"Grief," Dahl said. "Is the ultimate game-changer. Nobody comes out the same."

Kenzie rose and deposited the glass on a table. "And some of us never come out," she said, then affected a bright smile. "Well, if we're not snuggling down tonight I guess I better get to bed." She hesitated. "How's things with the ball and chain?"

Dahl reached for the bottle. "Ending," he said shortly. "Goodnight, Kenzie."

"Night."

She left the room quietly, unsure, on edge, wondering what tomorrow would bring.

CHAPTER SIX

Lyon bustled with good-natured excitement.

Kenzie waited halfway across a bridge that spanned one of the wide rivers dissecting the city, shrouded by shadow, studying the brightly lit auction house that stood on the other side. Soft light surrounded her. Couples passed by, arm in arm, whispering. The river flowed dark below, its lower banks concreted over and turned into a local communal area for kids and parents alike. Plush sofas and climbing frames filled both banks whilst adult-sized slides took people happily from top to bottom. Kenzie paused for a moment, seeing something she'd lost forever and sometimes wished for, but then Tremayne was at her side.

"You ready?"

She watched him carefully, never more conscious that this man would try to kill her instantly if he thought it would help his collusions. "We are. Don't forget, Tremayne, that your future depends on this going off without a hitch."

"Then let me work and move your ass."

He pushed by, followed by the three new guards. Kenzie fell in line, knowing Dahl was up ahead watching them all. The auction was imminent. The CIA device arrived too late and now they were forced to put on a show, sell the new item and use Tremayne's final confirmation call later to trace the seller. Kenzie had taken the time to study the relic, send pictures to the team, and consider what they had found out.

The investigation was ongoing, stuck in ancient history and veiled behind a thousand lies, but this item, as well as the others, was believed to be one of thousands of priceless objects hidden by the Incas in the sixteenth century. Immersed in murder, invasion, mystery and an unquenchable craving, the legend was of lost Inca gold that lay hidden somewhere in the high, misty mountains around Peru, Ecuador and Bolivia. With quests and treasure hunts and organized explorations going right through to the nineteenth century the fabled hoard kept its final secrets well—described once as "a treasure that could not be moved by one man alone, and nor by thousands", it vanished in time much like the Incas themselves. A cold trail, a new generation, a modern world was not the place for ancient artifacts that so-called experts said probably never existed anyway.

Kenzie was intrigued with the legend despite herself, and had urged Hayden and the others to hurry up with their investigations. The English girl, Karin Blake, was mentioned as being the Internet geek of the team. She should now have reached the end of her military training, but had not made contact with them. Kenzie didn't know what to make of that, knowing only that Karin was a genius super-geek who would probably have found all the answers to the mystery of the Inca treasure by now. The whole military training thing felt a bit off to her.

For now though, she marched across the bridge in Tremayne's wake and approached the glitzy auction house to be ushered quickly through the front doors. An opulent interior, a corridor lined with masterpieces, a chandelier-blanketed lobby and they were approaching the auction room. It all felt the same to Kenzie: the people, the luxury, the self-glorifying expressions. She would be happy to leave this world at her heels.

Joining late, Tremayne's lot had been slated to be one of the last. Kenzie sat through an interminable duration before their time arrived and Tremayne emerged from a shadowy corner to perform his deeds.

She watched. They still didn't care too much about the buyer, though Dahl wanted it all. Was it always the same buyer? For Tremayne, yes, but the seller used more than just a single middleman. He was clever, slick, streetwise. He'd been operating this way for over a decade and never given anything away.

Until now. What changed?

Tremayne played his part nicely. The lot was a golden vase of medium height, its origin obscured, its value understated for now. A supplementary payment would be made later. The seller kept everything safe this way, allowing him to retain total anonymity and avoid all contact with the criminal underworld. Kenzie saw the hammer drop at four-point-two million euros and studied the auction room. It had emptied quite rapidly as the night progressed, leaving only two dozen hardy bodies in attendance. She saw nobody she knew, nobody overly keen on the vase, nobody dangerous.

But the eyes of the world had turned to the Incan artifacts.

She watched as Tremayne disappeared into the holding area, accompanied by his new goons. She tagged along, watched the exchange of the vase, and waited for their car to arrive. She watched Tremayne the whole time. Once in the car he would make the call, and she held the CIA device.

"All good?" she asked.

"Smooth as Cleopatra's ass," he returned, clearly enjoying the excitement of the auction.

"You mean asp?"

"No. I really don't."

They waited, the moments stretching to minutes. Kenzie started to feel antsy, but quelled the jitters, staying professional. The F-Pace arrived and they headed inside. This time Tremayne rode in the back and she sat alongside him.

"You ready?"

"After this—we're done."

Kenzie didn't look away, didn't flinch. "You'll walk away."

"Without being shot in the back?"

"Or knifed." She couldn't help it.

Tremayne couldn't hide the flash of fear that widened his eyes. Quickly then, he fished out a phone and asked for the device. "How does it work?"

"Just attach it to the side. Give it a few minutes to pair and then make the call. The device will do the rest."

"This guy has major failsafes in place. And if he knows I'm looking . . ."

"Just do it. This is no time to lose your nerve."

Tremayne attached the small device and then waited. A blue light flashed. He pressed a button, speed-dialing the seller.

Kenzie knew he would keep everything the same as always—no small talk, no speakerphone, no questions. She hoped the device was as good as her team made it sound.

Her team?

A ring tone and then the call was answered.

"Yes?" A rich voice, relaxed and in control.

Tremayne cleared his throat. "Went off without a hitch. Ended up at four point two." He hesitated.

Kenzie leaned forward, a question on her face,

The seller said, "And?"

"Yeah, yeah, we're headed to the exchange now. I'll organize the supplementary and we're done."

"Excellent. What else?"

Tremayne looked surprised. Kenzie watched the blue light blink. How much time did they need? Seconds? Minutes? The top-flight agencies kept a very tight lid on what they could do these days.

Tremayne recovered. "Just wondering if you were about to offer me another . . . item. Y'know, to sell?"

"Ah, soon but not quite yet. As you intimated, we can't have too many items diluting the market now, can we?"

Tremayne muttered an affirmative.

"Goodbye."

The line clicked, a tiny death knell.

Tremayne blinked at Kenzie. "Kept him on the line as long as possible."

Kenzie clicked a button on her phone and waited for Dahl to answer. His voice was quiet. "I'm talking to the team now. And, don't worry, I have your position on GPS."

Tremayne leaned forward, so far that he invaded her space even in the back of the car. She took a personal moment to push his head away, barely refraining from cracking it against the side window.

"Conferencing the call," Dahl said.

Immediately Kenzie heard Hayden's voice. "So what are you saying? You pinpointed it but you didn't?"

Was she talking to Dahl? Then a man's voice answered her

question. "Hey, it's a prototype. But yeah, we pinpointed it to . . ." He coughed and Kenzie detected some embarrassment. "The mountains around Peru."

"Shit."

"Well, a little tighter than that. I'll send you the information."

"It's better than we had," Dahl said, as Kenzie watched Tremayne and his guards. They would be getting antsy now, wondering what was going to happen next. She waved Tremayne on, essentially telling him to make the drop and get it finished with.

"It is." Hayden sighed. "It is. We can work with this. Of course, I'd have put a pretty firm, friggin' guess that it would be the mountains of Peru."

"That would have been pure conjecture," Dahl said. "The treasure could have been moved over the centuries."

"I guess."

With the conversation winding up, Kenzie made her presence known. "We're heading for the drop here. Then we're done."

It was a signal to Dahl. "I'm on my way."

She broke the connection and slipped her phone in her purse, now more than ever acutely aware of Tremayne's reputation and his vicious instinct for survival. Darkness swarmed outside, interrupted by the ever-more-infrequent glares of streetlamps, traffic lights and lit road junctions. The neighborhood grew shabbier, the frontages now barred. She knew these places well. She'd once frequented them in many a city, after making deals. There was a time when she really believed she had found her vocation, a career for life. Now, more than miss any aspect of it, she hated what she'd become.

Trying to change all that. Was this the heart Dahl kept banging on about? The only people who'd previously shown faith in her were those who'd trained her to become a professional killer. She wasn't sure how to take Dahl's convictions because she had no real experience of trust though the last decade to base them on.

And before that . . . life was a haze of memory. Repressed. Unnecessary distractions, her instructors said. The things she could remember revolved around her family and how the men in authority had allowed them to pay a terrible price, a chunk of retribution leveled at the Israeli government but metered out on an intensely personal level.

Confused, lost, she held on to team SPEAR as if they were the shaky raft after a shipwreck. She wanted to belong, but knew she never would.

Twenty minutes passed before the F-Pace pulled to a halt outside a metal shutter. Its sides were rusted, its door pockmarked. Tremayne stayed put and then the door started to roll up, the sound an ear-splitting screech that made Kenzie grimace.

"Not the most subtle entrance."

"This guy doesn't do subtle," Tremayne breathed. "Nor does he have to. Cracktooth owns everything you can see."

Cracktooth? Kenzie watched, prepared and waited as the most dangerous moment of the evening approached. She wondered if Dahl had arrived, but couldn't count on it. She watched Tremayne exit the car, hand over the relic and then perform some kind of transaction on a portable tablet. All seemed well. A crooked-toothed, straggly-haired individual cracked a jagged smile.

Tremayne bent at the waist and then glanced back through the window at her, nodding, smirking and baring his teeth. The grinning man raised a gun.

Not like this. Not now.

She couldn't move more than a meter before the gun went off.

CHAPTER SEVEN

She flung herself full length, grateful that the car had a roomy back seat. A bullet shattered the glass, spraying the interior and her back. Another came immediately after, the noise overwhelming, the closeness to death a living nightmare. Kenzie squirmed, falling to the rear footwell. A third bullet punched through the back door, disappearing through the seat where she'd just sat. She heard Tremayne complaining that he'd "just bought the fucker", and then a noise above her head.

Cracktooth opening the rear door.

Kenzie pushed hard off her heels, angling her body through the door and hitting Cracktooth in the chest with her head. The blow wasn't hard enough to move, nor even stagger him, but it was packed with surprise, and brimming with fury.

She landed hard on the road outside, ignored the pain and rolled against his legs. A peripheral glance showed Tremayne turning to his guards who were exiting the car, no doubt reaching for weapons too. This was about as bad as it got.

Kenzie changed tack, rolling under the car.

She pushed with both legs, wrenched her arms, scraped her skin and tore her dress. The hot exhaust brushed her shoulder, an intense kiss that would leave a permanent mark. Material tore at her knees. She flattened herself as much as she was able. She saw Cracktooth's shoes move back and then his knees appear as he bent, making her writhe with even greater purpose. She saw other feet appear to the front of the car—the guards—then one set appeared at the side she was aiming for.

Now Cracktooth waved his gun under the car. She heard his laughter.

A shot. The bullet passed perilously close to her head, taking out the front tire. Tremayne cursed once more. Cracktooth could barely contain his mirth.

Kenzie squashed herself into a tight, flat shape and squeezed out the other side, then kicked at the legs that stood there. The guard was waiting, but hadn't expected the instant attack. He jerked forward, inadvertently pulled his trigger, and fired. The bullet slammed into the concrete next to Kenzie's head, the bullet as close as any had ever come to ending her existence.

Once, she'd have welcomed it. Not today.

"Ya get bitch?" A nasty, simpering drawl, spoken in French.

Kenzie saw but a single chance and only seconds of her life remaining. Using every muscle that had taken intensive years to mold, she whipped her body upright in a single movement, used the momentum to slam her forehead into the guard's and squinted as an explosion of blood covered them both. The guard collapsed, poleaxed. The gun slipped from his hands; straight into Kenzie's.

And even then, even with such inventive, skilled accomplishments, she was too late. A guard came around the front, gun leveled. Cracktooth was headed around back. Tremayne pointed a pistol at her over the hood of the car, still wearing that infuriating smirk.

"Not. Good. Enough," he mouthed.

The answer came in the form of a slicing, reverberating gust of wind, a high-pitched whine, and then a thick chunk of sound as a black, two-foot long Japanese blade somehow ended up lodged right through Tremayne's throat. The man's eyes bulged, his hands flexed and then he fell to his knees, already dead.

Kenzie didn't miss a beat.

All around her men stared, gasped, and one man let out a whiny guffaw. The Israeli fired her gun, sending the guard in front of her flying backward, then slid over the front of the car in an attempt to recover her weapon of choice.

The vehicle was high, slowing her, and she left smears of blood and skin across its smooth metal nose. Cracktooth had barely missed a beat, and now fired again, shattering the front windshield and covering her diving body with shards of glass. She hit the ground again, swearing and cursing, and asking for at least one of her impacts to get a little goddamn easier.

Aware of another object blasting out of the shadows she glanced up. Torsten Dahl hit like an avenging angel, hurling a trash can at Cracktooth and then following it up with his substantial body. The villain flattened like wet paper, folding and then smashing into the car, leaving a man-sized dent, rebounding off Dahl's muscle-bound structure and then folding again. Bones broke and that was the only sound. Cracktooth never uttered another word.

Kenzie saw two more guards, both looking unsure. Fighting the urge to grab the katana, she fired close to them and watched them run. Dahl appeared at her side.

"You okay, Kenz?"

"What do you think, Torst? That is no way to use a katana."

"It had the desired effect."

Kenzie found herself keeping an eye on the still-open metal roller door and uttered a silent congratulation. Here she was, a proper agent, watching their perimeter and looking out for her teammate. How the hell did that happen?

"So we really fucked it all up now," Dahl stated as he retrieved the katana. "The seller just lost a middleman and our only contact with him has gone. Hopefully, the team will be able to pinpoint his base in Peru."

Kenzie helped clean up, wrap the priceless Incan vase, and then walked with Dahl back to where he'd stashed a car.

"Tremayne may be gone, but he's not the seller's only buyer. And he's just one of dozens of high-quality facilitators out there. Remember, Torsten, I know them all."

The Swede offered her the katana, a nice gesture. "Tremayne's buyer? He'll be pissed. Maybe we can exchange the vase for information."

Kenzie nodded. "Yeah, but putting aside the incredible danger, isn't that a bit unethical? I mean, for a government-funded Special Forces team?"

Dahl waved it away. "Ach, nobody knows we really exist. Don't worry about it."

"Well then, the deeper we go, the worse, barely human animals we get in contact with . . . the more likely we are to learn more details about this mysterious seller. And who he previously sold to."

Dahl opened the car door for her. "All right then, Kenzie. I'm ready to go all the way in."

She paused, wondering for just a moment if he was flirting with her. Surely not. She met his eyes and wondered a little more.

The Swede offered a glint.

"What do you call 'all the way?'" she asked.

"Balls deep," he persisted.

"I do like the sound of that."

"Clearly. So start making calls. The further we penetrate this criminal underworld that exists around the smuggling and selling of ancient relics the closer we will be to unraveling this conspiracy. Let's get dirty on this one."

Kenzie swallowed drily, finding it hard to concentrate on work. If the Swede didn't stop using innuendos soon, welcome or not, she was going to have to jump his bones.

CHAPTER EIGHT

Drake trod the venerated streets of the historic capital of the Inca Empire, trying hard not to let his attention be stolen by the immense sight of the purple-blue mountains in the distance – sentinels guarding the Andes range around Cusco.

A man wearing a T-shirt beckoned the party as they approached a black SUV. The man appeared dubious, but then Drake knew they were probably a larger team than he'd imagined. The only person they had left behind was Lauren Fox, and then only at her request.

The breach between her and Smyth now seemed unrepairable. Drake would never pry, and had decided he was not qualified to offer advice; in fact he was most likely the one that needed it. So Smyth came and Lauren stayed. Drake didn't want to spin the dice on the outcome of that one.

The man nodded as Hayden approached him. "You Jaye?"

"Yeah, and we're SPEAR. You Eckhart?"

"Yup. I'd say 'get in', but y'all ain't gonna fit."

Alicia pointed at a nearby coffee shop. "We can catch up later."

The team split, Hayden climbing into Eckhart's back seat. Ordinarily, Kinimaka would have accompanied her but today the big man hesitated, unsure of his place anymore. Hayden closed the door behind her before anyone could react.

Drake decided Hayden shouldn't be alone, and walked around to the other side, sidling in alongside her. Eckhart took one of the front seats.

"All right guys, you come with good kudos. What exactly can your motley local CIA crew do for you?"

Drake knew they would be far from motley. They were operating mostly undercover and behind enemy lines, twenty four hours a day, seven days a week. They would be nothing less than outstanding agents.

"Nothing earth shattering," Hayden said. "We're interested in Cusco and the mountains around it. We have a vague tip-off that something bad is going down in the area."

"Vague?" Eckhart interrupted. "So vague it brought seven of you out here?"

"It's not the whole team," Hayden said in a spry manner. "We need to know the local bad cops. The more corrupt the better."

Eckhart let out a short laugh. "Y'all would be better off asking for a list of the good boys. It'd be a damn sight shorter."

"Really?"

He nodded. "Oh, they're not so bad as a rule." He tapped his fingers on the leather seat. "Petty, even. A few dollars here and there. A stint at the underground casino. A free wager on the ponies." He stopped tapping. "Y'might be looking dubious. But the low wage not only breeds corruption, it makes us see the solution as taken for granted. Believe me, Miss Jaye, I know."

"Owt worse than ponies, pal?" Drake asked.

"Man, you got a strange accent. You Australian? Anyhow, yeah, of course. The higher you go the worse the corruption."

"Stolen artifacts?" Hayden pressed. "Maybe by someone based out of town?"

"Nah, all of that crap used to go on *in* town. Safer for 'em and easier to network. Sorry."

Drake looked at a dead end, but Hayden urged Eckhart for more. "Give us three of the worst. The shadiest. The guys that you think might know more than you do."

Eckhart looked swayed and reeled off a trio of names, along with the places they tended to frequent by night. In closing, he promised to send over their mugshots by email. Hayden climbed out of the SUV and turned to Drake.

"Best we could do."

"It helps. It has to."

"Crap. Now you're sounding desperate."

"Odd thing, Hayden. I know this isn't exactly a world-saving mission and there are probably more important things happening right now. I know we could be called back any time. But this feels right." He paused. "Know what I mean? I feel like we're supposed to be right here, right now."

Hayden checked her watch. "You do? I wish I could agree, but I've been flying in and out of one mission or another for so long I can't say I really belong anywhere. Right now, DC feels more like home than anywhere else."

Drake stared at the coffee shop where Alicia made a face through the only window. He smiled, then remembered York, the place he once called home, and wondered if he'd ever return there. He still had the house and wanted to see inside it once again. See the old pictures, hear the croaking frog, look inside Ben's old room and check out the attic.

"I don't mean that I'm home," he said quietly. "I also don't know where that is anymore. One day though. One day."

"Ya think? When you're too old to fight?"

"When I'm too old to fight back," Drake amended and headed for the coffee shop.

After darkness fell they moved out, hoping an afternoon of preparation was enough to weed out the crooked individual they were after. Not knowing who that might be did have its drawbacks, but Drake was willing to bet at least one immoral serpent could be persuaded to point them in the right direction.

The three worst. Out of how many? The man they'd narrowed it down to was an ex-cop, squeezed out for brutality but never charged. Eckhart understood this man now helped run things from the outside, giving the corrupt authorities a thick shield of deniability. If this were true, then this man would have a finger in every pie.

Called only Joshua, he had been described as a cactus—short, prickly, and able to thrive in adversity. After the day's dirty business was done Joshua liked to retire to a seedy little bar on the dark side of the town, spending his ill-gotten gains until the place shut down in the early hours of the morning. From there, it was a short stumble to his apartment where he slept through the rest of the night and the next morning.

They found a quiet place to park and sent Yorgi into the bar.

Alicia gave him a parting pep talk.

"Yeah, Yogi, we're sending you 'cause you're a thief, you look like a thief and act like a thief. That's the bright side. So you're gonna blend in. Just try not to get chopped up." She waved. "Oh, and if you do get made, try that weird building climbing thing you do. See ya."

The Russian climbed out of the car. Drake spoke in Alicia's ear. "Encouragement, inspiration and great advice all in the same speech. Nicely done, love."

"He looked encouraged didn't he?"

"Oh, yeah. For sure."

Yorgi passed out of sight and checked his comms. This particular system allowed the microphone to stay open, so they heard everything in real time as it happened. Drake thought it useful since they were sending in a man alone.

Ten minutes passed in darkness, the only sounds the noise of the bar filtering through the comms. Only fifteen minutes to go before kick-out time. Drake heard Yorgi sigh. He heard men and women laughing drunkenly, the sound of a jukebox. Pricked his ears up at the sound of a scream, then relaxed when it turned into a fit of hysterics. A female spoke to Yorgi, no doubt propositioning him, forcing the thief to speak. Enquiries had revealed that this was a high-traffic bar, visited by out-of-towners, so Yorgi would be safe.

Soon, the warning came.

"Joshua is on his way."

Drake cracked the door, heard the others following. Hayden drifted ahead, stopping at a dark corner. Brick buildings lined the streets in all directions, their windows draped, barely any lights blazing. Darkness pooled along the center of the road. The only man walking it was Joshua.

"Brave," Kinimaka remarked.

"He does it every day," Smyth shrugged. "Familiarity . . . and all that."

"He won't be doing it tomorrow," Hayden said with grim determination. "Of that I am certain."

"First things first though," Drake whispered. "How to take him down quietly."

But Alicia was way ahead of him, sauntering out of the shadows and approaching the man with a smile. "Hey. Fancy a shag?"

Joshua's face was a picture, a goggling, staring, blinking portrait until Yorgi came up behind him and hit him over the head with a bottle. Alicia was on him before he could react, and the job was done.

Hayden nodded with satisfaction. "Let's see how tough this asshole really is."

CHAPTER NINE

Drake knew there were precious few times in a person's life when the crossroads presented itself. A juncture when all outcomes and all futures were uncertain. A person made a choice.

And the rest of their lives changed.

If only we could see these crossroads coming. If only . . .

Not that night they didn't.

Hayden dragged Joshua through the barely open doors and into the rear store of a shop the CIA used as a front. The store was sizeable, its corners obscured by towers of cardboard boxes. At one end sat a wooden desk, filing cabinets and a bookshelf replete with sheets of paper. At the other end, just a sink and kettle.

Hayden nodded at Smyth. "Grab that chair."

She waited for Smyth to comply, then threw Joshua into it. The man's head was bleeding where Yorgi had struck him with the bottle, and his eyes now swept every part of the room and every face before him.

"Who are you? Cops?"

"You speak English? Good. That'll make this much easier." Hayden again motioned to Smyth, this time to attach Joshua's arms to the chair by way of plastic ties. Drake noticed that not once did she look Kinimaka's way, and he fancied it wasn't because of their recent break up. The Hawaiian wouldn't be best pleased with what was about to happen.

Hayden's track record was not good when it came to holding back.

Hayden stalked over to the sink and filled the kettle. Alicia and Mai checked the outside, walked the perimeter, and reported all was well. Drake and Yorgi considered the inside, noted CCTV cameras and listening devices. Drake pointed them out to Hayden.

"Cover the cameras. Find the tape. Kill the ears."

He paused. "They already know we're here."

"I used to work for 'em, Drake. Believe me when I say—leave nothing incriminating behind. These things can hit you back years down the line."

It reminded him of Tyler Webb's menacing statement. He shrugged over at Yorgi and started on the main camera.

Hayden picked up a towel and stepped over to Joshua. His shortness forced him to crane his neck in order to look her in the eyes.

"You shouldn't fuck with me. You don't know who I am." Hard words.

"Y'know, I'm not even gonna play the game," Hayden said uncaringly. "I don't give a shit. In sixty seconds, I'm gonna ask you a question. Your answer will determine how much pain I then put you through."

Joshua hesitated, unsure. "In sixty seconds?"

Hayden wrapped the towel around his head, shutting him up and began to pour from the kettle. Water splashed all over the man's face and then to the floor. The struggle began, arms wrenching against ties and drawing blood, feet kicking at the chair legs and into empty space. Hayden didn't bother to hold him down and soon the chair had toppled over. She looked over to Smyth.

"Pick him up."

The soldier complied. Kinimaka came over to help Drake and Yorgi as they finished removing all the spyware they could see. Drake pocketed a tape and then listened as Hayden spoke once more.

"We're looking for someone from the mountains. Wealthy, prone to bribery, prefers to be left alone. Educated. A man of few words. Probably ruthless. Does it ring any bells with you, Joshua?"

A widening of the eyes, ever so slight, gave him away. The vigorous shake of the head, though, did him no favors at all.

Hayden had bound his face with the towel again before the denials shot from his mouth. This time, Smyth took the kettle and poured for a while. Gasps filled the room along with the hushed but violent struggles of the drowning man.

Another respite. Another rebuttal. Drake shuffled his feet and looked over when Alicia and Mai came back in. The two drifted separately, and it seemed to Drake that no words had passed between them. Their feud appeared to have lost some of its fire, but no doubt only because Alicia had been gallivanting with the other team for a while. Now that she was back . . . He shuddered inwardly.

Smyth kicked the chair over this time. Joshua tried to scream but only a jet of water burst from his mouth. Then came the coughing, retching and chest heaving.

"Can't hear you." Hayden leaned in close.

"It-it's . . . a—"

"Fuck's sake." Hayden didn't wait, but nodded at Smyth and the water boarding began anew. Drake frowned a little.

"Wasn't he trying to say something?"

"Dunno, Drake. Was he?"

The crossroads beckoned, a vast junction of possibilities, a multitude of outcomes. Drake saw what could be, but he didn't see all of it.

Smyth poured. Kinimaka stepped into sight. "Give him a break."

Hayden was already pushing Smyth's arm away. Maybe it was luck, or maybe she sensed his movement. As it was, she ignored him and stripped the towel away once more.

Eventually, Joshua found a breath. "It's not just me," he gasped. "We are the Cusco Militia. We are twelve. I am leader, but we are strong. You will all die horribly."

He spat at Smyth and then at Hayden, having no shortage of water in his mouth, and then spat at their feet. Rather than showing frustration or anger, Hayden only grinned.

"I'm happy that you wish to continue."

Kinimaka grunted and headed for the door. Drake felt for the big Hawaiian, but saw the far-reaching picture, and all the horrendous things that could transpire. They should continue. The Cusco Militia were probably well organized and well trained.

Hayden and Smyth performed their routine again, beginning to look more streamlined and content in their work as the hour progressed. Joshua spat out water again and again, choked until he almost passed out, made some joke about all the water helping to cleanse his practically dried out liver, and went under again. Kinimaka came back in, saw the ongoing struggle, and disappeared some more. Mai and Alicia stood next to each other, arms crossed, looking like they wished they'd prefer a bloody battlefield than such close proximity.

Drake sauntered over to them both, knowing waterboarding could take a while. " 'Ow's it goin'? Don't s'pose you saw a chip 'ole out there?"

Mai struggled, frowning. Alicia grunted. "Is that supposed to be an icebreaker?"

"Hellfire! Why would I do that?"

Mai put a hand on his arm. "Chip 'ole?"

"Chip hole. Fish and chip shop. Chippy. The house of the gods."

"Ah, and I thought I knew all your jargon."

"You don't know the half of it, Sprite." Alicia made a point of stepping between them to fetch the last bottle of water, removing Mai's hand by default. "Have you heard the noise he makes when you twist his—"

Drake coughed loudly. "Alicia!"

"Finger," she finished innocently, then started to remove the bottle top.

Mai, it seemed, had decided not to let Drake go lightly and, to be fair, why would he ever have expected her to? He guessed the only thing stopping her accelerating this feud into a full-blown battle was the fact that it was she who had left him, she who had needed time, she who hadn't been able to say if and when she was coming back to the team.

The Japanese woman moved incredibly fast, closing down the space between her and Alicia and plucking the water bottle from the other woman's hands. Then she took a long swig, smiling into Alicia's shocked face.

"Icy."

"That's the last bottle."

"Here," Mai proffered the open top. "I'll hold it still to make sure you don't choke too much."

"I don't swop spit with bitches."

"Oh, is that a recent lifestyle change?"

"Oh for fuck's sake," Drake said and turned away. "Stop twisting me bloody lug 'ole."

He hoped his disdain would have the desired effect and, for a while, it did. The team had been shaken hard lately. Dahl and Johanna splitting, and talking about divorce. Smyth and Lauren warring so badly that the New Yorker had elected to stay in DC. And then there was Hayden and Kinimaka, two people he'd thought were made for each other. He felt badly for them, seeing both sides and able to do precisely jack-shit about it. For right or wrong, couples made their own choices and moved ahead. It was just another one of those life-changing crossroads moments.

If only he'd known what was about to happen. Turning back then, he saw Hayden pouring and Smyth tugging on the towel. He saw Joshua's feet kicking and then heard them drumming on the floor. He saw Kinimaka return again and nod the all clear.

At last, they allowed Joshua to breathe. Smyth moved around to the back of the chair and whilst the corrupt man tried to catch breath, he kicked it forward. The floor came hard; Joshua's forehead striking concrete. Smyth pulled him back up, then bent down so he was less than an inch from the haunted eyes.

"You ready yet, or we gonna get started on the second hour?"

Joshua took a long shuddering breath. Blood from the gash across his forehead started leaking into his eyes. The man looked exhausted. Hayden made a point of heading back over to the sink and filling the kettle. About thirty minutes ago, on seeing her do the same thing, Joshua had asked for an Earl Grey. Now, he stared despondently at the ceiling.

"I will speak. You promise to let me go, I will speak," The words were ragged, torn from a bruised throat. "Ah, my head hurts so much."

Hayden spread her hands. "You sure? Don't want to hold out for just a while longer? Want an aspirin?"

Kinimaka stepped forward. "Quit it with the intimidation. Just let the man speak."

"Stand back, Mano. That way, you're not involved."

Drake moved to the Hawaiian's shoulder. "Let's hear what he has to say."

Joshua wasn't waiting any longer though, probably hearing the quiet friction all too well. He took one deep breath and began to speak. "We, the militia, see what goes on in town, we oversee most of it. There are many involved, from all . . . rankings." He shrugged. "It is what it is. I know of man you seek, though he is very careful. Money does buy anonymity if that's what you want and you have the deep pockets. He lives in the mountains, yes, but I don't know where. There are so many deep mountain passes nobody ever visits, even unexplored regions out there." He waved vaguely at the door.

"That's not going to be good enough," Kinimaka warned.

"No, no, I have not yet finished. He uses middlemen and his own people to pass messages, cash and other items. He buys from our town but sends only those sworn not to talk of what they know. Hey, guys, my forehead really hurts. Can you break bones in there? I mean, shit . . ."

"Wait," Drake said. "Rewind. You said 'his people?'"

Joshua cleared his throat noisily. "I don't know arrangement, but they do not work for him. It is more like they belong to him. For life. Maybe he has house like Charles Manson, eh?" He tried a grin that didn't even start to work, then continued, "The people that bring cash though, they not so clever. I talk, the militia talks, and they sometimes reveal too much, yes? I know they are closest to Kimbiri, and also know of Nuno and Quillabiri."

"Kimbiri?" Mai asked.

"It is a small village out there—" again he waved at the door "—in the mountains. Mostly self-sufficient. Remote. Traditional. Old Incan ancestors. We don't hear much from them."

The way he dropped his eyes spoke a different truth.

Still, Drake became upbeat. "More like it, pal. This is what we need, guys, so let's wrap it up. Wrap him up. And scram."

"Wait." Hayden lifted the kettle. "He's lying. Something's not right with his story."

Smyth stood at the crossroads. "Want a little more, bud?"

"That's all I know. All—"

Drake waved a hand in a delaying motion. "We got—"

Smyth was watching Hayden, who quickly nodded. He took a step back, raised a boot and kicked hard at the back of Joshua's chair. A man tied so tightly and unable to move will go down hard, and onto the same spot he'd already hurt, and if the choices at the crossroads stood against you—then that man would stop struggling almost immediately.

Forever.

CHAPTER TEN

The journey to Kimbiri was made by vehicle and by foot, the village not completely isolated but far enough away to make the trek feel like a tough grind. Dahl was informed of their destination and Hayden put in a call to Lauren along the way. This was after Smyth tried and got no joy. Hayden's call was answered on the second ring.

"Well, nothing looming," Hayden reported after she ended the call. "And Secretary of Defense Crowe has passed a nonimportant message on via Lauren. The new HQ will be ready in a few weeks."

Alicia perked up. "Really? The secret base?"

"Apparently."

Drake concentrated on the path they trod—a dusty, gravel-strewn cutting that ran between high verdant hills. Mountains stood cloaked in shadow behind the hills and white clouds scudded across a blue sky. Drizzle threatened a worsening, harder rain but had so far held off. The temperature up here was far below that of Cusco, requiring warmer clothes, but the team had packed accordingly. Drake hitched his backpack higher, taking care not to disturb the generous cache of weapons and ammo the CIA had supplied them with.

Hayden shrugged as Alicia continued to stare. "Crowe didn't say. Here's hoping."

"Yeah, we really do deserve a secret base."

"Are we there yet?" Smyth grumbled.

"Not yet, baby," Alicia said in mothering tones. "Would you like to play I Spy to help distract you?"

"I'll play anything if it warms me up." Kinimaka shivered. "I'm friggin' freezing up here."

"Not quite Waikiki beach?"

"Not exactly. A tad cooler."

The path led them across a flat plateau that stretched for a mile to all sides and then up the side of a steep, grassy hill. At the top they traversed past several rows of crumbled walls, an old settlement perhaps. Hills and mountains always lay ahead, and all around. Sparse trees dotted the landscape. The path was no wider than a horse, and for safety's sake forced them to travel single file. Drake noticed Mai near the front and Alicia close to the back, a picture replicated by Hayden and Mano. How would they ever repair the rifts that had started to form in the SPEAR team? Should they even try?

Or break away?

But he didn't want to think like that. Putting one step before the other, he walked with the men and women he'd come to view as family. The only family he could properly remember. A sad fact, and regretted. Everyone should remember their dad, the ways he helped and laughed and fought for you when you were young. Everyone should remember their mum, the times she cheered and uplifted you. Everyone should remember those eternal family moments.

But Drake . . . he didn't. The past was past and gone.

More hills, more trekking. The team followed a GPS map toward a set of coordinates, having programmed in the easiest path. The readout finally declared they were less than a mile away.

Descending another extensive, rolling hill they saw a mostly flat plain below, its contours made up of shallow dips and long stretches of tableland. At the center of this plain a small village had taken hold, a hundred or more houses built from brick and tiles nestling within the dips or against the small slopes. Walls ringed each house and the village itself, some crumbled, others as high as a man's chest. More houses were built together or closely adjacent as if space were a factor.

Within the village they could already spy people.

Hayden paused and studied the team. "We need a spokesperson."

Alicia shrugged. "Don't speak Inca."

Even Drake cringed a little. "The predominant language is

Spanish, though out here . . ." he shaded his eyes with his hand as the sun broke free for a brief, blissful moment.

Mai was making a show of staring at Alicia. "I fail to see any circumstance where you would be the best spokesperson."

The Englishwoman opened her mouth, a retort already formed, but then hesitated. "Well, the Sprite has a point, I guess."

"Maybe someone will speak English," Kinimaka said hopefully. "Failing that we can use hand gestures. Or send someone back to town for a translator."

Drake agreed with the Hawaiian. All they needed from Kimbiri was a helpful hint, an indication of where the mysterious man's house might be. The mountains were too vast and dense to check any other way and the trails that crisscrossed them too treacherous and plentiful. Short of staking out Cusco for his next shopping trip, they really had no choice. And not enough time.

"Let's try," he said and walked steadily down the path. Surrounded by the vibrant scenery and bracing day he could almost believe the team were content with their lots, but nothing could be further from the truth.

Smyth walked alone, head down, having refused all offers of help or concern since Joshua died. Drake understood it was a testing moral situation that the soldier found himself in. On the one hand Joshua had been part of the Cusco Militia, no doubt immersed in more excessive endeavors than they would ever know, but it had been Smyth's blow that killed the man. Joshua had been tied down—no heat of battle struggle. Hayden also seemed a little subdued, recently trying and failing to bring herself up and out of the doldrums. To Drake, it was a team problem; a great, blood-curdled whirlpool of moral decisions, repercussions and guilt. It couldn't go unchallenged.

Drake knew the event was a big, barbed thorn of fate. The moral standpoints would be discussed elsewhere. Joshua was a cold-blooded criminal, a killer with no conscience. Drake tended to afford his kind less understanding.

As they drew closer to the village, several inhabitants scooted away. Others chose to hide. Drake watched them with concern. Surely they didn't look that threatening. Weapons were concealed and flak-jackets were covered over. Kinimaka was at the rear; Hayden at the front. Those women he could see wore shawls, hats and skirts in a variety of colors; the men jeans and leather or denim jackets. Some wore baseball caps. They were a weathered looking people, happy with the elements and their place in the world, content with their community.

But today Drake sensed something was different.

Hayden paused on the outskirts, gave the team a warning look. "Something ain't right here, guys. Be careful."

Without any hint of threat, they prepared as best they could.

Closer still, they viewed the brick houses and carved out trails between. The strong walls, the livestock wandering around. Families sat huddled in the entrances to their homes. Men walked toward them down the wider main street and Drake recognized fear in their eyes. He saw a woman on her knees, wailing, head held in her hands. He saw a family gathered around her, misery so entrenched in their features it might have been carved there.

"Slow down," Mai told them all. "Something has happened and we're not a part of it."

She pressed forward, concerned, as the rest of the party slowed. Drake stayed as close to her shoulder as he thought reasonable. Alicia unconsciously dropped back, joining Kinimaka. Smyth continued to show little interest, milling around the center with Yorgi and Hayden.

Mai addressed the approaching men. "We can help. What has happened here?"

Drake tried not to wince. It was natural that Mai would be the one openly concerned. She had traveled half the world to help Grace, Chika and find her parents. She had left everything behind, including him. Mai couldn't stand to see innocent people persecuted, or in pain, only seeing her young self in those situations.

Confusion lit the faces of those closest. One said, "help?" in a halting voice, another nodded. It was the young that guessed the language and a boy that then ran off, presumably to fetch somebody. Suspicion still filled many eyes and the tears of the family never stopped. Drake understood they should not approach them. They couldn't hope to know what had happened here. These people, despite their hardiness, were still a vulnerable folk; stationed out here in the wilderness and away from even a half-corrupt authority. Self-supportive they may be, but even independence attracted its own set of dangers.

In the end a tall, willowy woman approached, jet-black hair drawn severely back, a black hat atop her head.

"What do you want here?" Her voice was authoritative and high-pitched. "Who are you?"

"We came for your help," Mai said. "But I now see you have some problems." She then bowed slightly. "I am sorry. Who are you?"

"The children's teacher," the woman said. "Why do you think I always speak at the top of my voice?"

Mai smiled politely. "I am Mai, and these are my companions. We seek a man that lives in a house somewhere in these mountains. But now . . . our problems appear trivial. Can we help?"

"Why?" the woman said, then immediately looked embarrassed. "I am sorry. Forgive my impoliteness. If one of my children spoke that way I would inform their parents. Hello—" she held out a hand "—I am Brynn."

Mai shook. "We are soldiers," she said simply. "Searching for a lawbreaker."

Drake saw no clear threat in these people, only fear and mistrust. He liked Mai's basic, nondescript termination.

"No lawbreakers here," the woman said instantly.

"We know," Mai answered. "We came only to ask for help."

"How ironic. On this day."

Mai must have noted a shift in the woman's eyes, for she glanced over at the seemingly bereaved family. It occurred to Drake that they should probably back away from this place and leave for good, but that same odd feeling he'd been having since they disembarked in Cusco—that sense that they were in the right place, doing something important despite the overall status of this mission being marked as low—sparked up inside once again.

They were meant to be here.

"I'm Drake." He stepped out from behind Mai and offered a hand. "Matt Drake."

Brynn shook, met his eyes, and then stared back at the family. "You come to us on a sad, sad day."

He took several moments to study the terrain, the village boundaries, and saw nothing untoward. It was the soldier's instinct, assuming these people were under some kind of threat, but it could just as well be a personal loss.

"I am sorry," Mai said. "We did not mean to intrude."

Drake was so thankful it was Mai and not Alicia that had stepped forward to talk. The Englishwoman's first impulse was always: head-lock, her second: ask questions. But then, she'd been forged by danger; in one threatening situation or another as far back as she could remember.

"Thank you," the woman said. "We should move away from here."

They followed her through the village, being watched from doorways and windows and by groups sitting by the side of the road. A goat wandered by and Brynn paused to let it pass. Drake turned from a cold gust that chipped at his face as the sun vanished behind an ominous raft of dark clouds.

"Here." Brynn had led them to a roughly circular patch of ground that appeared to be the center of the village. Older people sat around on wooden stools or with their backs against gray stone walls. Brynn took a seat halfway up a slope, shading her eyes as she looked to the mountains.

"You seek a man who lives there?"

"We do."

"I am no elder," she said, then stopped talking. "No leader. But destiny does have its way."

Drake didn't follow. Mai sat as the woman offered the space beside her. "Bad luck may portend good fortune," she said. "But you have to find it within the darkness."

"And you are good fortune?"

"I don't know," Mai admitted. "Not to all."

Drake saw Smyth getting antsy, and guessed what the soldier

was about to do. Impatient, he would stride in, boots and all, and achieve nothing. He rose, walked over and put a hand on Smyth's chest.

"Give her time."

"This is a waste of time."

"No, mate. It's where we are right now. And where we're meant to be."

Smyth made a bewildered noise. "Eh?"

"He's saying we don't walk away from people in need," Alicia spoke up. "And maybe, for once, he's right."

"Thanks, love." Drake turned back and smiled at Brynn. "We're here," he said. "And always happy to talk."

Brynn smiled back. "Maybe you are good luck after all."

Drake fought to keep the smile in place. Throughout the struggles of the last few years he could hardly describe the SPEAR team as a 'good luck' charm. A diplomatic man would say that bad shit and bad people happened everywhere.

A cynic would say it followed them around.

Matt Drake said they put themselves in the way of it, and tried to help good people out of bad situations.

"How can we help?"

CHAPTER ELEVEN

Time passed and the day grew colder. Kinimaka broke out the supplies and handed food around. The villagers regarded them all with suspicion, though some of the braver ones—mostly the very young—approached with interest on sighting the snacks until their parents pulled them back. Drake sent smiles all around and wished he could at least part-communicate. The hand gestures he tried just didn't work. The villagers kept their distance.

The woman whom they had seen and heard crying grew quiet after a while, and they saw nothing of her. The deep silence that covered Kimbiri drilled down to their souls, filling them with wonder. The sky was huge and empty save for clouds; the hills and mountains free of human interference and fiercely individual.

Brynn returned with a man and a woman in tow. The man was old and walked with a limp, the woman almost his age, still smiling at the people she passed despite clearly suppressing a hurt. With difficulty she faced Mai and Drake and offered them a smile.

"We are pleased to meet you."

Mai looked between the man and woman. "We are soldiers and not blessed with manners. We are also looking for someone and short of time. If we can help you, please let us know."

Drake saw what he assumed were the heads of the village, both nod in time. Brynn would already have passed on the previous conversation. It made no sense to backtrack.

"I am Emilio," the man said, speaking through Brynn's translation. "This is my wife, Clareta. We speak a little English, but it is easier to let Brynn speak for us now. You understand?"

Mai nodded. "Of course."

"Until recently, we would not have spoken so openly to

outsiders," Brynn explained. "We are a village of the Andes and we happily keep our distance. Not because we have to. Do you understand that?"

"I do," Mai said, and Drake agreed.

"But we have already broken our silence. We have already admitted we need help. That makes this easier and respectable and right. I know you understand. Two weeks ago we visited Cusco, and then again one week ago. Before that, twice more. I do not use the word desperate, but . . ." She looked away to the mountains as if seeking inspiration or courage.

Mai sat unmoving. "Why visit Cusco?"

"In the night they come. They snort and snuffle around our walls. They breathe noisily against our windows. They slaughter our livestock for fun and bathe in blood. They walk the dark streets of our village and mate and cry and cackle there . . ." Brynn held her breath for a moment, brimming with emotion. "And then they take one of us. Man or woman. They take one away and we never see them again."

"They?" Mai asked first. "Who are they?"

Brynn's face was ashen, her eyes terrified. "Monsters."

Drake gave the area an involuntary double-check. "When you say monsters?"

Brynn shuddered. "I speak good English," she said. "I know what I mean."

Drake thought about asking for a description, but saw how fearful the woman was and decided to return to that particular subject later. "And you went to Cusco for help to tackle the problem?"

"Yes, of course! We swallowed our pride and our privacy and went to the city. It was after the second night that we reported it. They did not laugh at us; they did not suspect us. Instead, they did nothing at all. Four times we have journeyed there and four times they have ignored us. Now . . . last night they came again. What do we do?"

Brynn's last comment was an outburst of despair. Recognizing that, almost immediately she cleared her throat and pulled her coat tighter, looking away.

"I am sorry," she said.

"You have no reason to be," Mai said.

Drake reined in the anger. "You reported each incident to the police and they did nothing?"

"I do not know the Cusco police," Brynn said. "Maybe they investigate. But we do not see them and every time we go it is same man. And they have no previous reports on file. It is as if . . . as if they do not care."

"How many people taken?" Kinimaka now came forward and knelt before Brynn.

"Six." Brynn forced out the word through a raw throat.

"Over how long?"

"Six weeks," Brynn said. "And every night we fear."

"Do you have any clues," Hayden asked, "where the monsters come from? Where they take your people?"

"Most of us . . . most of us are so scared." Brynn cried a little. "That . . . that we hide underneath our beds or cower in closets. Most of us . . . can't take not knowing who they will come for next."

Mai didn't hesitate, but laid a hand on Brynn's shoulder. "There is no shame in being scared."

"Some of the men . . . they watch through high windows or the eaves. They see a little of what happens in the dark. They see naked, black-smeared, odd shapes. No features. They see monsters and even they are afraid."

"And they do not act?" Smyth said, for once careful to keep emotion out of his voice.

"Not against so many. They count hundreds."

Drake was shocked. "That many?" He covered his confusion and a dozen questions by nodding at Mai.

"And when they leave they go that way." Brynn nodded straight at the mountains with their winding passes. "They take our people there and not one has returned."

Drake stared at Hayden. "You think the cops are paid off?"

"Either that or criminally lazy."

Kinimaka added a new disquiet. "Are there other villages in the area?"

Brynn nodded. "Nuno. Quillabiri."

"Do nightmares follow us around?" Yorgi asked. "We come here to find bad seller of Inca relics and find even worse. I do think we are cursed."

"Speak for yourself, Yogi," Alicia said. "I broke my curse."

Mai didn't react; concentrating all her focus on Brynn, she leaned over and took the woman's hand whilst staring the village leaders right in the eyes.

"If you want our help," she said. "You have it."

Smyth groaned.

Drake couldn't help but wonder what kind of hell they'd just walked slap-bang into.

CHAPTER TWELVE

Splitting forces, especially when the coming night held such monstrous promise, was never a good idea, but Drake backed Hayden when she suggested it. The nearest village to Kimbiri—Nuno—was only a thirty-minute walk to the south and a potential target for some kind of raid tonight. They couldn't be certain until they talked to the villagers and decided to leave four in Kimbiri and send three to Nuno.

Hayden found herself wanting to walk alone whilst Drake and Alicia passed the time with a little harmless banter. This worked at first, but she knew almost immediately that she needed company. Her own thoughts were as dark and deep as mountains at night, and as confusing as their myriad passes. And just as dangerous.

Why did she always destroy relationships? In the heat of battle, she'd told Mano how she felt, and in no uncertain terms, wrecking their bond, but it had been her simple desire for space that caused the outbursts. Not a fundamental need to be rid of the Hawaiian.

For years now, he had been there. Every battle, every conversation; every goddamn bullet. At her side—a shadow. She feared now that she'd used his moral stance to push him away, citing that she knew better—for the good of the nation. Maybe she was right, maybe he was right; it didn't matter. What mattered was how they both came out of it.

As for Mano, she had no idea. She didn't deserve to know where he was. And she still needed her own space, needed to find something. Trailing along these mountain roads inspired a much-needed sense of solitude, and she soon fancied that Drake and Alicia were leaving her alone on purpose. They knew a little of her relationship track record, which was not good. They didn't know it all—which was better. Suffice to say, it was the same old story.

More breakages than a boxful of kids' toys.

The cool air surrounded her, the vast mountain range standing still and ancient, one of earth's extraordinary sanctuaries. One could say anything to these silent sentinels and never be judged. One could stare into their primeval, hushed immensity and, for a few moments, slough off every problem and worry you ever acquired.

They walked for a while, Hayden twisting and turning through past and present and an odd kind of future where every single moment was a shard of uncertainty.

"Cheer up, love," Drake interrupted her. "Could be worse. You could be Alicia."

"Fuck off, Drakey."

Hayden smiled, thinking: *How the hell do they do it?* They both must have fears, worries, regrets. Compartmentalization worked to a certain point, yes. But it could hardly deal with the terrors they'd faced and put down, the personal ordeals they went through every week.

It could be worse.

Sure. It could. Of that she had no doubt. Of them all only Dahl had children. Only Dahl was married. Shit, that guy was fucking superhuman.

And deserved better than his current lot. But who knew, maybe it would all come around. She saw they had been walking twenty minutes and looked ahead to where the village should be.

"Just in the lee of that mountain?"

"Yeah. Not quite where I'd put my village, but I guess there's a reason."

"To keep the weather off?" Alicia speculated.

"An avalanche would soon change all that." Drake motioned at the snow high above.

"Always an answer."

"It comes with intelligence and free thinking."

"Probably. But I'm sure Yorkshire was excluded when those options were offered."

Drake stared. "Who are you? Dahl?"

"Yeah, sorry. Been around you lot too long."

The Yorkshireman laid a hand on her forearm. "And staying around."

Alicia offered a smile, their exchange something Hayden had once never thought possible. Alicia had always been so flighty, so intensely focused on the next horizon and the next job. Somehow, she'd found a kind of peace. And embraced it.

Hayden sighed inwardly and spotted the jumbled huddle of homes up ahead. The trail dipped and then ran along flat ground for a while, green swathes to either side, before splitting among the houses and ending up against the mountain. Hayden had already seen young men watching them, and walked easily, steadily, offering no threat to these people.

The villagers back in Kimbiri had told them that one of the elders spoke decent English and the younger people could get by, so they were reasonably confident their questions would be understood. They were not welcomed along the way, even when they started to pass among the houses. People stood around or rose from their work to watch the newcomers. Hooded eyes studied them and then met with the next pair. A scraping of digging tools made Hayden's ears prick and sent her gaze to the right.

Two men stood atop a short slope, holding a pitchfork and a spade.

Drake nodded at the nearest youth. "We're here to help. Do you speak English?"

So far, no real sign that these people were being terrorized. Hayden began to think maybe they'd wasted their time by coming here. They should have dealt with what they knew rather than second guess and spread their resources. But it stood to reason that Kimbiri wouldn't be the only village affected.

Alicia half-turned. "Pretty soon," she muttered. "We're gonna walk headfirst into the mountain. Any ideas?"

Drake grinned. "We could ask them to take us to their leader."

"They're not aliens. They're Incas."

"They're not friggin' Incas either." Hayden looked around. "Surely someone—"

"What is it that you want?" A man stepped out of a house up

ahead. He was tall, gray-haired and slightly disheveled, as if he'd just thrown his clothes on. He carried a knobbly stick to help him walk, and scratched irritably at a ragged beard. He squinted hard at the newcomers.

"What?" he asked again before they could get a word out.

"We come from Kimbiri," Hayden explained. "Brynn sent us, the teacher? And Emilio and Clareta—the elders? We would like to help."

The old man spat into the muddy road. "Can you plant vegetables?"

Alicia shrugged. "If by plant you mean put headfirst down in the dirt, then hell yeah, we've dug a few vegetable patches in our time."

Hayden had little time for repartee today. "Kimbiri is beset by . . . savages," she finished a little lamely. "Every week they come. The police will not help. We came to see if you were the same?"

"Every week?" The old man spat again. "Who are you?"

The team introduced themselves as best they could. Hayden watched as more and more people gathered. She didn't know what she'd been expecting, but a group of stern-faced, freshly washed, brightly clothed individuals wasn't it. For their part they stared at the newcomers with interest and mistrust. She had hoped for someone friendly like Brynn to step forth, but the town withheld judgment for now.

"And why are you here?"

"We came first to Kimbiri seeking help," Hayden explained. "We were searching for a house in the mountains owned by a reclusive man. We hoped they might know its whereabouts."

"And they offered up this savage story?"

"No. We walked into their grieving."

The old man squinted hard. "Explain."

Hayden took a long breath and told him what they'd seen only hours earlier. His expression changed gradually, clouds of emotion altering his features from mistrust to disbelief to fear and finally to anger.

"Why have they not told us?" he barked. "They make the trek to Cusco; they talk to cops, but they do not inform Nuno."

Hayden knew pride no doubt had its place in Emilio's and Clareta's decision not to seek help from Nuno. But there was a more telling question to ask.

"And have you informed anyone?"

The old man's words caught in his throat, his expression softening. It was only a moment before he took a long look around, studying the other villagers, and then came back to Hayden.

"We have weapons. We fight. But they do no good. We . . . we thought we were the only ones."

Hayden held out a hand. "Well, now you have help. What is your name?"

"I am Conde." He proceeded to speak rapidly to the assembled throng, hopefully explaining the facts. Hayden watched them all closely in case he might be ordering an attack, but in many she saw relief entering expressions and a relaxing of muscles. She waited for Conde to finish.

"We expected them to come last night," he said when finished. "But it seems Kimbiri suffered. Tonight?" he shrugged. "We will fight."

"You have fought before, you say. Can you tell us who these people are? What they look like?"

"People?" Conde was back to snarling again. "Do you think we would be so frightened? Do you think we would allow people to come among us? To take our friends and families? These are not people." He all but shuddered.

Drake stepped forward. "What have you seen, old man?"

"El monstruo. It is el monstruo."

Hayden fought back a shiver. She didn't have to ask Conde to explain. "Has anyone ever gotten close?"

"First Desi, then Ordell. They were taken. We have not seen them since." Hayden heard a woman's wail at the mention of the last name.

"How many others?"

"Eight," Conde said. "Every week for two months now."

Drake looked back at her. "So Nuno was hit first."

Hayden sent a look into the distance. "Maybe. There is another village, is there not, Conde?"

"Yes, Quillabiri. But that is a way from here."

"And more?"

"Small settlements. Many without name. Two dozen people in each one, maybe a few more. We are a hardy, private folk."

Hayden wondered how far this went. She wondered how they had come across all this, out here in the colossal Andes and if she should turn her phone off right now. That way they couldn't be forced home before they were done. The US political machine had no priority out here, but a new Secretary of Defense would never accept that.

"Eight lost," Conde offered up with good timing. "Five men. Two women. One boy," His face twisted with emotion. "In the old days our ancestors used sling and shot. We have no enemies, not here. We are not fighters. We live a meagre, content life. But we have boulders, stones and we can make a bow and arrow. Yes, we have a rich history. A mighty empire. A sniveling conqueror. Betrayal. Murder. Gold. There is not a man nor woman here that does not know it. We speak Spanish and Quechua, and a little English. Mostly, we farm. We know what happens in the big cities—drug trafficking, weapons trading, judge-hooding. I say all this to help you better realize that we are not hillbillies." He laughed at the strange word. "We are not uneducated and ignorant. And that you know when I say el monstruo, it is precisely what I mean."

Hayden nodded. "We understand."

"We handle our own problems. Self-discipline and the control of one's emotions is of high value here. We do not have a counterculture such as do the big cities, and we do not need western values. This is Peru. What is left of it."

"Culture resists change," Drake said. "My own land is a traditional place of bacon butties and fish and chip shops, but the interlopers keep trying to find a way in."

Conde nodded, despite obvious confusion. Hayden tried to turn the conversation back around. "Can you describe el monstruo?"

"It comes shrouded by its friend, the darkness. It uses shadows for cloaks. It is silent, as silent as the seconds after death. It has little form. Do you see? Though we see signs of a body and crooked limbs, it has no face."

"Masks?" Drake guessed.

"No masks. Only a smooth hint of nothing."

"Fuck me." Alicia glanced up at the mountains. "I bet you have fucking spiders too, don't you?"

"Vampire bats as large as men." Conde nodded, almost smiling. "And the terrible alpaca. We have many of them."

Alicia shook herself. "Just steer me the hell away from them."

Hayden fixed Conde's eyes with her own, giving nothing away. "You fought these things? Did you ever hurt one?"

"Oh, they bleed. They bleed thick and red. But the place where they fall is always empty the next morning, so perhaps they cannot die. And they outnumber us. So many."

Hayden stepped away, having heard enough and confident that Nuno was beset by the same problem as Kimbiri. And how many others? She dared not guess. The burning pyre of questions grew and raged, the flames becoming angrier. Where were the people being taken? What happened to them?

And could they cut one operation short—put it on hold even as Dahl and Kenzie fought merciless enemies across Europe to progress it—to jump right slap bang into another?

The seller was out here too though. Guarding his trove of ancient relics, what had been written about as the greatest hoard the world had ever known.

"This time," she said. "It's not about war, or bullets or terrorist bombs, and it's not about us. This time, it's about a few villagers in the mountains. And it's just as important as all the others. Are you agreed?"

Drake's lips turned up at the corners. "We're right where we ought to be."

CHAPTER THIRTEEN

As a ghost-ridden gloom descended across the haunted mountain range, Drake stood shoulder-to-shoulder with the craziest woman he had ever known.

"You think they'll come tonight?" she whispered, clouds of breath escaping her lips.

"I hope so," Drake said. "There's nothing I'd like better than to dish out some comeuppance to a band of cold-blooded killers like these. But I do wish Dahl was here."

Alicia made a show of staring at his groin. "Why? Did your balls fall off?"

"He'd love this. No complications. No guesswork. Just plain, old fashioned retribution and a chance to help good people out. Maybe save their loved ones."

Hayden came up behind them. "We're as ready as can be," she said. "They're armed with a mixture of farming tools, knives and even a saucepan or two."

"Bows and arrows?"

"A few. In the right hands. And on the right roofs."

"Then we're ready."

"One thing is for sure," Hayden said. "El monstruo won't be expecting us."

"Don't say that." Alicia stared at the gathering dark, the bruised mountains, the fading shapes and the gray clouds. "They can't be monsters."

"You scared of men without faces, Alicia? Vampire bats? Alpacas?"

"Shit, aren't you?"

Drake knew his face was shrouded. "A little."

"What the hell is an alpaca anyway?"

"Imagine a llama but ten times more ferocious."

Alicia shuddered. "It's healthy to be scared."

"Don't let Smyth hear you say that."

"He wouldn't hear. Smyth's a mess right now, and so is Lauren."

"The team is split," Hayden agreed. "In more than just a physical way. And I'm sorry I contributed to that."

Drake shrugged. "Personal is personal, love," he said. "We're soldiers, cut and dried. When we go to work it's nothing but professional."

A chill wind rolled out of the mountains, passing through them. Drake found himself wondering what it had encountered along the way, what kind of wild creature it might have brushed past. The lofty heights of the Andes stood in perennial stillness, but the lower ranges harbored a multitude of claws, fangs and beings that wished harm on others. A deep silence hung over the village and he knew nobody would get a moment of sleep tonight.

"You hear that?" Alicia said suddenly.

"What?"

She listened. "Maybe nothing. Maybe a falling rock."

Drake remembered Brynn's words. *They come down out of the mountains.* His Glock was holstered but ready; his new H&K hanging loose at his side. They couldn't just shoot anybody in cold blood, but he relished getting close to some of these "monsters".

Every day some upstart met his match. Some ruthless killer got his just desserts. And some overbearing trailblazer was taken down. This was about to be one of those days and a lesson learned for all the cowards that preyed on those that could not defend themselves.

And monsters? They found equals too.

He listened hard but heard no sounds. The contrast of the vast mountain range and the arcane stillness it produced to the concrete jungles they usually fought in was immense, and off-putting. Drake had positioned himself upon the highest roof overlooking the point where the village was normally infiltrated, but lookouts were everywhere. All primed, all ready. They were crouched down, partially concealed.

Alicia squinted at the shadows that surrounded the village of Nuno.

"What the fuck is that?"

Drake cleared his throat, rather than answer. He was not a gullible man but the shape that crawled inside the shadows was not normal. Human beings didn't move that way. It was a snap thought, but as authentic as rock, as earth, as dirt. It was a primeval truth, and triggered a primeval fear.

The closeness of Alicia and Hayden calmed him, the old training centered him, enabled him to look through more dubious eyes. But still . . .

It crawled like a spider, limbs rising sharply and then quickly creeping along. It had legs and, probably, arms. It was coated all in black, but had no real form in the dark. It moved swiftly, a hungry tarantula, causing the hairs along the nape of Drake's neck to stand up. It scuttled along at such a rate, and unlit, that he could make no decision so quickly and now saw exactly what the villagers saw.

"Monsters."

They came as a pack, crawling along one after another, side by side, and they made no sound, but when the villagers saw them they began to backpedal and to scream.

"Holy crap," Hayden breathed.

"There's nothing holy in that," a voice said from behind them, making them start. "It is el monstruo."

"We're badly prepared," Drake acknowledged. "We gotta hope that noise wins the night, pal."

"Noise?"

Drake hefted the H&K. "You say meet el monstruo. I say meet el Kock."

Hayden shone their meagre flashlights from the roof down into the street as those villagers that had not taken flight lit torches and put tinder to a small bonfire built in the main square. Light was their ally now.

Drake aimed at the skies.

Hayden's flashlight lit the backs of the sneaking creatures. The extra light picked out material and glistening flesh. It picked out more form.

"I think . . . I think they may be human."

Drake saw the creatures converge on a house, scramble around its base and then bang at the windows as if testing for an entry point. They didn't stand on two legs, but reached up from the ground, balancing on one appendage. So far, they'd done nothing illegal.

He shrugged. Two villagers huddled in an empty doorway—a man and a woman, both dressed in thick, bright clothing—and now the man thrust the woman behind him as the creatures swarmed around and spotted them.

"You see that?" Hayden whispered in his ear.

"Got it." He watched through the scope.

Alicia commented from another direction. "I got at least half a dozen of the mothers sneaking right below me. Looks like a trail of giant ants."

Drake watched one of the creatures scuttle full-pelt at the man in the doorway and then leap straight for his throat. It reminded him of a documentary he'd once seen where a large spider leapt unexpectedly at a man's face, understandably scaring the hell out of him. The creature struck the man who, despite his obvious fear and revulsion, struck out. The creature still hit however, sending him staggering back against the woman, who screamed. Drake decided enough was enough.

"Let there be noise."

Gunfire rang out inside the village. The residents had been warned it would happen and how to take cover. Drake stitched a line in the brickwork across the top of the door and watched for the creatures' reactions.

Bodies froze and heads rose, almost as if sniffing the air then, in slow motion, a hundred heads all turned upwards, finding Drake, Hayden and Alicia.

"Fuck, that's creepy," Alicia hissed.

"I can't fire on them," Drake said. "They haven't done anything except look scary."

"Well, it ain't Halloween," Alicia said. "And imitating giant spiders is felony enough for this girl." She fired downwards between the creatures, her bullets chipping at the few paving flags down there or sinking straight into the earth. Instantly, the creatures broke for it, swarming around the building or up against its vertical side. Drake had a sudden, irrational fear that they might be climbing the brickwork, scurrying up to launch an attack at them.

He jerked away, then checked himself. *Stop being a knob!* But it was the lack of sound, the silent communications, the faceless and almost formless bodies, the horrendous way in which they moved. With tough discipline he forced himself to look down the side of the building, saw the creatures pressed up against it or banging at the wooden door.

The door splintered. This was an empty house; its occupants sheltering elsewhere for the night. Hayden walked over to the hatch they'd left open that led inside. "Shall we?"

Alicia grimaced. "I'd rather guard the roof."

Drake made sure the man and woman were running safely and that the bulk of the creatures were heading toward their house. "Party animals are all here. Let's do this."

"Creature feature would be a better description," Alicia pointed out.

Hayden walked into the house first. "Stay here, Alicia. Use the comms. We need to know if the villagers can't handle the rest of them."

Drake followed their boss, happy that candles still flickered to light their way. Down a short flight of stairs and into an attic, diagonal beams of wood holding the roof up and spiderwebs everywhere. A door stood open that led to another staircase and down to the first floor landing. He ran toward it, descended the steps and then froze, listening.

"What the—"

A scratching sound came from the closet to his left, fingernails or claw-tips being drawn slowly across a wooden surface. It was slow and deliberate and highly distracting. Hayden watched the landing as Drake flung the door wide open.

Darkness leapt at him, striking him hard and bodily around the upper chest. He toppled backward, staggering, losing his grip on the rifle. A slick, fleshy body landed on him, grease smearing his clothes and hands as he struggled, and giving him no grip whatsoever. The attack was soundless, but this close up, finally he knew that this was not el monstruo, not a creature born of a black pit.

It was human.

Skull, face and neck were covered by a thick, stretched balaclava with the tiniest of eye and nose holes, the rest of the body naked save for a pair of shorts, and covered in some kind of filth or gunk or oil. It slithered all over him, stinking, panting, striking and smashing at him. He pushed it away, but like an attack dog it was tenacious. Its fingers had some kind of material attached that gave helped them grip, same for the feet probably. Drake swiped out and caught a wrist that was quickly snatched away. But not before he saw the oddest thing.

"Hayden, it has . . ."

More then scuttled up the stairs, running low and fast—a nightmare swarm that belied human movement. They were trained, sticking together; they were violent, raised with cruelty; and they were driven. Somebody made them like this.

Drake punched swiftly, forgetting the grappling which clearly wasn't working. These things felt pain then. His opponent flinched away, grunting.

Drake kicked out at what he assumed was the head, feeling relief when it smashed against a rail and then stopped moving.

Hayden faced the swarm. Drake shuffled to her side and the two stood together, filling the landing, as the creatures came up. Then they were scuttling and jumping, rearing off two feet and launching themselves through the air. Drake tried to bat one aside but the body was too heavy, smashing him to his knees. Hayden met another head on, striking it with her elbow and crying out herself with pain. But the blacked-out body fell away, not moving.

It was instantly replaced with another.

Drake felt a punch and then a two-fingered jab to the throat. When he caught the wrist he flinched again. The two-fingered jab had been done for only one reason.

This thing only had two fingers. The previous attacker had only four. Signs of battle? Another flailing about at Hayden did so with the stump of a wrist. A fourth appeared to possess only half a foot, but maybe that was an optical illusion.

This day just gets weirder and weirder, he thought. Not because of the missing body parts but because every single attacker was missing body parts.

He swiped another away, sent a creature tumbling back downstairs and taking another four out with him. Arms and legs waved, and greasy black stains marked the bare wood and walls. Drake found his Glock and fired another warning shot. This also had no effect whatsoever. Did they even know what guns were? Shit, that was not a good thought. Hayden fell back as a fist slammed her face. The figure jumped but Drake hit it bodily out of the air with his shoulder, sending it over the landing and crashing below. Bones snapped. Finally there came a noise, a scream, exploding from one of them; a high-pitched keening whine as if metal were being put through a wood-chopper. Drake saw blackened bodies shooting away from the screamer. He blocked another attack, fired the Glock again.

No response.

He kicked another down the stairs. Alicia's voice came across the comms. "About eight of the mountain-spider-things are converging on the house where we stashed most of the bloody villagers. Shit, we need to move, guys."

Drake stared hard at the crush of bodies and then nodded at Hayden. "Going through now. Come right down and join us, love."

CHAPTER FOURTEEN

Securing his weapons, Drake waited half a minute and then began to barge right through the middle of their attackers. The grease that coated their bodies, and an odor of stale sweat filled his nostrils immediately; their quiet grunting only accentuating his distaste. Hands and feet jabbed at him, each missing a finger or a toe. A tight black mask came down fast, striking his cheek, the features beneath flattened and obscured. The man might as well have had no nose.

Hayden came behind, flinging others aside and trying to keep up the momentum. They needed to be fast and hard, move without mercy to get through the crush. Alicia cried out as she raced across the landing and then hit the last of the climbers, fighting them for the first time and making her own characteristically loud impressions.

Drake winced as he reached the halfway point down and faced a woman, her right arm missing from the elbow. She swung it at his face, missed, and he threw her at the wall, seeing blood and oil spurt in an erratic pattern across the paintwork. He kicked the next man in the chest, using his height advantage; picked up another and upended him over the bannister. Hayden followed at his heels, clearing the way for Alicia who ended her opponent's day with sharp, precise jabs, knees and kicks.

Around the bottom of the stairs and the crawlers were exiting rapidly. Like a swarm they poured out the front door, a few steps ahead of Drake. Revulsion stuck in his throat, but he knew what these things were now—just not what made them the way they were.

An errant creature rose up on two legs, black and jabbing like a rearing, threatened arachnid. Drake dove in with an elbow and was then rolling outside, into the street, among them. An elbow struck his face, a knee glanced off his ribcage. One of the figures crawled right over him without stopping. Drake rolled and rolled until he hit the grass verge on the other side.

Alicia, on her feet, offered a hand. "Playtime done for today?"

"Aye, love. How's it looking?"

"There's too many of them for this rough and tumble shit. We need to start tying 'em up or something."

"Should have known you'd come up with that. What position do you prefer?"

Alicia ran at his side as they jogged quickly toward the supposed safe-house. "Oh, Drakey, don't tempt me."

Hayden caught them up. "No way could these guys have known which house we chose," she said, catching her feet as the path sloped. "No goddamn way."

Alicia made a squeaking noise. "Mountain spider!"

Drake kicked out at a black figure that sprang at them from the shadows, all raised elbows and knees, hands jabbing like fleshy daggers. "Fuck's sake, Alicia. Stop calling 'em that. Makes it worse."

Then he turned to Hayden. "You think there's a spy in their midst?"

"Makes sense. Easier all round. A local that wants something is far easier to plant than an outsider."

"Well." Drake breathed deeply as they converged on the creatures that surged around the house. "Let's make sure we catch one of them."

Alicia made a noise of distaste. "Instead of Glocks and HKs," she moaned. "We should have brought cans of Raid."

Villagers stood in the windows and filled the door, which had been broken down. They held spades and garden forks and a dozen other man-made implements. One creature writhed on its back, a long wooden handle sticking up out of its stomach. Another bled profusely, struggling to keep balance because it appeared to only have one arm. The darkness, the black clothing, the way they crawled . . . it all spoke of el monstruo.

But what kind of man— Drake stopped the thought for a moment. His next words would have been, *bred them*. But they weren't bred. They were adults; they were full grown; they were . . .

The attack was unconvincing, uncertain. Drake, Alicia and Hayden usually entered the fray with guns blazing, fighting weapon with weapon, but these assailants were unarmed. They hadn't hurt anyone. Drake found himself twisting arms and grabbing material where he could find it, throwing men and women aside, punching those that were stronger and generally barging the rest out of the way. Soon, their hands and clothing became coated with the oil. Their skin stank. Drake grabbed a limpid binding of hair, felt the grease squeeze out all over his knuckles and flinched away. The owner whirled and charged. Drake fell to one knee and sent them flying over one shoulder.

Then the screams began.

A cluster of assailants was overrunning the doorway. One of them disarmed a woman and pulled her bodily from the step. She fell, crying out, her fellow villagers trying to reach her but tripping and falling themselves. The black creatures dragged her away, leaping and jumping at her as if she were a magnificent treasure, starting to squeal with pleasure now that they had found their quarry.

At the side of the house another knot found another victim, and started the same routine.

"We can't let this happen." Hayden's face was fixed and the Glock came out. She headed around the side of the house.

Drake turned to Alicia. "Try to stop her killing anyone. I'll sort this out."

He started to run after the beleaguered woman, but then the villagers came rushing out of the house; buoyed and daring with their new helpers. They jabbed at the creatures with their weapons, eliciting screams and grunts and keening wails. Drake reached the woman, dealt out several crushing blows, and took a couple of bruising strikes. The woman ran to him, fighting creatures off. Drake pulled her out of their midst, now helped by villagers who sank sharpened edges into greasy flesh. Drake saw one creature caught along the throat; the jugular opened up and a fountain of blood shot forth.

No.

But the frenzy was on the villagers, and he could hardly blame them. They fought the things of nightmare, their worst dreams made reality this past few months, and the rage of release was irresistible.

Drake dragged some away. The creatures hesitated. He saw Alicia at the other side of the house and Hayden too, then heard the boss fire her gun. A creature twisted and writhed. The rest of the horde reared back; an incredible sight to watch and so unnerving Drake caught his breath. For a second the world went quiet.

The creature with the severed neck bled out. Others nursed breakages quietly. The woman they'd tried to abduct held a hand over her mouth to keep from sobbing. A man that might be her husband enfolded her in his arms.

Then the creatures came to some kind of decision. As one, as if possessed of mental telepathy, they scuttled and raced toward their fallen, gathered them up and carried them away from the village. They ran by paths and roads and between houses. They made no sound. The only thing they left behind was blood. Drake watched the horde vanish, an undulating black pack, greasy and spidery, all arms and elbows and legs, many of them amputees. He watched them swell and heave into the dark that surrounded the village and then beyond that, across the flat plateau, under the silver-shod fields, toward the silent majesty of the mountains.

Alicia met him a few steps in front of Hayden. "Dude, I sure do hope they don't call us back to DC anytime soon. 'Cause we ain't fucking going."

Their boss still held her weapon but now slid it back into its holster. "I second that enormously."

Drake said nothing. Since they arrived in Peru he'd somehow known they had a deeper mission. These remote, vulnerable villages needed help and they needed the SPEAR team. They were out here until they won . . . or died.

CHAPTER FIFTEEN

Kenzie knew that the deeper they delved into the filth that surrounded and filled the criminal underworld the better chance they had of finding Tremayne's buyer and at least one more of the seller's middlemen. Of course, there was nobody more qualified than she.

"Haven't heard from the team in a while," Dahl was saying as he paced the hotel room's floor back and forth.

"We have our own problems." Kenzie reluctantly ripped her gaze from his tensed body and stared over at the priceless Inca vase they had appropriated. "Based on my queries so far the supposed ultimate buyer of that thing is a violent, criminal superstar—a real piece of work that thinks he's God's gift to law breaking. The other players might be happy to give up the middlemen, the corrupt authorities and locations of previous items, but they want something out of it."

Dahl stopped and shrugged. "Of course they do. What?"

"They won't say. But they can point the finger at all involved."

"They won't say?" Dahl repeated, deeply surprised. "What kind of criminal won't say what he wants out of a deal?"

"The kind that wants to meet." Kenzie sighed. "Tonight. Two nasty little rats known as middlemen. We'll try to get a bead on Tremayne's renowned buyer, the real rock star, but it's gonna be hairier than an old woman's armpit in there."

"Sounds like the most violent meet in history," Dahl said.

"Well, I'm sure there's been worse." Kenzie coughed without giving anything away. "But I have met both these guys before. They come armed to the hilt, as edgy as your white cliffs, puffed up to the max with self-importance, and ready to kill as instantly as bad coffee. I'm not sure I want to deal with them again."

"But they don't know you've changed sides . . . wait . . . *my* white cliffs? For fuck's sake, Kenzie. Do you not yet know that I'm Swedish?"

"Swedish?" She looked surprised. "Are you sure?"

Dahl started to turn an odd shade of red before realizing Kenzie was baiting him. Only then did he take a breath, relax and sit down.

"You've been pacing for an hour," Kenzie said. "There are other ways to work off extra energy, you know."

"I am married."

"Not for long," Kenzie muttered, but loud enough for him to hear. "The old battle axe still in touch?"

"If you're referring to Johanna, the mother of my children—" Dahl walked over to the window and stared into the gathering darkness— "then yes. She may have changed her mind."

Kenzie snorted. "Oh, the mother of my children," she repeated in a mocking voice. "That squaw has you turning up, down, inside and out. She'll be the death of you."

"You're saying I'm not focused?"

Kenzie looked away. "Maybe."

"On the job? Or on you?"

"I am the job, Torst, believe it or not. And not just because we're tracking relic smugglers. My life . . . is one big job. Morning till night. Dusk till dawn. There's nothing else."

"Then change your fucking life," Dahl said, shrugging it all off and then walking over to check his weapons and Kevlar. "People do it all the time."

Kenzie smiled without humor. "Not those with a price on their heads. But don't worry, that's next week's problem, right? Tonight holds a whole different set of evils."

Dahl half-turned as he worked. "Maybe you could explain what's about to happen."

"All right. I've been buyer, seller and agent in the past. Tonight, we have two pretty vile middlemen. Both wanting something out of the meet. Both will expect a good deal and neither know the other is coming."

"Crap."

"Yeah, and they'll be as tooled up as Bosch, baby. It'll have to be game faces, hints of violence and understated threat. The kind of language they all understand. Keeps everything in check."

Dahl nodded. He knew the game. "What do we have to offer them? And don't say the vase."

"Oh, no. I'm keeping that for when we find Tremayne's buyer. They're middlemen. You just have to use your imagination."

Dahl finished with his preparations. "Not something I'm renowned for."

"Then we'll improvise," Kenzie said. "Pass me the list of those previous sales."

Nice lay languid and dispassionate under a leaden sky. Drizzle fell in erratic bursts as if it couldn't make up its mind, coating the streets with a slippery film of water. Dahl and Kenzie watched the pub as it closed for the night, then saw the workers head home and finally the night manager. The Swede's watch said 2 a.m. Kenzie counted off the minutes.

"Here they come."

A sedan pulled up at the curb in the empty street, tires shedding water and crunching to a stop. The rear doors opened to discharge four men. Then the front passenger door released another. Kenzie knew they'd be packing, but the amount of hardware they carried bulged under their jackets and weighed their belts down. She stayed silent as they approached the pub's front door and then produced a key, gaining entry.

"Must be a front," Dahl said.

"Easy to procure. And a safe meeting place. Unless something goes sour . . ." Kenzie stayed put until another car arrived, disgorged its passengers, and then started to tick itself quiet. Another minute passed.

Dahl turned to her. "We ready?"

"Let's kill 'em."

Dahl sighed and followed her out into the rain. Kenzie strode across the road, staying visible, and walked right up to the front door. It opened for her. A man stood back in the shadows.

"Hey, asshole, you gonna invite us in?"

"It sounds like her!" a voice shouted. "Be careful, Abel. She is moutarde."

Dahl snorted quietly. "Mustard? You're yellow? You come in a jar?"

"Hot, darling. Hot. And that's disgusting."

"I didn't mean it like—"

But then they were through the door and inside the pub. Dahl fell silent. Kenzie appraised the place in six seconds—the empty bar where a shooter would be hidden, the spaced out tables arranged to shield the bar's owner, the goons arrayed in strategic positions, the half-open doors and darkened corners—she was a veteran at this kind of meet. The owner though—he ought to be a retiree. Seventy if he was a day, Cyrano was a criminal who would never give up, an old man who knew nothing else. His face was a furrow, the deep carvings not all wrinkle, and the pockmarks not in the least from old age. Wiry and lean, he still cut an image, eyes twinkling as if thought he deserved to take her around the back for a little fiery relief.

"Kenzie," he drawled in French tones. "It has been too long."

She crossed to a corner, the windows and a wall at her back. "Cyrano. So long I thought you might be dead."

"You will die before me, young girl. And no sword today?"

"Katana," Kenzie corrected. "Do I need it? Do I cry myself to sleep? Do I fuck."

"I am sure you do and need all those things and more. But we now have business to attend to."

She became aware that Dahl was staring at her instead of the room. "What is it?" she hissed.

"I don't know. I'm sure I've heard something like that recently. Just . . . can't . . ."

"Focus," she hissed angrily. "On the here and now."

The third man in the room attracted her attention. His name was Patric and he was a fat oaf; a sweating pig of a man that relied on his sidekick—Paul—to look out for his interests. Well, Paul and a dozen well-armed guards.

"Patric," she said. "Those gym sessions working for ya?"

Half a dozen chins wobbled as the man pretended mirth. Rather than answer though, he nodded in Paul's direction. Paul said, "We are not here to trade insults, bitch. And I did not expect Cyrano. What do you have for us?"

Kenzie zipped the various retorts that came to mind, deciding to let it flow. This sure as hell wasn't the time or place for bickering. Maybe another venue, another life. Both these men were utter lowlifes, capable of selling their young for a tidy profit. Both deserved a little visit from her weapon of choice.

One day.

She quickly pushed her little outburst of earlier and her tongue-lashing of Dahl to a distant corner of her mind.

"Tremayne is dead," she said simply into the silence.

Fingers twitched close to triggers. Both middlemen were surrounded by a force of guards, all toting machine pistols close to their hips. The atmosphere and their lives rested on a knife's edge which, Kenzie figured, could be used to cut the very air.

"Do we know what happened?" Cyrano asked, voice cracked with age.

Kenzie shrugged. "Bastard came across someone more ruthless than he. It happens."

Her knowing smile helped light the room.

Of course, they wouldn't know which way to take it. Patric grunted, shuffled, and made a gesture to Paul, his front man. "Ask her what she wants from us."

Kenzie regarded him with disdain. "What I want is Tremayne's buyer. You know, for the Inca vase? What I want is his location. And information on who else I might be able to . . . facilitate a few sales through." She failed to mention she needed leads on the identities of all the other buyers, past and present and authorities involved. But one step at a time. One lead always pointed to another.

"You have more of the Inca relics?" Cyrano stepped forward in his greed, the perfect target.

"I do." Kenzie nodded as Dahl shifted slightly, preparing. "Two more vases and a great shield. Just like the one Tremayne sold in 2014."

Recognition swept across Cyrano's face, which Kenzie was grateful for. She saw Paul lean in to Patric and whisper. A sudden tension made her muscles go hard. One wrong move. One wrong word. One misunderstood intention . . .

She cleared her throat softly. "Either you can help me or you can't. But we are here to do business, nothing else."

Dahl watched everything like a state-of-the-art CCTV camera, sweeping back and forth and registering every minute movement. She felt him move, heard the soft breath coming through his parted lips. She sensed the coiling of muscles.

Cyrano sent one of his men to the bar. "I need a drink. Would you join me, Kenzie?" He offered nothing to Patric.

"Not tonight," she said with as much promise as she could muster.

"And your large but silent friend?"

"He's my manservant. He does not drink."

Dahl said nothing, totally focused, which gave Kenzie hope that they might make it out of here with the barest amount of blood on their hands. Cyrano frowned, but then shrugged it all off.

"Whatever. But show me the proof that you can acquire these vases. And which one of us gets the shield?"

Kenzie had always known these men would finally fix on that point. "The one that brings me Tremayne's buyer's location first."

Cyrano nodded and Paul grunted, as if he'd been expecting her answer. Patric fired another question through his sidekick.

"Why is this man so important? The buyer of the Inca relics?"

"That is between him and me," Kenzie said quickly, forcefully.

"And if I make it my business?" Cyrano growled.

Kenzie didn't hesitate. "Then our deal is off and I go with Patric." They were on prison rules now, where he that threatened hardest usually won the day, but he that threatened hardest must be able to back it up. Sooner or later, he would be called out.

"But Patric is slow and oh so fat," Cyrano said with a chuckle. "He could not service a paid whore, let alone a sword-wielding goddess like you."

Feet shuffled quickly. Men moved. Guns flew out of holsters and belts. Cyrano let out a huge guffaw.

"Ha ha. Ha ha. I am joking. Let us see what we can do, eh?"

Kenzie barely breathed. Even scratching an itch here and now would incite a blood bath. Tension stretched tauter than a high wire, thrumming in the wind.

"Seriously, you are not so fat, my friend. I have seen fatter. You see? I am full of compliments today." The old man smiled as if the most stressful thing he would do tonight would be rolling over in bed.

Dahl's hands were on his weapons. Kenzie had already decided which way she would dive when the shooting started. It just needed one nervous trigger finger, one goon who'd already snorted a line too much today. Cyrano tipped back the double whisky his man brought him, savoring the taste.

"My liver loves this stuff," he said with a grimace. "So, Kenzie . . . what are we to do?"

All this time Patric bristled in a corner, surrounded by his men but still immensely visible. Sweat dripped from his brow. The sidekick, Paul, flexed the fingers of his right hand in anticipation.

"We should deal," Kenzie said quietly. "With any other outcome—nobody wins."

Cyrano nodded. "Of course. Except the police. Interpol. FBI—"

She stopped the old man's prattle. "We came to deal. It is on the table. Decide now or don't. I am ready either way." She focused on Cyrano with a significant gaze.

Patric nudged Paul. As the room relaxed a smidgen, the sidekick brought his machine pistol up quickly, sighting on Cyrano. "If you move, old man, I will turn your brains to wallpaper paste."

Kenzie fumed inside. Fucking relic hunters. You just couldn't trust 'em an inch. "What is it now?"

"We want both vases and the shield."

"Of course you do. You're a fucking gangster." She shook her head, now unsure if there was going to be a way out of this. She should have known better, being an ex-gangster herself. How often had she seen the spoils and gone after them wholeheartedly, jealously, with aggression in her heart? The same heart in which Dahl saw some kind of integrity.

Dahl now coughed and drew himself upright, moved his own hands away from his weapons. "I urge you all to remember that it is we that hold the artifacts. Our commodity. Our rules. We want the buyer, other buyers and the corrupt ties involved. I suggest the first man to get his ass in gear stands a better chance of winning."

"Hallelujah," Kenzie moaned. "And that should be man's only motto."

Patric laid a meat slab on Paul's shoulder. The second man spoke as if receiving the speech through his subconscious. "You bring the English to a French bar? Are you mad?"

Kenzie knew it was a joke, but had reached the end of her tether. Her guns, one in each hand, targeted both leaders. "Fuck this," she growled. "Make your decisions now. Deal . . . or die."

Both men looked down the barrels of her guns and smiled.

CHAPTER SIXTEEN

In the aftermath of battle, a quiet peace and reflection reigned. Drake wished they had done more to assuage the villagers' fears. Wished they had unmasked—or unclothed—at least one creature to categorically prove it was human. Just human.

But the illusion remained, as clear as natural water, that the black-clad figures were not human.

He shivered despite every facet of his training. He shied away from it despite every year of experience. Yes, they possessed arms and legs, a heart and a head, but normal people did not move and fight like that. They did not work as a horde like that. This was something . . . something abnormal.

He walked now in the cold light of dawn, following the bare trail back to Kimbiri. Alicia and Hayden were with him, and the old man Conde with three of his friends. The idea was to let the elders meet, discuss, and help with the solution. Drake's main hope was that Kimbiri also hadn't been beset in the night.

"We are grateful you helped Nuno last night," Conde said to Hayden. "None of our people were taken for the first time in months."

"We are happy to help," Hayden told him. "Very happy. But you have to understand that our actions now raise a new question . . ." she paused, and Drake knew by her expression that she was thinking how best to delicately phrase her next comment.

"How will the mountain-spiders react?" Alicia said bluntly.

Conde stared at the Englishwoman whilst Hayden sighed. "What do you mean?"

"You don't get it, old man, do you?" Alicia went on. "Right now they're probably hanging around in their webs, licking their wounds, eating flies or something. But they've never been attacked like that before. Beaten away. It won't stop them. It'll make them come at you harder."

Hayden held up a hand. "We don't know that for sure. Alicia's speaking from a soldier's point of view. It's what she would do. The creatures are a major unknown quantity, so we have to prepare for the worst scenario."

Drake took in the scenery as they talked, which always lifted his spirits. Empty spaces ran as far as the eye could see; green slopes and forested hills, extensive mountain ranges and clear blue skies. He breathed deeply, savoring the freshness, enjoying the depth of silence that inhabited these lonely places. The trail ran ahead, undulating gently. He took out a bottle of water and drank, noting it was his last and wondering if there might be some fresh mountain stream where he could refill. Then he laughed at himself. Talk about getting carried away.

Alicia nudged him. "You with us, Drakey?"

"Yeah, just reminds me of home that's all."

The blonde snorted. "Really? Well, shit, I don't see any power stations. Or steel mills. Or even chocolate factories, for that matter."

"Nah, but I heard these hills are crawling with alpacas so watch your bloody back."

Alicia narrowed her eyes as she studied the hills and mountains. "Nothing's moving out there."

"Ya think? Alpacas are shifty. They blend. They crawl. They can be upon you before you know they're even there. The whole pack."

"How come I never heard of anything as dangerous as that?"

"I guess you're not a mountain girl." He felt a moment of real concern. "On the other hand, of course, the creatures or their bosses or whatever are probably watching." He tried to penetrate the far, high passes with his gaze. "And if the village does have a spy . . ." He shrugged.

"Nobody left during the night or this morning."

"That doesn't mean they won't. They'll play it safe. Fetch water. Hunt. Whatever it is they do." He half-laughed, realizing he had no idea how the villagers subsisted beyond farming the land. "Of course, we're being stupid. A spy would have a cellphone."

"Not much service out here."

"A satellite phone," Drake amended. "Maybe we should ask—" He clamped his mouth shut, realizing he'd been about to finish the sentence with the words "Karin to trace it." A torrent of past images rushed through him; images of people they'd lost and faces long gone. Kennedy, Sam, Jo and Ben. They lived only when he remembered them now, only when he let them.

"I wonder where Karin is?" he asked.

Alicia seemed to catch a tension in his voice. "What do you mean? Training, isn't she?"

"Karin finished her training two weeks ago. Nobody I know has heard from her since."

Alicia pursed her lips. "You know she's Army now, right? They could have sent her out on an op."

"That wasn't the deal. And it's basic training. Not Shaolin Monk 99th Dan."

"It's basic army training at Fort Bragg. Special Forces. Rangers. That ain't basic at all."

"I guess . . ." Drake tailed off.

"You're worried about her, I get it. But this is Karin. When she surfaces she'll get a hold of us." Alicia grinned. "She's family."

Drake grinned back as a cold rush of wind scoured his face. Of course, Alicia was right. What surprised and elated him was her newfound reasoning, her ability to see the good in people where until recently she'd have found only the negatives in that conversation. It convinced him to pull ahead with her and whisper something else. "And something else has been bugging me for a while now."

Alicia crinkled her nose. "Ah, Matt, I know exactly what you're gonna say."

"You do? How could you?"

"Because it's on all our minds. Branded there with a hot iron. I think of it as Webb's legacy. I wonder who's embarrassed all the time. Who cries themselves to sleep. Who killed their parents. Who is dying." She took a breath. "But most important—who's a bloody lesbian?"

Drake shook his head. "It's not you, is it?"

"Depends on the female. I guess I could be persuaded."

Drake considered asking for a list, then remembered the track of their conversation. "So you do wonder about Webb's legacy?"

"We all do. No doubt."

"It should be . . . addressed. It shouldn't hang over the team forever."

"Yeah, but then I guess you weren't one of the people Webb spoke of. If you were . . ." She shrugged.

Drake nodded in agreement. "I guess you're right. The other side, of course—Webb has a stash of nasty revelations somewhere which we haven't even started searching for."

"I prefer not to think of it. Joking aside, some of those revelations could kill us. Or put us on the run from the law." She looked worried.

Drake saw Kimbiri appear up ahead and fought off the feelings raised by Webb's legacy. Villagers had already seen them and were hotfooting it back to the houses. As they grew closer he saw a crowd gathered on the outskirts, Kinimaka, Smyth, Mai and Yorgi among them. His heart lifted to see his friends.

He slowed, allowing Hayden and Conde to catch up. Kimbiri's villagers stood stoic, their faces weatherbeaten and grim, their outlook worse. As the two groups came together the wind started to blow harder, scouring the lands and exposed flesh, tugging at warm clothing as if in anger. A howl went up among the distant mountains, causing most sets of eyes to glance up there.

A wolf maybe. Or something else.

"The mountains," Conde said. "Kept their secrets for millennia. I wonder why they couldn't keep them just a while longer."

"These things aren't from the mountains," Drake said. "Not until recently. They're man-made."

The two groups joined and exchanged greetings. Brynn stepped up to help translate for her people as Hayden quickly explained the events of the night before. Nobody seemed surprised and nobody expressed concern other than in their faces. Hardy lives bred hardier responses.

"We have all lost people," Conde said. "Now we need to find them. And end the attacks on our families and their homes."

"The creatures will be planning their next move," Emilio, the leader of Kimbiri, said through Brynn. "A response or a harsher attack. We cannot trust anyone. We tried the police of Cusco. Nothing happened. We try again." He shook his head. "We are alone. But these people. These soldiers. They have helped, yes, but even they are here for something. What is it that you want, soldiers?"

Conde looked a little uncomfortable with the question, no doubt since it was his village the soldiers had helped the night before, but Drake saw Hayden take it at face value.

"As we said, initially we came to the mountains to ask for your help. There is a chateau in this area, and a man that lives a quiet life. We believe he is stealing and selling local treasures. If you know of him . . ." She spread her hands.

No reactions were forthcoming. Brynn said, "It is a large area."

Hayden shifted. "We are soldiers. But we shouldn't be here. Sometimes, we operate without sanction, and without a local government's knowledge. The truth? This was supposed to be a quick in-and-out op. We never expected to stay."

"So the Americans are coming?" Conde asked. "To save us?"

"Ah. No. Our bosses don't know we stayed," Hayden admitted. "Nobody is coming. They wouldn't risk it even if we asked."

"And we could be called back at any moment," Smyth put in harshly. "So let's say we get on with this, eh? Some of us are missing our . . . friends."

"We do not need your help," Brynn said with a great deal of pride. "Now that we know of Nuno's position, we can join our forces. We can fight them off."

Drake studied the assembled faces, the fear, the youth, the rictus-like smiles that barely held up. "It will not be easy."

Alicia fiddled with her jacket. "They are strong because their numbers are strong."

Brynn's gaze never faltered. "We can win."

At that moment a young man stepped forward. Drake guessed he would be in his mid-teens. The youth stood right before Brynn and held her stare with his own. In halting English for the benefit of the soldiers he said, "At night we hear . . . screaming? Yes, screaming . . . from the mountains. We see far away lights . . .

marching. The creatures bring the darkness, but they vanish toward the lights. Those mountains . . . are haunted."

Drake nodded. "I understand why you might think that."

The youth whirled, grabbed Drake's arm and pulled. "No! They are haunted. Do not go there. You have to believe me!"

Alicia reached out for the youth but Mai was quicker. The Japanese woman knelt on the floor so their eyes were level. "Have you been up there, my friend? Have you seen the ghosts?"

The quivering started in his shoulders and went right down to his knees. Mai held on tight, practically holding him up.

"What have you seen?"

"Evil," he whispered, biting his lips until the blood ran red. "The most terrible evil."

CHAPTER SEVENTEEN

Alicia fought hard to sift through the swirling eddy of emotion that pounded at her. Only recently returned from a side mission in the Caribbean where she'd lost one of her own, she still struggled to process the young man's death. Thrust into this new operation, at first a swift mission, now more akin to a rescue or search and destroy exercise, she had begun to feel a little overwhelmed. And with the presence of Drake and Mai, and the ongoing complications within the team, she battled the increasing urge to cut loose.

You can't abandon the villagers.

Is that the only reason you're staying?

No, she stayed for Drake and the rest of her new family. Even friggin' Mai. Because even the runt deserved some loyalty. She stayed because she felt and embraced a duty to do so. Nevertheless, she couldn't help but worry about her other team and how they were coping. It didn't help that the lands around here were as hostile as the goddamn enemy, and even the wildlife was deadly. Not that she'd laid eyes on anything yet. Only heard the distant cry of wolves.

She ended up sitting with Kinimaka. "How's it going? Hayden still being a bitch?"

The Hawaiian was retying his laces, probably to make sure he didn't fall over them. "You can be very blunt, can't you?"

"Shit, piss off. Me? Nah, I'm a motherfucking princess."

"Funny. I've never seen that quality."

"You should look a bit deeper. Outside, yeah I'm nasty. Dangerous, hot and immensely shaggable, but inside . . ." She paused, thinking. "Well, I dunno. Maybe ask Drake."

"Hayden and I are done, to answer your initial question."

Alicia heard a call, then rose and offered a hand. "Then move on."

"Easy for you to say." Kinimaka heaved up, using the house at his back for balance and then gauging it as if to make sure it wasn't about to fall down. "Moving on for me means literally moving on."

Alicia looked to where Drake and Hayden were assembling a team. "The team would be damaged without you, Mano."

"You left. Once or twice."

She winced. "Yeah, and I came back."

"We always worked well together."

She steered him toward the group. "You two made a good team before you started doing the Pork Sword dance. You could be still."

"She's not the same."

"We all change, Mano. Get used to it. But she'll change again, have no doubt. And maybe you'll be there for that." She gripped his arm as they came within earshot if the group. "If you want to be."

Alicia took in the scene. The SPEAR team stood around in reserved silence, weapons prepared, packs full, warm coats and hats and other equipment at the ready. The young man that had seen the mountain's ghosts stood with his head held high and his eyes wide, looking every which way except toward the mist-shrouded heights. Two grown-ups were with him—the boy's parents. The debate had centered around the boy's knowledge and necessity, but when Hayden finally pointed out that he'd be safer with the team than back at the village, the tone soon changed. Several volunteers were offered. A new debate threatened to start up. It was Mai and Brynn that pointed out that the morning was wasting away and if the trekkers didn't want to be out after dark then they should get going.

Alicia fell in next to Drake, looking into the village from the outskirts. Narrow paths wound between houses, funneling the winds. Most of the inhabitants and Conde stood in the crowd of watchers, facing the mountains and its terrors. In truth, they had placed an awful lot on the boy and his daring past act, but even Emilio and Clareta vouched for him, and the way he spoke convinced them even further.

He knew something. And some kind of trauma was keeping him silent.

Alicia kept a sharp eye on the terrain as they headed for the lowest point between two mountains. Their slopes looked brown from this distance, almost barren, but the closer they came the more she began to see an abundance of small green bushes and trees. Clear trails meandered up toward the heights, passing a few brave, solitary farmhouses along the way. The ground was rocky, uneven, threatening to give way at every step. They traversed the path between mountains and then began to climb the eastern slope, rising gradually. The village grew small below and then the trail wound around to the northern slope and it fell out of sight.

Hayden called a brief watering stop and took the time to ask the boy if he'd been able to keep his bearings. For the first time he looked confident and a little haughty.

"Of course. I was born here."

The morning waned and soon became afternoon. Deeper into the mountains they went, one slope merging with the next until even Alicia had to concentrate hard to remember the way back. Trouble was, everything looked the bloody same once you were up here. A deep chill saturated the air, making her draw her jacket close around her.

"Any chance we can stop for a bite to eat?" Kinimaka panted at last. "I'm famished."

"Seconded." Alicia slapped Drake across the shoulders. "Did you pack the sarnies, dear?"

The Yorkshireman sighed but dug out a pack of rations. They wouldn't eat the villagers' food; not until they had to. Three gulps and the meal was gone. Kinimaka looked nothing less than miserable. Smyth was chomping at the bit, eyes probing the landscape as if his head were in the game, but Alicia guessed where his thoughts were really at. Yorgi was keeping quiet as usual and Mai was staying close to the kid, offering support where need be. Alicia thought of a few motherly digs but decided now was not the right time.

The mountains held jealously to a depth of silence that had a striking resonance all of its own. Alicia felt small and insignificant, walking among its timeless slopes, an emotion she hadn't entertained for some time. She kept her eyes on the vast landscape.

"Do you think the kid's lost?" she asked Drake quietly. "We've been out here for hours now and he made this journey at night."

"It was here," the boy then said aloud. "It was all around here."

He pointed toward a cairn off to the right, a man-made mass of stones in the shape of an upside-down ice cream cone.

"I was close. Too close. I heard one of them talk. Just one. He called this the Feasting Trail."

Alicia glared at the waymark as if it might be intimidated into giving up all of its secrets. "What the hell does that mean?"

"I hid here," he said, pointing near the base of the stones where the grass was flattened. "Over a week ago. I told nobody. I . . . I . . ." His lower lip quivered.

Mai bent over, placing a knee on the yellowish ground. "You are safe now. You can speak. Tell us what you saw, my friend."

Haunted eyes fixed solely on hers. "The trail went that way." He gestured without looking. "Winding upward and marked by torchlight that flickered. Because the lights were bright I could make out what was underneath . . ." He swallowed, looking white and sick.

Drake shared a glance with Alicia. She gestured toward Smyth and Yorgi. "Maybe you guys should secure the perimeter. Just in case."

The boy struggled to speak, tears in his eyes. "Body parts," he forced out. Each standing torch lit a pile of . . ." He choked and Mai told him not to go on. Alicia drew a heavy breath and followed the trail with her eyes. They should see signs of scorching up ahead—something to follow—and perhaps even some remains. She didn't voice the obvious questions—whose bodies? Were they the creatures or were they the villagers? Or perhaps others? It was enough that the boy had led them here after witnessing such a horror.

He wasn't yet done.

"Far, far along," he said. "Up there. The lights glowed bright and were steady. The Feasting Trail led that way, though I went no further. In my nightmares I see it as their home."

"Did you see what happened to the body parts?" Kinimaka blurted out. "I mean—it's an odd way to mark a trail. Are you sure they were real?"

Hayden frowned at the Hawaiian, about to admonish his thoughtlessness, but the boy latched onto Mano's words. "I watched only for a little while before I ran, but the mountain spiders or whatever you call them, stopped by each fire and lifted the remains. That's how I knew what they were. They seemed . . . they seemed to carry them away."

Alicia felt revulsion twist her face. "Senseless and twisted," she said. "I don't understand this at all."

"They are the ghosts of the mountains," the boy said. "I told you so."

"Ghosts don't leave a trail." Mai stared into the middle distance. "Let's see if these guys do."

Together, they headed out, gathered protectively around the boy. Smyth found a small hole in the earth a hundred meters distant. The grass was spotted black all around, the dirt charred. With utter care now they moved forward, easily finding another three torch-holes. The path bent outward toward the edge of the mountain.

Coming around the curve of the slope they saw Yorgi had stopped and was staring at the ground. Alicia, Drake and Hayden went forward, leaving the others behind. The Russian looked up as they approached, distaste on his face.

"Another hole in the earth," he muttered. "And this."

Alicia cursed inwardly. A blackened foot lay on the ground, partially rotten; the flesh torn and ragged. Hayden pinched the bridge of her nose.

"What the hell is going on, guys?"

Smyth came up, glaring at the foot as if it were a rattlesnake. "When in the mountains," he said. "Keep your gaze up high."

Alicia saw it then; above them and clinging to the side of the next rocky rise, perched on the slope of the mountain several hundred meters distant.

"Is that . . . a house?" Drake asked. "Too far to make it out properly."

"These things have to live somewhere."

"I was thinking more like a cave. A nest, maybe."

Alicia didn't want to ask if he was joking. The house appeared to be built on three levels, with towers jutting at either end and a front wall from which a steep pathway delved down toward the valley below. "We should get closer," she said. "Do a proper reccy."

Hayden checked her watch. "No time for that," she said. "Unless you wanna be out here for the night. In any case, the boy doesn't and we must respect that."

"Plus," Drake nodded, "I think they've already seen us. Just saw the glint of binos. I don't like it, but I think we should all head back to the village and dig in. hopefully, they won't raid tonight, but we should prepare."

"We know where they are now." Smyth's lip curled with satisfaction.

Alicia regarded him. "You fancy going in there? I know I don't."

"It's a den of evil and no mistake," Kinimaka said. "We should prepare for anything. Anything at all."

Alicia turned away, seeing Mai still shielding the boy from the worst of it all. "It's the villages around here we should worry about," she said. "We can't protect them all."

"Information," Drake said, "is the key. Surely somebody knows all about this house and who owns it. Someone in Cusco. Shit, it could even be our chateau."

Hayden coughed. "You only just made that connection, dude?"

"Well, now we have a location and pictures." He pulled out his cellphone and took several snaps. "Looking at the position it must have a helipad. Unless the guy's a . . ." he stopped, staring, then finished. "A recluse."

"With an army of pet spiders," Alicia added. "That terrorizes the local villages."

Drake shook his head in disbelief. Alicia knew exactly what he was thinking. *We stumbled into some mega-crazy shit this time.*

CHAPTER EIGHTEEN

They returned to Cusco the following morning, having spent an uneventful and sleepless night in Kimbiri. Alicia, Drake and Mai ranged far and wide during the dark hours, but never saw any lights in the mountains, and no signs of trouble falling upon Nuno. The return trip was perfunctory, focused and businesslike, the vistas and the cool winds making no impression on the team. The focus was all on what they would do in Cusco.

Hayden reminded them of Joshua and the Cusco Militia, now eleven strong and made up of influential people from all walks of life. Smyth gave the ground hard eyes when reminded of Joshua, full of conflict. Kinimaka remained quiet, offering no counsel. Drake again found himself wondering how it would all wash out.

"The CIA gave us a list," Drake reminded them all. "Two men haven't been questioned yet."

"I'd like to get to the heart of this militia," Hayden said. "And wrench it out. What they're doing to the villagers is unacceptable."

"At least," Smyth grunted.

"A return visit to the CIA?" Alicia suggested.

"Let's start with the two we already know about. The CIA might be wary after Joshua," Drake led the way back to a vehicle and then sat in the back as Smyth drove. The team were understandably subdued, their thoughts and emotions being tugged a dozen different ways.

Cusco sprawled before them under a leaden sky, its far reaches climbing a gentle incline. They bypassed the tourist areas and headed straight for the rougher parts, seeking out the two men—one called Bruno and the other Desi. Earlier information had given them a place to look and clear photographs. It took a monotonous hour to find Bruno's pad, and then the humdrum task of surveillance began.

Nothing moved in Bruno's house. The drapes were drawn, the doors and gates all locked. "Night birds sleep late," Hayden said, and sent Yorgi and Smyth out for sustenance and drinks. There was a time when Kinimaka would have volunteered—today all he asked for were donuts.

They split surveillance—one team on Bruno, the other on Desi. The houses were only ten minutes apart. As morning became afternoon and then wore on, Drake began to worry. The return trip to Kimbiri wasn't long but they wanted to be back before nightfall. Mai voiced a similar concern and then Alicia finally saw her last thread of patience unravel.

"Fuck this," she said. "I'll wake the bastard up."

The purpose of the stakeout wasn't only to establish Bruno's position, it was to determine if he was alone.

"Wait. He could have—"

A voice crackled over the comms. "Still nothing here."

"Let her try." Mai waved Alicia out the door. "He'll think she's a hooker."

"That's the idea, Sprite. You'd best stay here since I'm thinking quality stands a better chance."

Drake winced at both digs. The pair hadn't had much opportunity to fight through the last few days, but the antagonism certainly hadn't diminished. The team prepped as Alicia strode up to the front door, removing her jacket and stuffing her weapons behind her back, into her waistband. It was makeshift and it was messy, but would hopefully distract Bruno for the few seconds required.

Alicia pounded at the door, undoing her shirt now. Drake slid out of the car, surveying the street. Very little moved up and down the road; parked cars stood at the curb and a few dogs barked. A young child rode a scooter in the distance.

"Shit, how far's she gonna go?" Kinimaka asked a bit worriedly.

Drake looked up. "Alicia? All the way, mate, as usual."

With the shirt unbuttoned half way, Alicia popped the button on her trousers, letting the two ends hang apart. She tied her shirt up, struck a pose and pounded again. Let her hair down. Pouted. By the time a figure moved behind the front door's opaque glass panel she was inching down her trousers and when Bruno shouted out she simply put both her lips to the glass and kissed hard.

"You wanna open up, big boy? Then you can open me up."

Bruno had the door unlocked in less than a second, falling over himself as he made out the blond figure. On seeing her properly he drew breath. Drake saw his lips move but couldn't make out the words. Alicia held all the man's attention as Hayden, Mai and he closed in. Their weapons drawn, they paused at the side of the house, and heard Alicia's spiel.

"How much? Well, I dunno, man. You alone? How do you measure up in the sausage department?"

"Yeah, I'm alone and better than most." A throaty reply.

"Well, whip it out, big boy. Let's take a look."

Funny how Alicia even managed to turn the tables of prostitution so that she was the one in charge. Drake wasn't surprised though. Of course she would. The second Alicia started laughing he knew it was time to move. The team surged around the corner, weapons raised, then ran past Bruno, pushing the man back into his own house. Mai and Hayden wasted no time checking the interior rather than relying on his word, but the rest of the small space was empty. The inside smelled of sweat and beer. Alicia opened a few windows, pretending to choke. Drake drove the man back into his own sofa, allowing him to fall, but kept his hands in plain sight.

Hayden approached him from the right. "Bruno. We know you. We know the rest of the Cusco Militia. But you're a lucky man today. Tell us what we need to know and we'll let you live."

"Americans?" Bruno grunted. "Americans go fuck yourselves."

Drake heard a crackle over the comms and listened as Kinimaka explained how the second team had cornered Desi at the dark end of a side alley. Their interrogation would have to be short and discreet, but it was ongoing.

Alicia stalked over, raised a knee and planted her foot on the sofa close to his groin. She leaned forward. "What? You don't want me now?"

"Dunno. You don't sound American."

"Funny guy." Alicia slapped his face so fast he didn't even blink. But he did raise a hand to his cheek in the aftermath, eyes watering.

"I normally charge extra for that," Alicia assured him with a smile.

Hayden leveled her Glock at his face from the other side. "No charge for this," she said. "I'd be happy to do it."

Mai came to Drake's shoulder, making him suddenly hyperaware of the concentrated female strength present within the room. These were the strongest women he'd ever met and, sometimes despite even themselves, the best intentioned. He watched Bruno's eyes flit from one to the next, finally settling on Drake as if seeking a male connection. But Drake only shrugged.

"Tell 'em what they need, pal," he said. "Maybe you'll live."

"But you are going to hospital," Alicia growled. "That's a given."

"I have done no wrong!"

"We know about the Cusco Militia." Hayden tapped his temple with the Glock. "Pay attention."

Bruno looked like a rabbit trapped in the headlights. "You know what happened to Joshua?"

"They'll never find the body," Hayden said shortly. "What will happen to yours?"

"I am small part." Bruno showed them an inch gap between thumb and forefinger, making Alicia laugh.

"I already saw that." She snorted.

"In militia," he said desperately, looking from Hayden to Alicia to Mai. "Not even enforcer. I transport." He mimed the driving of a wagon and then a long, winding road. "I plan. I deliver."

"Logistics?" Drake said. "I guess that makes sense. Most of what these guys are into will need moving around, from goods to bloody people."

"You are one of the twelve though," Hayden said. "So you will answer our questions."

Bruno nodded unhappily.

"The chateau in the mountains," Hayden said. "Who the hell owns it?"

Bruno frowned excessively. "The sha . . . two?" He wrapped his tongue around the word thickly.

"The big house," Drake amended. "On the side of the mountain."

"Ah, it is said to belong to quiet man called Dantanion. Never see him. He send his people to town."

"We already know that." Drake wondered now if they might be able to tie both cases together. "Do these people try to sell relics? Inca treasure?"

Bruno shook his head without hesitation. "No. They buy food. Only important things. To live with." He struggled to describe it but Drake guessed he was trying to describe the everyday essentials of living.

"Soap," he said. "Medication . . . tablets? Food. Drink. Clothing. That sort of thing?"

"Yes, yes. But mostly best they can buy. They have much money."

"And these people?" Alicia said. "Would you say they look less like human beings and more like . . . spiders?"

Bruno gawped. "I do not know what you mean. They young and old. No talk. No smile. Just people."

Alicia looked around at Drake. "Two separate cases?"

Hayden coughed. "How many houses exist out in the mountains near Kimbiri and Nuno?" she asked. "I mean modern, expensive ones?"

"Or indeed, modern, humble ones," Mai added with thought.

"Only one that I know of," Bruno said. "Dantanion's. Cusco knows of the house but not the owners. All the rest—homesteads. Farms. Old families."

Drake saw the tension in the shoulders, the tightness of the lips and the way Bruno refused to look anyone in the eye. He supposed it could all be down to Alicia's treatment of his manhood, but somehow doubted it.

"You're lying," he said. "You know more about this Dantanion's house than you're letting on. Give it up, mate. It ain't worth upsetting Alicia for."

The blonde's boot planted itself in his chest and then traveled dangerously lower. Hayden backed it up with another thump of the temple, the Glock striking dully.

Bruno winced. "You will not believe me."

"In your defense I totally understand why you might think that, but tell us anyway."

Bruno shifted uncomfortably, glancing down at Alicia's dirty boot. "I know little of Dantanion. They say so little. He is tall; he is good; he is a god. He is their leader. He provides for all. Yah, yah." He made his hand talk. "Yah, yah. For sure he is a mystery. To have such power over people."

"Go on." Alicia ground her heel.

"Ow. Be careful, bitch. This Dantanion—some in Cusco believe he is today's Dracula," Bruno started laughing. Drake noticed, however, that the noise was forced. He watched the man carefully.

"So the dopey twats think he's drinking blood, eh?" But the memories of the Feasting Trail and what they had found there prodded his mind like the smooth knob of a stripped bone.

"Not that. Not blood." Bruno stopped laughing now, and a slightly hysterical intake of breath filled his lungs. "That house. It has been there for a three centuries . . . clinging," he struggled with the word as if he'd heard it from another, "clinging to the cliffs like some . . . some ravenous spider from before history. Three times, it has been home to men. Three times." Bruno swallowed drily. "In mid-1800s thousands of Chinese came here, and one legendary noble. Fingers like knives, they say. Face like plastic that warped. Always wore a red and gold robe. He owned the house and filled it with peasants; threw them from the walls for his pleasure. Burned them for fun. Brought with him this, opium? Something like that. They say clouds melted the snow above his house. But when he started taking locals—not Chinese—somebody started a revolution. An attack. They killed the man and shunned the house, leaving it empty for a hundred years."

Alicia leaned back, amused. "First he won't talk. Now you can't get a word in edgeways. Must value his hazelnuts."

Hayden picked up on something. "You say the house is three hundred years old? But it looks modern."

Bruno nodded. "Dantanion used his people to make it new," he said. "Even use local builders before cut off."

"Who else owned the place?" Mai wondered.

Bruno blanched. "Drug trafficker. It was what you call? House of horrors?"

"Haunted?" Mai tried.

"No, no. He made it house of horrors. I heard from my grandfather, who cleaned there. Whole rooms full of blood to wipe down. Chains and hooks in roof, still with flesh . . ."

"Ok, man," Hayden interrupted. "We've heard enough of the damn house. What about this Dantanion who lives there now? His people? What's going on there today?"

"It is . . . shameful. Appalling." Bruno shook his head, adamant despite Alicia's warning look.

"Worse than what you just told us?" Drake forced a laugh. "C'mon, pal."

Bruno sniffed, eyes as wide as Frisbees and glazed over with fear. "Flesh eaters," he all but whispered. "They eat the flesh of the living."

Drake stared, mouth open but every cognitive process dammed. Alicia pulled her boot away as if Bruno was suddenly diseased.

Hayden pinched the bridge of her nose. "What did you say?"

"You hear me, lady. You hear me well. A cult of flesh eaters. That is what lives in that house now. And you wish to go there." He spat to the side.

"And Dantanion is what?" Drake found his voice. "The Cannibal King?"

Bruno nodded, not seeing the sarcasm only wallowing in fear. His whisper was barely audible. "That, yes. Exactly that. Not a man. A demon. A flesh eater and a chief. In Cusco they warn their children to go early to sleep lest Dantanion the Mountain Demon comes to claim them."

Alicia audibly gulped. "And the spiders?"

Bruno frowned, and then his voice dropped several octaves lower. "What spiders?"

"Never mind," Hayden said quickly, much to Drake's relief. No matter what you believed, no matter the realities you saw, there were always certain scenarios and creatures and beliefs—so powerfully felt by others—that challenged all you knew.

"You say members of this cult, of Dantanion's house, come to town?" Somehow Hayden was maintaining her focus. Drake saw again why she ran the team. "On errands. It seems to me that he has to get these people from somewhere. And . . . replenish . . . them. Now, Bruno, you provide transport for the Cusco Militia. We know for a fact that the cops are in Dantanion's pocket. What's the story?"

Bruno shrugged slowly. "I do not know whole story. Just because I am militia, doesn't mean I know everything. But militia . . ." He cringed a little, clearly worried about how much to reveal.

"Tell us," Hayden said. "Or I'll feed you to fucking Dantanion myself."

"They're into everything. Drugs. Weapons. Prostitution." He paused. "Human trafficking."

Drake read between the lines, more on focus now that creepy story corner had passed. "So Dantanion sends out an order? Kinda like we would order a takeaway? And the militia delivers."

Bruno nodded.

Hayden looked interested. "How often?"

"Nothing is regular. No plan." Bruno was starting to look even more fearful as he sensed the questioning was coming to an end. Alicia swapped boots, adding to the anxiety.

Drake wasn't sure what Hayden was thinking, but he laid it out for the team. "So Dantanion pays off the cops, who leave him alone. The militia provide people that maybe get brainwashed into this cult. That about it?"

"Yeah, that's it."

"And Inca relics?" Drake thought it might be worth mentioning again. "Nobody trying to slip a sword or a shield through?"

"We haven't touched the relics in years," Bruno said. "Tourists are everywhere. Government comes down hard if one gets . . . caught up. Most sites are guarded now. It's just too much trouble."

"Not even a vase?" Alicia pushed. "Or one of those phallic symbols?"

"Steady on, love," Drake said. "I'm all the phallic symbol you should need."

"Well, you're not bad. But sometimes a girl just fancies a change, you know?"

"Nothing." Bruno looked between them as if sensing madness. "The militia leave the treasure hunting to the crazies."

That made Drake smile. "The crazies are right here, mate, on your doorstep."

"Even closer than that." Alicia shifted her boot. "We're right on your bollocks."

Hayden leaned about as close to Bruno as she could get. "Don't get comfy, militia man," she said harshly. "We have to get along now, but we know you. What you do. Where you've been. You belong to us now, and we will be back. I have a feeling you're gonna be useful."

"I will try," Bruno said without much enthusiasm.

"You'll be there when we call," Hayden said. "Unless you want me to drop you off, trussed and parboiled, on this whacko's doorstep."

"She will do it too," Mai said.

"Damn fucking right I will."

CHAPTER NINETEEN

The man in the tight-fitting Gucci vest and jogging bottoms ignored his desk as he entered his office. He already knew what would be waiting there; knew from a hundred other days when he'd gone in. Every time he left the office the sous chef rotated the delicacies.

Dantanion crossed over to the window and the view. It filled him anew; it stimulated him, gave life to fresh plans and dreams. Mountainside filled his vision, from the valley below to the heights above. He placed two fingers against the glass as if he could touch its very essence. But the mountains didn't speak to him—the community did.

People working far below. People working next door; in the offices and kitchens. In the bedrooms. In the future, he hoped not to have to procure new people from the filthy hovel of Cusco—he hoped to be self-sufficient.

A plan for the decades, then. And new ways to stop the mass becoming bored. The village raids were unnecessary, but useful for now. It kept the peace; kept the status quo. Gave the masses a goal to work toward and a way to unwind. Dantanion thought about the latest development—a group of armed men in Kimbiri. Was it random or had the villagers hired help? Were his people in Cusco involved? Who were the soldiers?

Dantanion took time to think it all through. Thinking made him hungry. He glanced over at the wall clock—black rim and golden filigree, the hands stood at 4 p.m. It would be a waste of a good appetite to start snacking now. Dinner was in an hour.

The burner cell in his pocket started to ring. Dantanion narrowed his eyes, sensing bad news and feeling the weight of a bad omen settle across the house, weighing it down, pushing at the deep foundations. With trepidation he answered.

"Hello?"

"Tremayne is dead," a voice said. "The last relic is lost."

Dantanion was a man of deep composure and spoke softly. "How did this happen?"

"We are not sure. Hijackers, we think. They have the relic but have disappeared. Now, others are asking questions."

Dantanion stared into space. "What kind of questions?"

"They seek the identity of the seller. These relics—they are lava hot right now. Untouchable. Too many, too soon. And the people that ask—they are previous middlemen."

Dantanion hadn't seen that coming. He wondered if they could discover his identity. They were ruthless criminals, these middlemen, as capable as any agency. And he only dealt with the best.

"Come home. Your job was to watch Tremayne, which is clearly now complete. Come home and let us feast to your health."

A hesitation. "You don't want me to try tracking the hijackers?"

"I assumed you had tried that already."

"Well, yes. A big, skillful man and an athletic woman. They finished Tremayne and vanished. They must be talented to thwart our efforts."

Dantanion was briefly reminded of the supposed soldiers now residing in Kimbiri, but decided it was all too coincidental. The incidents couldn't be connected. Besides, he had a man in Kimbiri already collecting information.

"Come home," he said, ended the call, and destroyed the burner.

The relics were essential to their existence here, and thus worth any kind of risk. This was all fine when the flags fluttered on your side; but when the wind fell and the material started to catch around the flagpole, then you were looking at a tough unraveling operation. Where to go next? The market for these incredible relics was intensely small, but supremely lucrative. Dantanion knew there were only a handful of people across the globe he could use.

Most of them were now untouchable.

The relics.

Critical items. Without them his astonishing new world would die very quickly. The money they accrued was vital, but it poured out of his account like water being emptied from a sink. Dantanion was not a man without means, but even his small fortune drained within a year as his community quickly grew. Like a spark to a flame and then a bonfire he could not stop the conflagration, the spread of amazement and love he felt for this newfound society. But as it grew, like any content population, the dangers to it increased. Somebody out there always wanted to take your happiness away.

Whilst surveying and preparing the caves beneath the house for more and more people, Dantanion and his helpers had come across a hidden treasure so vast they could barely believe their eyes. It had lain there for centuries, hidden, untouched. Squirreled away down some narrow passage leading off another narrow passage and another.

It had claimed two lives, but those bodies had ended up fulfilling their destinies. Dantanion blessed them, prepared them and then helped eat them. Below, in the extensive cave network, he housed most of the people, fashioned a medical center to help newcomers switch to a new form of meat, and taught the bravest of his followers how best to occupy their time if they wanted to stay unseen, remain aloof and yet be utterly worshipped at the same time.

He taught them to be monsters.

His vision. His world. When he saw them work together for the first time, scuttling and crabbing and making grown men scream, he felt wonderful. The sacrifice they claimed tasted so much better for it.

The relics!

Ah yes, his mind shied away from the real truth. And the real truth was in that vast treasure hoard. Some careful research and many months passed. Playing devil's advocate with himself he would not at first believe the truth. He questioned it, wrestled it to the ground and stomped on its head.

But the truth won through. The more he read of the old legend the more he believed it. Atahualpa was an Inca king who was captured in his palace, in modern-day Peru, by the Spanish invaders—Pizarro in particular. The Spanish were greedy and brimming over with an insatiable envy for the astounding Inca wealth. The Incas themselves, if they hadn't partaken of dozens of years of internal warfare, might have been better placed to force the Spaniards to retreat. Atahualpa, as great a king and warrior as he was, was taken—locked away by the merciless interlopers. Dantanion recalled reading that a ransom was asked for and willingly raised.

A roomful of gold. Collected piecemeal and properly arranged for Pizarro and then transported over the mountains. But, for reasons unknown, as the world's greatest treasure rumbled ever closer, Pizarro reneged on the deal and put Atahualpa to death. The Incas lost their king and the Spaniards lost their gold. Legends tell that the gold was buried deep in some secret mountain cave, and there it stayed.

To this very day.

Dantanion knew it was the roomful of gold as soon as he read about it. Though not left in situ, the sheer amount of gold, the way it was hidden as if thrown away in anger, and later certain identifiable pieces, told him all he needed to know.

Eternal wealth. Eternal happiness. Solace, solitariness and a new society with common ground, forever.

Dantanion delved further, understanding that such a vast wealth would be commandeered by someone far less scrupulous than himself as well as those that possessed a right to own it. Either way, he would be out of pocket. So, for the good of the community, he found a way.

History surrounding Atahualpa's gold was rich. The Inca king had been well renowned. A Spaniard named Valverde claimed to know the location after Atahualpa's death, became rich and drew a map to the infamous Derrotero de Valverde. And although lost until the 1850s, such a legendary fortune could never vanish entirely from the world—resurrected again and searched for by a man named Blake, the last person ever to set eyes on it.

Never a man led by fancy, Dantanion was pleased to see that Atahualpa's gold was no mere story. It had existed for real, was recorded in the Spanish chronicle, and it was also reported that a large convoy of gold was en route to Pizarro. Beyond that, mystery shrouded the whole effort, and Dantanion doubted that it would ever have been found if not through sheer luck and a desperate desire to make the caves below his house habitable.

And the pieces it contained? Oh, how . . .

Quickly, he derailed his train of thought. Here he sat, facing a new and drastic dilemma, and all he could do was track his gold back to the Inca kings. They had lost; they had died. Internal strife and warfare had weakened them. But not him. Not Dantanion. The kingdom he built would prosper and grow.

A series of small chimes rang out from an old clock he kept on the table.

It was time to eat.

CHAPTER TWENTY

Dantanion made real conversation with nobody, so it was always with a great air of introspection that he made his entrances. The mind never stopped turning, the conveyor belt of ideas revolving without end. It was no slice of chance that had brought him to these mountains—the Incas had practiced cannibalism as a major part of their culture—but he didn't believe in fate either.

Instead, he believed in solid hard work.

But he changed clothes now. Donned the suit and the long robe, entered the feasting chamber slowly and regally like the leader—like the king—that he was. The long, solid oak table sat empty, surrounded by his people who all bowed as he walked by. A ceiling-height, room-wide picture window to the left had been draped by blackout curtains. Candles flickered in sconces all around the room and now servants brought in more candles, placing them at strategic points on the table.

Dantanion stood at the head of the table. Silence greeted him. Servants bowed and waited, every muscle held rigid.

"It is a good day for a feast," he said.

It started proceedings. The people bowed again and then turned to their neighbors, talking quietly. Many stared at Dantanion, hoping to see a smile of a slight nod. They knew he was reserved and even a brushing over with the eyes often brought out a woman's blushes or a man's smile. He blessed a few now. The servants brought out table mats, then cutlery that Dantanion inspected for its sharpness and brightness. As always, it was perfect. The man he had chosen for Kitchen Master was easily the equal of his impeccable head chef.

Next, they brought out empty skulls and set them before every man and woman. Some were filled with water, others with wine. Dantanion accepted a refreshing rosé. His palette changed from time to time, but his hunger for human flesh never dulled.

Today, they had cooked an offering from Nuno. The individual had been properly tended, worshipped and prepared.

Dantanion followed his own ritualistic mix of cannibalism—a perfect link where endocannibalism and exocannibalism met. The first was a form that proved one's power over one's enemy, performed a final humiliation on them and took revenge. The latter was more reverential, enabling one to inherit the strength, proficiencies and achievements of the consumed individual. Dantanion saw the new ritual as a necessary act—an exploit to help make the community bond, to give it power, to furnish it with skill and knowledge, and to make it strong and able to fight for its lands.

There were other rituals that required more belief, but not tonight. For this was a night of feasting and merriment.

Dantanion sat back, worry temporarily eased, as a pungent bouquet of charcoal, oils, dressing and cooked flesh wafted into the room. The far door was open. The servants entered carrying the offering between them—a selection of thigh, chest, breast, neck and brain. The serving tray was a serving table, four servants to each side and walking slowly. Around the sides of the table were arranged the delicacies and after dinner pickings—fingers, toes, shavings of flesh they called "unmentionables", ears, a tongue and other treats—all sautéed with a minimum of dressing to impart maximum flavor.

Carefully, the servants placed the serving table upon the main table, ensuring it was equally rectangle. Dantanion dismissed them and then held aloft the skull that contained the rosé.

"With this feast we gain the strength to overcome our enemies, replenish and renew our knowledge, expand our skills and accept new successes. We give thanks to the offering for giving their essence and all that they were, to nourish and sustain us."

The community intoned, "We give thanks to the offering for giving their essence and all that they were, to nourish and sustain us."

Glasses raised and were drained. Servants rushed to refill.

Razor sharp knives were raised, their blades glittering red and gold by the light of the flickering flames.

By ritual, Dantanion took the first cut.

CHAPTER TWENTY ONE

One more opportunity to put her life in her hands. One more chance to make amends. One more dance with Torsten Dahl—and then she could happily die.

Kenzie corrected herself very quickly. She didn't want to die. At least not today. Not whilst the Swede wavered between sex and love, and not whilst his lonely wife decided between love and divorce.

The choice, however, was well and truly out of her hands.

Fully prepped. Fully loaded, they came. Dahl toting two Smith and Wessons, a HK semi-auto, and Sig-Pro semi-auto handgun. The extra ammo weighed his small rucksack down. Were they expecting trouble? Kenzie grimaced.

She carried similar weaponry, but with the addition of an old friend.

Dahl eyed it now as he pulled the car over into a dusty lay-by. "You really think you need that thing?"

Kenzie sighed. "Tell me, would you leave your penis behind if you were going on a date?"

Dahl faltered. "Umm . . ."

"No, of course not. Because sometime during the night it might be useful." She cracked open the car door, pulled the katana out of the back seat and slipped it smoothly into the scabbard attached to her back. "Same here."

"Fair enough then," Dahl muttered.

Kenzie smiled to herself, then took in the view. They were parked in the hills above Monaco, having spent the best part of the last two days in the resplendent city of Monte Carlo. Just beyond the wheels of the car the cliff dropped away, rock and scrub and boulders littering the way down toward the topmost tier of the city. Below, the French Riviera's most famous streets meandered through the main town, passing by casinos, restaurants and designer boutiques, with the sparkling jewel of the Mediterranean spreading as far as the eye could see.

"I could imagine being on one of those yachts," she said, shading her eyes against the sun and the glare. "Lazing in the harbor."

"Yeah." Dahl paused for a moment to look. "Just a small one though. Nothing ostentatious."

"Of course," Kenzie acknowledged. "Nothing over ten mil."

They both laughed and shared a look. Being alone and having to rely on each other these past days, spending the nights talking and imbibing, had created a strong bond between them. Kenzie would take it further, but Dahl continued to hold off for his marriage, and now she respected him even more for that. Despite all the shit they went through, time and again, some of these people still managed to hold down normal relationships.

Good fortune to them.

Kenzie did stare hard into those blue eyes though, enjoying the spark of friendship she saw there. "It's been fun, Torst. Sharing this mission with you."

The Swede smiled, and then turned serious. "Agreed. So let's concentrate now, end it and go home in one piece."

She continued to drink in the view. "You thought Cyrano and Patric were bad? This guy, Treacle—he's pure evil."

"I can't accept that name."

"He will try to kill us today."

"Many have tried." Dahl moved to her side. "Yet still we stand."

"Love your faith. Maybe being with you will save me after all."

"Always thought so."

"I'm so glad we had this time alone."

Dahl placed a hand on her arm. "You seem certain we're about to die. I never saw that in you before. Is there something you're not telling me?"

"If I had known the almighty buyer of these Inca relics was Treacle I'd never have come," Kenzie admitted. "Now we know he's not only the buyer of almost every relic the seller has offered, he's the buyer we double-crossed back in Nice when we killed Tremayne. And he knows that. If I'm being honest . . ."

Kenzie's brow creased in thought. "I would bet hard that Treacle ended up with every Inca treasure, even the ones he didn't buy, if you get my drift."

"I know you're scared of this guy, and that's not something I've seen in you before."

Kenzie studied the view as if it might be the last thing she would ever see. "Time's almost up."

Their small lay-by, a parking area by the side of the road, might hold four cars if they were parked nose to ass. Dahl had purposely chosen the furthest space to allow a fast getaway. Directly before them now lay one of Monaco's renowned tunnels, carved and cut out of the rock face and leading steadily down toward the bay.

"You think this Treacle person will reveal the line all the way to the seller?" Dahl asked. "Cops? Politicians? Generals? The whole lot just to possess an Inca vase?"

Kenzie cast an eye to the trunk where they had hidden the treasure. "Why not? He's the only person on earth that will know. Plus, he holds most or all of the other pieces. If we're to retrieve them we need him to trust us at least a little bit."

"But you said he would try to kill us."

"Yeah, for sure. Treacle has to do that for appearances' sake. An evil reputation must be maintained."

"Ah, of course. Never thought of it like that."

Kenzie wiped her brow as the sun blazed down. Below, where the tunnel ended and the road swept down toward the town, she could see a toll station and three black SUVs inching through. Two came up fast, their engines roaring whilst the third rolled along at a relaxed pace as if taking in the sights. The first two approached, their engines loud through the tunnel, emerged and pulled off the road, parking behind Dahl, facing the other way. Blacked out windows revealed nothing.

"Keep it skin-tight," Dahl said as the front doors of both vehicles cracked open simultaneously. "We take your lead."

Kenzie loosened the katana at the same time as letting her right hand dangle over her concealed handgun. "I'm ready."

"Surely they won't cause a scene out here. It's too public."

Kenzie said nothing. Treacle was ruthless to the point of absolute ignorance and indifference. The fact was, it was more than a lack of morals, it was a total lack of giving a shit. In Treacle's world, only Treacle ever mattered. All else was expendable dross.

Four men emerged from the two cars, all wearing cut-off T-shirts, sunglasses and baggy jeans. They carried weapons openly, grossly—not just small pistols but machine guns and rifles. One man bounced a hand grenade between both hands whilst smoking a cigarette. Another two bodyguards jumped out of the back and then the man himself appeared.

Blond, shaggy hair, tall, toned body. Late forties, and with a shit-eating grin. Just as she remembered him.

"Awwight, Tweacle?" he drawled smugly. "Lovellly day for it?"

"Still pretending you're a Londoner?" Kenzie shifted only to gain a better vantage. "Have you forgotten you told me you were from Brooklyn?"

Treacle nodded. "Yeah, yeah, Tweacle, I remember. Did we fuck too?"

"If we did you would remember."

"I dunno." The blond head of hair shook. "I fuck a lot."

Men spread out around the cars and the lay-by. Kenzie had noticed that the third vehicle still hadn't emerged from the tunnel. Probably waiting on the other side as a precaution. Cars passed by slowly along the road, hopefully most of them missing the deadly exchange.

"You ready to deal?" she said.

"'Course I am. I'm a dealer aren't I?"

"We have what you want. Do you have the information?"

"This Cyrano." Treacle clearly wanted to slow it down. "Man's a buyer too, yeah? Man found me, now thinks I owe him," Laughter blasted from the offensive mouth. "Wanker . . . and why didn't he want the vase?"

"He did. But we needed you."

" 'Course, 'course," Treacle clearly knew he was important. "Makes sense. But why should I lower meself down to deal with a bint like you?"

"Because I have the relic." Kenzie ignored the offensive word. She'd heard much worse. "And you want it."

"I remember you." Treacle moved closer, his men scrambling to move with him. "Right bitch you were. Angling to gazump me, you were. Bad all over and hot because of it. What happened?"

Kenzie shrugged.

Treacle included Dahl in his gaze for the first time. "Tweacle," he acknowledged the Swede, then spoke to Kenzie. "This big boy bang the bad outta you?"

Not yet, Kenzie wanted to say. *But I will keep trying.* Instead she flexed her fingers and rolled a shoulder, drawing attention to the weapons. "We going to chat all day or deal? I have a roulette table just shouting my name out."

"You and me both, Tweacle. You and me both. How 'bout you give us a flash? That'll please the boys and speed things up."

Kenzie drew her katana faster than a man could draw breath. "How about I chop their knackers into cutlets?"

Treacle coughed, wincing at the image. "Steady on, steady on. No need to be shirty. That's a helluva a blade you got there, Tweacle. Makes me feel almost inadequate. Almost." A sickly smile.

Kenzie made sure the tip of the sword pointed at the floor and was as shielded from passing traffic as was possible. "Who's controlling the new thread of Inca artifacts? Where's it coming from? Who's involved? Now, or we walk."

"You kiddin'? I'd love to watch you walk away."

Treacle's men guffawed. Kenzie waited.

"Tell you what, Tweacle." He held up a thick file and flapped it at her. "I'll make you a deal. You live, you get the information. You die, I'll strip and defile your still warm body. Meet me at the Casino de Monte Carlo in an hour."

The buyer's self-confident grin twisted into a leer of hate. Dahl was fastest of all, drawing a Smith and Wesson and firing into two midriffs. Men twisted, falling. Kenzie swung the katana toward Treacle's arm, but the man was fleet and danced away. Her upswing took a bodyguard across the abdomen, sent the gun he held clattering into the dirt. She continued her swing, allowing the momentum to turn her body and become a mad dash. The car doors were open. A bullet skimmed past her ass. Treacle cheered. Kenzie dived into the front seat as Dahl crouched alongside the wheel and took several pot shots.

"Get in!" Kenzie shouted. "Bastard wants to play, I'll show him how the Mossad fucking play!"

Treacle disappeared into the back seat of his SUV, guards following. Dahl came around and jumped behind the driver's seat. "What the hell is going on?"

"Foreplay," Kenzie muttered. "Now make this bastard squeal."

Dahl gunned the engine. "Which way?"

"Into Monaco, of course."

Dahl scowled. "Where there's a cop on every corner."

Their car squealed as its tires spun in the dirt, spitting gravel out the back straight into the close-parked SUV's rear end. They could hear the pepper-shot clatter even above the engines.

"That'll knock a coat of paint off his insurance," Kenzie joked with a grin.

"Shit, you're enjoying this, aren't you?"

Kenzie stroked the pommel of her katana. "What's not to like?"

"How about near death?" Dahl loosed the car and squealed out into the road, cutting a fine arc and leaving a trail of rubber in his wake.

"Made friends with that asshole a decade ago. He doesn't scare me."

The entrance to the tunnel yawned ahead. Kenzie remembered the third SUV and told Dahl. Behind them, the other two SUVs made a great show of turning around.

"Y'know," Kenzie said as they raced into the tunnel, darkness and then interior light replacing the sun. "All of a sudden, this doesn't feel right."

It was a short tunnel. Already they could see the end.

"You think they're waiting at the other end?"

"No. I think—"

The enormous sound of an explosion and cracks appearing along the roof of the tunnel, the fireball and the flames, told her she hadn't been thinking along the right lines at all.

CHAPTER TWENTY TWO

Kenzie slapped a hand to her mouth in shock. No way was this tunnel going to collapse, but the force of the detonation was sending rubble smashing down from the roof and rolling down the sides. Lights flickered and died, the only illumination intensely bright from the end of the tunnel. Heaps of debris already blocked the way and more was falling down. She saw boulders the size of her head bouncing into the pile, their edges jagged and deadly. She saw an oncoming car swerve to avoid the wreckage, smash into the sidewall and come to a sudden halt, the front end smashed in. She saw the third black SUV parked in a lay-by far ahead.

"There's the asshole who did this," Dahl said at the same time. "Must have rigged some dynamite or something."

More cars were pulling up ahead, people climbing out of their cars and pulling out phones. Kenzie opened her door and started to move.

"Wait!" Dahl launched himself across the front seats, grabbed her shoulders and pulled her back in. She felt the power, the sheer strength of the man and then ended up staring at his chest from less than an inch distant.

"What's the issue?" she said in a muffled voice.

The sound of a hail of rocks smashing down onto the car roof and her door gave her a terrifying answer.

"Oh. It's raining rocks. Why didn't I think of that?"

"Not part of Mossad training?" Dahl swung the door shut and climbed off her.

"Not whilst I was there."

Another hail of rubble clattered down onto the roof. Kenzie saw the first indent appear—a V-shaped delve in the headliner.

"To be honest," Dahl said mildly. "I was expecting more of a sexist comment."

"Were you? From me? Well, Mr. Muscles, you'll be happy to know I've decided to let you and Missus Muscles get back together. I guess you deserve another chance."

Dahl took his eyes away from their dilemma for a moment. "This time . . . it will work."

"I hope so. I'm no marriage breaker."

A rock the size of her fist smashed against the windshield, causing the glass to give and a spider web tracery of cracks to race away from the epicenter.

Then she saw all four doors of the SUV open. Armed men wearing T-shirts jumped out, looking up at the shattered tunnel entrance. One of them spotted their car and pointed.

"We're gonna have to risk it," Dahl said. "These people up ahead are gonna get hurt."

Kenzie kicked at her door, forcing a small pile of rubble to topple away. An errant stone fell from the roof and bounced off her shoulder, causing her to wince in pain. Just the shadow of what could have been. Dahl squeezed out the other side. Between them and the exit now stood a knee-height pile of rocks and a steadily pouring pebble-and-shale shower.

"Move!" Dahl shouted at the milling car drivers. "Get out of here!"

He ran hard for the exit and Kenzie followed, spurred on by his bold moves. The stony waterfall bounced off them, drawing blood here and there but not even slowing them down. The final obstacle was more serious. Dahl paused.

Raised his gun and fired. "Only way to get 'em all moving."

"It works for Jessica Ennis and Usain Bolt." Kenzie peered over an unsteady boulder.

Dahl turned to her. "You're a sports fan?"

"Only my entire life."

"And what are your thoughts on the Swedish football team?" He fired another shot as people raced for their cars or decided to duck behind them.

"Didn't know they had one. In truth though, I'm more of an athletics girl."

"Fencing?"

She watched the blatant enemy advance. "Get out of here. They poke each other with matchsticks."

"I hear there's some skill involved."

"Yeah, probably when they glue them together to build a tower."

With the coast clear, Kenzie used the rubble pile as a barricade and leaned over, gun in hand. Four enemies ran at her, machine pistols poised. She took the first shot, bullet blasting wide. The return came at once, lead stitching a line across the tunnel above her head. Running and firing wasn't their strong suit then. Dahl took his time, kneeling and aiming; his first shot sent the lead man jerking to the side. Kenzie fired once more. Again her bullet found thin air instead of hot flesh.

"Not one for the clay pigeon event then?"

"Up close is where it's at. Your wife will probably agree."

She kicked herself for her bluntness, striving for a more agreeable manner. It was the damn Swede that was trying to bring on the change. He shouldn't bear the brunt. A clatter of gunfire sent her beneath the barricade, with bits of stone spitting off the top. One bullet managed to blast right through the piled stone and shattered the front grille of their car, reaffirming just how fragile her grip on life remained. She saw Dahl fire once more and curse, then popped her head up.

Three gunmen still coming, guns switched to auto.

Instinct sent her ducking, covering, scrambling to the left to change position. A man jumped over the barricade, shooting down at the position she'd recently occupied. She rose fast, swung her shoulders and unleashed the katana.

The blade chopped down through his arm, parting him from the gun and sending a look of horror across his features.

"What?"

"You tried to kill me first." When the next man climbed over she wasted no time and no mercy shooting him in the head. She saw Dahl fall away from a man who jumped to the top of the entire barrier, gun blazing, then somehow manage to kick the rocks out from beneath him. The barrier shivered and then collapsed, the man falling among the stones.

Dahl finished him, then waved at Kenzie. Together, they flew over the rubble and charged the SUV. It saw them coming and turned to speed back down the hill. Dahl faltered. Kenzie stowed her weapons and took a wild look around.

"We have about thirty minutes," she said. "Then we lose Treacle forever."

Dahl grunted. "Oh, I love hearing those sentences we never expected to utter," he said. "But they work better with kids. Put the dinosaur back in the conservatory." He was casting around, searching for the bare bones of a plan as he spoke. "Granddad, Mum and Dad say we can't talk about your fat belly anymore. Shit, I just trod on a crocodile . . ."

Kenzie took a moment to stare down the side of the nearest cliff, over Monaco. "Time's ticking."

"Yeah, and so is that beast."

Dahl sounded so happy, Kenzie immediately whirled her head around. The Swede was galloping—no, more like frolicking—in the direction of a deep blue car with an imposing shape. Kenzie chased after him.

"So this makes you happy? A Maserati?"

Dahl's head spun around so fast it almost turned three hundred and sixty degrees. "You like cars too?"

"I've sometimes been called a petrolhead."

"I knew there was something about you. Who gives a fuck that you're a trained killer? If we can talk about cars for an hour, we're mates forever."

Kenzie made a pained face as she caught up to him, not entirely sure she wanted to be the Swede's "mate". Not in the sense he meant anyway. Her father had been a car lover, and thus so had her brother, but good memories of them caused bad endings to re-emerge. Like predators, they were never far from the surface.

Dahl smiled at the man behind the wheel. "Sorry, mate. Need your car. I really will try to treat it well, but failing that, please know these things are happiest being driven hard."

Kenzie opened the other door and popped her head inside. "Aren't we all?"

The man, eyes already wide, noticed the katana and leapt past Dahl, leaving the driver's seat open. "Cheers, mate," the Swede called and jumped in.

Kenzie seated herself in the passenger side. "Nice of him."

"Fasten your seat belt."

"Yes, Dad."

A dirty, deep growl came from the exhausts as Dahl trod on the accelerator, returned to the barricade so Kenzie could hop over and retrieve the Inca vase from their old car's trunk, spun the car around and sent it shooting down the hill toward Monaco. Kenzie guessed they had about twenty minutes to reach the casino.

"Best step on it," she said. "See what a GranSport can really do."

Another tunnel stood ahead. Dahl floored the gas pedal all the way through, breaching the redline of the rev counter, seeing the kph climb past one hundred and fifty, and feeling his mouth fall open as the animalistic roar of the tailpipes resounded between concrete walls.

"That's a great friggin' sound," he breathed.

Kenzie took the time to prep their weapons. The road dipped and plunged, sending them through two more tunnels and along a palm-tree lined road with the blue Mediterranean sparkling out to the right. The Maserati blasted past slower cars, its speed and power making a dangerous passing maneuver safe and easy, whipping past the great scenery on its way down to Monte Carlo. The mountain road twisted and turned, dangerous drops to the right one minute, incredible dwellings the next. Cliff faces rose above, dotted with expensive homes. The glittering bay sprawled below, a shimmering accompaniment to the star-studded streets, casinos and hotels it bordered.

Dahl blasted past the outskirts of the city.

"You know where the casino is?"

"It's on the Grand Prix circuit."

Kenzie scowled. That wasn't really an answer, but she guessed to his mind it said everything. The Maserati growled past the bay, shops lining the left-hand side of the road where markings for the F1 starting grid covered the asphalt. Then the road began to climb steeply, first straight and then to the left. Dahl followed it around, slowing as they reached the top and nodding to the right.

"Casino's behind those bloody hoardings. Looks like workmen have blocked the main entrance off."

They followed the route around and drove past a pair of policemen to get to the casino's other entrance. Kenzie laid eyes on the famous venue for the first time. The casino occupied the short end of a long rectangle; the Hotel de Paris one of the long sides. The facades were stunning blocks of intricate architecture, the entrance to the casino made dark by a jutting overhang. Cars were arranged in front of the entrance, all facing outward in a semi-circle. Crowds milled all around; tourists seated with cameras as if camped there for the day.

Dahl dumped the Maserati next to a blacked-out AC Cobra. "Balls, if we had time I'd snap a picture just to piss Drake off."

Kenzie stashed the katana, figuring the casino staff might have issues on sighting the trusty blade. The pair then locked their handguns and the vase in the glovebox and got lucky by finding that the owner of the car kept his key in the center console. Along with the tracker device. Not clever, but useful for now. Dahl grabbed the key and they left the car cooling, heading for the casino steps.

"Four minutes," Kenzie said.

"Perfect."

Inside, they crossed a wide inner sanctum, surrounded by dark wood paneling and golden fittings, to a small, barred booth where they purchased tickets to enter the casino. Past a security check and they were inside a wide room filled with blackjack and roulette tables and lined by two restaurants. Kenzie sauntered over to one, looking for all the world as if she were inspecting the menu, whilst scouring the room for their enemy.

Treacle sat alone at a roulette table, a pile of chips before him.

"Finally," Kenzie sighed. "He's getting serious."

She wandered over, counting the men around the room that were probably part of his entourage. Twelve. Fuck it then. She'd faced worse odds with Dahl.

"Ah, don't sit, darlin'," Treacle said. "Pretty ass like that should always be seen."

"One more sexist comment from you and the odds of landing on red on this table will suddenly be incredibly improved."

She seated herself next to the slime ball. "Talk."

"You did good. Real good. Now, Tweacle, listen up 'cause I will say this only once." He opened his mouth to speak, then took a proper look at her. The oily gaze then switched to Dahl.

"Where's the vase?"

She desperately wanted to say "In the jam jar, Tweacle", but kept the comment to herself. "Outside. In the car."

"Understood. Bags are searched an' all that. Awight, listen up. Seller's been at this caper for a decade. Sellin' this, that and the other. All Inca shit, y'know? An' when I say shit, I mean only the fuckin' best. Real trophy pieces. I got 'em all, one way or another. Comes from that Gold Room stash, an' I been tryin' to track this mother down but I got zilch. Nothing."

Kenzie followed as best she could, understanding the general gist of it. Dahl was close enough to listen too, watching over Kenzie's shoulder.

"Seller's a clever bastard. Goes by the name Dantanion. Lives in some chateau somewhere with his pets."

Kenzie envisioned kittens. "His pets?"

"Don't ask me, Tweacle. Some kinda cult. Has an army, by all accounts. That's why he needs the dosh regular. Shit, girl, it took me five years to strip away all this info, little bit by little bit. Better be worth it."

"Oh, I'll personally make it worth your while."

"Grrr. Awight then. Cusco in Peru is where all the cover up gets done. It's as close as I came to the treasure, girl." Treacle shook his head and gambled on black. "Fifty-fifty chance, eh? So, I got names." He reeled off more than half-a-dozen names which Dahl, efficient as ever, jotted into a small notebook. "We're talkin' major officials there. A judge. Top cops. Ex-cops. A physician. Property developer. Knights of the realm, all."

"Says the Queen of Egypt," Dahl commented drily.

"Whatever, dude. I got some major info on that bird too, ever you want it?"

Kenzie blinked despite herself. "Say again."

"You don't know? Thought you were a relic smuggler? Shit, it's about to go down hard all around the world, starting in Egypt. Nasty bastards from all over the world are headed there. Small armies being shipped in, they say." He shook his head, the blond mane shaking wildly.

"Why the hell—" Dahl began, then clammed up quickly.

"Why? You never heard of the earth's four corners?? The horsemen? Ancient warriors? Seems it's the biggest thing yet, mate."

Kenzie brought the odd tangent to an end. "You gave us the chain? And you say these objects are part of the Gold Room?" She couldn't keep the disbelief nor excitement out of her voice. She knew the Inca legend off by heart.

"Ah, yeah, now you're getting hot for me. Or Atahualpa's gold. But you'd best take a cold shower, baby. This Dantanion's a clever bastard. Once he gets wind you're on to him, he'll switch. Move it all elsewhere."

Kenzie nodded. "Then why are you telling us so easily?"

Treacle smiled from ear to ear. "'Cause I'll end up with it all anyway. One way or another." He flicked his last chip onto the table, leaving it where it landed. "And I'm a major twat. I enjoy conflict."

Kenzie thought they might be the truest words ever to leave Treacle's mouth. She followed his original statement to its cleanest outcome. "You think the Peruvian government will end up with the artifacts and you'll be able to acquire them?"

"Better that than all this cloak and dagger, one piece per month bullshit."

To a criminal it made sense. Kenzie saw the logic. She figured they'd rinsed all they could from Treacle's dirty laundry, at least on this subject, and pushed the chair back. "You done here?"

"Ready for my reward."

Kenzie moved away from the table, knowing exactly how Treacle would react and how he would follow her, and felt a jab of relief when Dahl gallantly and purposefully pushed in right behind her. Not that the criminal's comments particularly bothered her, but it meant she could properly concentrate on what happened next.

Outside the casino.

CHAPTER TWENTY THREE

Sunlight, gleaming cars and swarms of bystanders greeted her eyes as she left the Casino de Monte Carlo. A true assault on the senses. To the right, hundreds of people were seated outside the Café de Paris, whiling the day away. The blue Maserati still sat behind the black AC Cobra, a couple of young photographers angling for the best picture of the two together.

Treacle pressed beside them, uncomfortably close. "Point the way, Tweacle."

Kenzie saw bad choices everywhere. Bad outcomes. But she walked toward the car and sent a glance over at Dahl.

What to do?

The Swede always stepped up and today was no different. Kenzie knew he'd be factoring the crowd of people nearby and all around. Treacle's goons walked close by, ignoring everything except what their boss wanted—expendable robots. Kenzie imagined all the options flashing through the Swede's mind, as they were flashing through hers. The training always stood at the forefront of your mind—didn't matter how many years had passed since you used it for good. She might be a dirty-faced, broken-down, trod-upon angel, but she was still an angel.

In the end, she saw only one outcome. Dahl walked to the blue Maserati, took out the key and used it to remotely open the passenger door. Dahl reached inside and stared at Treacle.

"I give you this, you walk away. Agreed?"

"'Course, Tweacle. 'Course we will."

Kenzie had never disbelieved someone so much in her entire life. She stopped at the passenger door, which was also unlocked.

Dahl lifted the bag with the vase inside, unzipped it and took the Inca relic out in the street. Treacle swallowed hungrily, eyes alight.

"That's it. We're good. Now hand it over."

Dahl allowed the vase to fall from his hand, watched as it fell toward the concrete and Treacle's expression changed from greed to terror.

"Noooo!"

Dahl caught the vase on the top of his boot, holding it in place with expert balance. Treacle's mouth dropped open so that his jaw almost hit the ground.

"For fu . . . don't you know what that is? Stop it, Twea . . . stop it!"

Dahl reached out, caught hold of Treacle's chin and tilted his face upward. "If you cause trouble. If you try to hurt us or anyone else, I will hunt you down and break you down. Into dust. Do you understand me?"

"Yeah, yeah, Tweacle. Now for fuc—"

Dahl squeezed until the jawbone creaked. "Do you understand?"

A big goon then muscled his way in right next to Dahl. The three men stared hard at each other, unspoken comments flashing between them. Dahl kept his hold on Treacle, then flicked the vase high into the air.

"Kenzie."

Acting fast, she sprang around the car, eyes on the revolving relic. Dahl threw Treacle into the small space between the front of the Maserati and the back of the AC Cobra, then took hold of the big goon and threw him down there too. Out of sight they fought and struggled.

Kenzie pushed a bodyguard aside, never once taking her eyes off the priceless possession. As it tumbled down toward her outstretched hands she had to slide across the front of the sports car, gliding across the paintwork, to catch the object and then slid down the other side onto two feet.

The vase was intact. Dahl had an arm around the big man's throat and was bearing down on Treacle, keeping both of them pinned. Cords stood out in his muscles. Kenzie showed the vase to the rest of the goon squad.

"Don't move."

Hidden from almost all prying eyes, Dahl smashed the big

bodyguard's face into the Cobra's stainless steel exhaust, giving him an impression to be proud of, then rolled him underneath the car. He dragged Treacle upright with a grip around the neck. Pain lit the criminal's eyes. Sweat rolled down his face.

"We're leaving now," Dahl whispered venomously. "Don't forget what I said."

He jumped into the driver's side as Kenzie ran around the car and opened the passenger side.

"The vase!" Treacle wailed, and trigger-fingers became clearly itchy.

"I'll leave it by the curb." Kenzie pointed to the other side of the square. "Best be quick."

Dahl gunned the engine, sending the Maserati drifting around the arc directly in front of the casino and then slowing for Kenzie to place the vase in the road. Then they blasted away, heading for another hill and another street lined by designer boutiques.

"Where to?" Kenzie shouted, trying to catch her breath.

"Well, we're done," Dahl said, watching the road ahead and the rearview for signs of pursuit. "We have all the information we're gonna get. I guess it's time to rejoin the team."

Kenzie felt a surge of disappointment. She'd never say it aloud, but had enjoyed the last few days with the Swede, working together and building their bond. She'd privately hoped it might last a bit longer.

"You sure? We could try to find another buyer."

"Peru is clearly the place to go," Dahl said. "And the team are there already. No doubt taking it easy in the mountains. Playing soccer with the villagers. Dantanion is out there somewhere, and the Gold Room. It's time to learn about the Inca treasure and seek out this cult. The action's only just begun, Kenzie."

Ah, so he was thinking she was worried life might become boring.

"Great," she said, sitting back. "Good to hear it."

CHAPTER TWENTY FOUR

In darkness, they waited.

Drake stared at the mountains, purple and huge and stained by drifting shadows. Breezes played across his face with icy fingers. No flickering lights met his gaze, no shaded insanity loomed large, but he knew—knew in his soul—that the monsters were coming.

Dantanion the Mountain Demon would send them.

He crouched atop a low roof, watching the ways into Kimbiri. Alicia crouched by his side.

"This has to be the creepiest op we've ever been on," she said softly.

"They're just people," Drake said. "Nothing more or less."

"You're kidding? They're bloody cannibals."

"Well, yes, I guess. It's not something you come across every day."

Alicia shifted. "Now that's one stupid statement, Drakey. I thought cannibalism died out years ago."

"The Incas used to practice it. Aztecs too. It's not like we're in the wrong place."

"I'd really like to be in the wrong place. Just this once."

Kinimaka occupied the same roof as them. "This is for the people that live in Kimbiri," he said. "We could head up to the mountains, camp there. Reccy for days. But who would help the villagers then?"

"Same people who've been helping them all along," Alicia muttered. "No-bloody-one."

"If they come, they'll be better prepared this time," Drake pointed out.

"Oh, that helps." Alicia shook her head, patting her H&K for the eighth time. "Man, do I hate spiders."

"They're not—"

"Whatever. Just glad I got me this can of Raid."

She held up a blue can she'd bought in Cusco earlier that day.

Drake laughed as he had when she'd purchased it. "So it's a spray or shoot situation?"

"Later maybe. Let's get the fighting over with first."

Shadows deepened. A crescent moon rose over a far peak, casting a silvery glow. The trio shivered up on the roof. Directly across they saw figures move: Hayden and Smyth. Another roof concealed Mai and Yorgi. They could not be more ready for an attack.

Villagers manned other vantage points. Those that couldn't fight were tucked away safely in the only basement in town. Kimbiri was ready.

Drake saw movement first, just a huddle of shapes flowing over a rise in the distance. At first he thought his eyes might be deceiving him, but Kinimaka spoke out too.

"They're coming."

Alicia petted her rifle. "If I see pointy teeth I'm gonna scream."

Drake smiled to himself, unable to imagine Alicia Myles being scared of anything. But then everyone had a skeleton or two in their closet—and the SPEAR team more than that if Webb's statement was anything to go by. They hadn't had time to sit down and discuss it yet, and nobody had been forthcoming. Was there worse to come? Quite possibly depending on Smyth and the murder of Joshua.

He switched the distractions off. Good news was better to dwell on anyway. They'd received a message today from the Mad Swede. Both he and Kenzie were on their way to Peru with information. Drake looked forward to seeing the big idiot again, but only because it gave him someone to take the piss out of.

His earpiece crackled. "Enemy sighted about a mile off."

"Got 'em," he said. "Remember, we don't know what to expect this time."

Flickering torches illuminated the outskirts of the village. It had been weeks since the power died here; and nobody came to help. Villagers had tried in vain to locate the problem, but it seemed something more fundamental might have happened.

Someone in Cusco wanted Kimbiri forgotten.

Drake saw the first shadows slink into the light like creeping wolves, a limb stretching at a time, bodies low to the ground. Nothing appeared to have changed—black clothing stretched over all flesh including the skull. Limbs moved awkwardly as if each was about to break. The spidery movements gave every watcher an involuntary shiver.

"God help us," Mai said over the comms.

Drake watched closely. The team stood at the center of a moral dilemma. No shots had been fired. No proof was evident. An individual had tried to carry off a villager last time—but that didn't give a soldier free rein to fire upon the group. So far, all they were guilty of doing was a bit of crooked crawling. *And looking shifty*, he thought. Behind the main large group which had paused as it approached the flickering lights, a line of black-cloaked individuals walked normally. These carried the lights, and probably illuminated the way down the mountain passes. Of course, their faces could not be seen inside the cowls—which were mere black holes that could lead to a new kind of insanity. The line they made was twenty strong, and they did not move.

"I really don't like this," Kinimaka said.

Drake's fingers flexed over the reassuring metal at his side. "Aye, pal. Never seen anything like this in my life."

As if by telepathic signal the creepy horde exploded into action. Not as a mass this time, but instantly separating and coming at the village from as many different directions as possible. They broke off in twos and threes, scampering between houses and along rutted lanes, crawling through gardens, hugging walls like enormous slugs, scuttling close to the floor without space between them so they resembled one, terrible, giant spider.

Doors could be heard smashing, windows opening. And that gave the SPEAR team some leeway. Hayden rose from her position across the street and shouted at the top of her voice.

"Stop, or we will be forced to fire on you. This is your only warning."

Blank, featureless faces turned slowly and looked upward. Drake suppressed an eerie shiver and readied his weapon. Were these people really cannibals? Were they seeking a sacrifice?

You're a long way from home, matey.

Cold winds gusted by, the mountains watched impassively and the wild, untamed lands spread far and wide. The rooftop was exposed, dirty and unsafe. But they were soldiers and they were here to do what they did best—protect the people. Help the villagers in their time of need. It wasn't only a duty; it was a calling.

Still, the faces were pointed up at Hayden, disconcertingly quiet and immobile. In stillness, they watched. Hayden stared back and seemed at a loss.

"What the hell am I supposed to do now?" she whispered over the comms.

"Go down there," Alicia whispered back. "We'll watch."

"We'll all go down there," Drake decided. "Maybe we can talk some sense into these muppets."

At the edge of town, where the darkness held sway, twenty black-robed figures with twenty burning torches shifted their weight, making the flames flicker and the black smoke billow.

And right below, Drake saw the unmistakable movements of enemies reaching for weapons.

"Cover!" he cried.

Kinimaka hurled his bulk to the ground, making the roof creak ominously. Drake and Alicia paused just one extra second, concerned to see what manner of weapon the creatures pulled out.

Not believing their eyes.

"You gotta be kiddin—" Alicia managed before the first thick black arrow whistled overhead.

Drake met her eyes. The two were lying flat on the roof, protected by the height of the house but still vulnerable. Alicia blinked rapidly.

"You believe this?"

"Because Incas," Drake said, as if explaining the answer to a fundamental question.

"You tryin' to be funny? This ain't the time, Drakey."

"No. It's just like the answer to every motoring related question is simply: Because race car. This is Inca country."

A shaft struck the corner of the roof and tumbled onto Drake, its momentum spent. He picked it up and took a look. "Nothing special about 'em," he said over the comms. "Rudimentary, no metal at all. I can't tell if the tips are poisoned though, so take care."

He looked over at the other roofs. Arrows lanced through the air and the gaps between houses, a deadly wooden shower. Unreality washed over him. If some crime lord was trying to unbalance them with peculiarity, then he was doing a damn fine job of it.

Rushing noises from below told him the creatures were on the move again, searching for victims. He rose fast, wishing there was more light. It would be too easy for these things to hide in the dark shadow and take pot shots.

Other figures rose all across the rooflines. Hayden leaned over and took the first shot. An arrow flew past her face. She fired again. A figure shrieked and then fell, twisted all wrong. Drake lined another up but a twitch in the dark made him duck away. The arrow parted the air where his head had been. Crawling forward, he peered over the edge of the roof, took aim, and sent a bullet into the ground an inch wide of its mark. Gunshots filled the night and the villagers clasped their weapons, unable to help for now but desperate to save their kin and their way of life.

"Time to move," Mai said. "We have to get among them."

Drake agreed. The real battle was in the streets, not up on some low rooftop. Crawling fast, he made his way to the ladder at the rear of the house and hesitated as Kinimaka reached it first.

"You go, bro." Kinimaka heaved out a sigh. "Ladders and I just don't get along."

Drake swung onto a rung and climbed down, Alicia a foot above his head. He jumped off into darkness, checking for enemies around the narrow alley and seeing nothing. Rifle ready, he moved off just as the ladder creaked alarmingly to signal the steady descent of the big Hawaiian. Indistinct shapes flashed across the far end of the alley, becoming larger as Drake moved closer. Alicia breathed in his ear.

"Look out for teeth."

He nodded, focused ahead. Bows and arrows might be rudimentary but they could kill as well as any bullet. And who knew what other weapons might be still concealed? He paused at the exit, hugging the wall and looking around. Something low to the ground squeaked and sprung up at him, arms and legs striking hard, surprising him more than anything. The training was usually to look above ankle height, and the black-clad figure had been crouched incredibly low. A spindly elbow smashed his head back, bruising his cheek, but he managed to hold on to his weapon. As he fell back he registered another shape creeping across the wall at head-height, clinging to a row of trashcans, before launching at Alicia. She fell back, grunting, striking the opposite wall and trying to get a grip on her attacker. Drake managed to get a secure grip on his own assailant and threw him bodily against the wall, hearing bones crunch. Kinimaka jumped from the third rung of the ladder, coming down full force on Alicia's opponent. The creature fell without a single sound, obliterated.

Drake ran out into the street, spotting a bow-and-arrow wielding man and firing first. The bullet struck; the body fell. He spotted Mai and Yorgi to the right; the others coming up the main street. Darkness flowed toward them.

"Come on!"

Drake found himself kicking out at the low-scuttling pack, striking what he assumed and hoped were ribcages, thighs and shoulders. Some collapsed or flew backward, smashing into their colleagues, upsetting the entire pack. Chaos took hold. Dark creatures rose fast, weapons in their hands, and now Drake saw an assortment of knives, scalpels, a sword and even a scythe.

It was the scythe that swept toward him, blade glinting red with reflected torchlight. Drake danced back into a deeper dark, then jammed the barrel of his rifle into the figure's stomach, doubling it over. The scythe fell.

Alicia was battling alongside, face to face with a man, his features partially hidden but thankfully all too normal. Drake heard her sigh of relief above the din of fighting.

"It's truly just a man."

Drake elbowed another. "Ya got a good look at the choppers yet?"

"No, hang on."

And then what Drake thought would be a punch, a tilting of the head and a second sigh turned into a terrible, sharp intake of breath.

"Oh, shit. Jesus, Drake. Fuck off!"

Alicia punched and kicked and threw her opponent across the width of the street, freaked out; acting crazy. "I was joking!" she cried at the swaying man. "Joking, you hear!"

Drake lifted his own enemy by the chin, ignoring the empty, staring eyes and the hard jabs to his body. With force he managed to wrestle the face mask over the lips. A punch to the nose made the mouth open and exposed the teeth.

Incisors. Sharp. Filed to a point. Other teeth made sharp with a rasp or similar tool, perfect for cutting through tough flesh.

His stomach churned. The man wriggled away, leaving Drake grasping at thin air.

Until now, he hadn't truly believed.

Another sprang at him, leaping off the ground and hitting his legs. Then another, striking his midriff. Drake went down beneath the combined weight, still struggling to believe all he had seen. A knife appeared low down, thrust up at his abdomen. The tactical vest caught the worst of it, but the blow still hurt and brought Drake back to the real world. He kicked out at the covered, faceless head, saw it jerk back and fall away. The figure grabbing his midriff slid up his body now; it was the same man whom Drake had already exposed.

Teeth came fast at his face, blood tipped.

Feeling the same revulsion as if a giant creepy-crawly had landed on him, Drake gripped the throat and smashed the man again and again, bloodying the teeth even more and the nose too. Squirming, spitting and snarling, the man forced his head closer, fighting like a furious animal, his weight a deadly restriction. Drake saw more coming, their masks up, teeth and noses and eyes exposed, crawling at him from left and right, grinning with feral pleasure, limbs twisting in awkward angles as they crept in their unnatural way. Chilling faces filled his vision.

Then a boot came down inches from his nose, a trusty, worn, old boot that he recognized. Alicia stomped on the head of the closest, kicked another in the teeth, booted a third's skull from behind, burying his face in the earth. She jumped among them, striking down at the crawlers, forcing them away. Drake rolled into space, staggering up. Blessed cold air and sky filled his senses. Alicia fell to one knee as two creatures caught her right leg.

Drake stumbled as an arrow bounced off his ribcage and pain exploded from the impact.

Kinimaka was a train. A pounding, runaway juggernaut of a man, stomping and ramming his way through the crowd of attackers. An arrow struck his chest but made no visible impact. Those that crawled, he broke their bones; those that crouched, he made them fly and stagger and stumble into brick walls and ungiving sidewalks and each other, turning the melee inside out.

Alicia pointed her gun. "Fuck this shit."

Drake watched her back. The attackers scattered as she fired. Kinimaka threw three into nearby walls, then watched them crawl brokenly after their brethren. Drake now saw first-hand how strong they were. Two reached down to pick up their fallen and drag or carry them away.

A dozen of the creatures then crouched, poised, and leapt up at the three soldiers. Drake braced for impact, determined not to go down under the impact. But as they waited, as they prepared to make like a formidable wall, the town's villagers came screaming past them, picks, spades and shears flashing and smashing down. They hit the creatures head on before they could leap, forcing them back, breaking them this way and that. Some screamed in fear as they fought, others in release—at last they had found the courage to fight their nightmares.

Drake took a moment to survey the rest of the street. Creatures were being beaten back. Hayden fired close to them, still reluctant to kill. A flurry of arrows fell among the SPEAR team, striking Smyth's and Mai's shoulders and driving them to their knees. Mai spun on a knee as a blade flashed at her, caught it at the handle and twisted it from its owner's grip. Then she returned the weapon, point first.

The man's companion shoveled him up as another engaged with Mai. Smyth headbutted a creature, then came up staggering, forehead crossed with four large spots of blood. His flesh had met sharpened teeth. The blood began to flow and Smyth brought up a hand to wipe it away, still reeling.

Mai protected him, pushing him away toward Hayden. The boss spun three times, firing on each rotation and hitting her enemies center mass. The battle was well and truly engaged. Black-clad figures fell and groaned and were dragged away.

Drake saw Yorgi use his buildering skills to leap from a garden wall to a trashcan and off a drainpipe to land on the back of two aggressors, bearing them to the ground where Mai finished them off. Then the Russian thief employed similar skills to escape a set of fangs. Drake fought down disbelief once more. An arrow sent Yorgi to the ground but bounced away, bruising being the only outcome.

What the fuck have we landed ourselves in the middle of?

Never in all his years of world-weary labor had he experienced anything like it.

Blackness separated from blackness to his right like two items glued together being pulled apart. It was something incredibly tall. Seven feet? And it pointed a bow and arrow at his heart.

Drake drew his Glock and fired, a gunslinger against a demon; his bullet striking as the arrow flew; the shaft nicking a scrap of flesh from his arm. The tall figure disappeared back into the darkness from whence it came.

Drake fought off two more, shot another, then saw the bulk of the attackers beaten back by the villagers. Men traded blows, catching knife thrust on spade blades, using shears to force bodies backward, a garden fork to thrust away a scuttling spidery attacker at ground level. The creatures hissed endlessly, like steam escaping a narrow vent. Alicia kicked at one that snapped at her feet, but it only kept coming.

"For fuck's sake!" she cried. "Why can't you fight like normal people?"

But they were backing off, vanishing into the shadows one by one, melting away toward the mountain passes and the ghostly hills. They took their arrows and their secrets with them; and they also took their dead.

Drake stood in the main street of Kimbiri, glad to be alive, surrounded by villagers who talked happily of their win and tended to their wounded. Shouts came up that nobody had been taken.

The SPEAR team assembled, walking over the shafts of arrows and cast-off knives, picking their way between pools of blood, embarrassed at being thanked by the villagers and hugged until their chests hurt.

"You don't have to thank me," Drake said for the dozenth time. "We want to be here."

Alicia peeled a woman away from him. "He's taken," she said. "All the other guys are free if you fancy one. Oh, and the women."

Mai stared with venom. "One day you will regret all this."

"One day." Alicia glared back. "Maybe."

More people came up, shaking hands and clapping shoulders. The villagers chatted away, happy, and Brynn translated where she could—though most facial expressions were translation enough.

Drake felt more than a pull, a tug of compassion toward them.

They were fast turning into an extended family.

CHAPTER TWENTY FIVE

He woke the next morning with a naked Alicia wrapped around him. There might be better ways to awaken, but right then he couldn't think of any. Their house had no heating, but the duvet and their bodies kept them warm well enough. It was still dark outside the uncurtained window but a quick glance at his wristwatch reinforced what he already knew.

Slowly, he stroked Alicia's naked flank, letting his fingers travel from waist to thigh and back again.

"We have ten minutes." He leaned in close.

Alicia spun around and locked his neck in between her thighs. "Then make yourself useful. Tap twice on the bed when you need air."

Drake performed satisfactorily enough to be ridden hard for four of those ten minutes, which then satisfied both of them. They rose together, washed, dressed and threw down some rations before pouring coffee. Yorgi and Smyth were sharing one of the other rooms and wandered down just as Alicia rose to refill her cup.

"Hey guys," she said. "Who—"

"Quit it," Smyth growled as he stumped by.

"Whaaat?" Alicia tried to play the innocent.

Smyth stood looking out the window, through the cold glass at the slowly rising sun. "Who would have thought what madness lives up in those mountains?"

Drake raised a mug. "We can't let anyone else be taken."

Smyth ate as he stared into the dawn. "Gonna be a long day. Like every other recently."

Alicia reseated herself. "And night."

Yorgi leaned against the door frame. "Last night was so crazy." His Russian accent thickened the more tired he was.

Drake thought about the mind-numbing creatures and the

weapons they used; then recalled the courageous assault by the locals and finally thought about their overwhelming gratitude. These people weren't taking the soldiers for granted—they appreciated every scrap of help.

"We won't let them down," he said.

"Hard to watch a couple of hundred folks every minute, twenty four hours a day," Smyth grunted just because he could and, Drake imagined, because he hadn't heard from Lauren in a while.

"But we will do it," Alicia said, showing her changing side. "Because they need us, and deserve us. They are good people."

"Be easier when Dahl and Kenzie get here," Drake said.

"Well, Dahl anyway."

"He believes she is inherently good. And I believe in him. Their European trip was successful and he said he couldn't have gotten anywhere without Kenzie."

Alicia opened her mouth to voice a retort, but was interrupted by the back door opening and the rest of the team entering. All looked cold, tired and weary; even Mai, who normally spruced up no matter the circumstances.

"Oh, that's a nasty sight first thing on a morning." Alicia shielded her eyes and looked to the morning sun as if for inspiration.

Mai almost managed to answer, but Smyth's low, troubled growl cut her off.

"So guys, who here has thought about Tyler Webb's statement?"

Silence fell across the room, deeper and more profound than the new dawn.

A few members of the team looked over at each other. Some stared at the walls or the floor. Others continued watching the mountain peaks catch fire.

"Maybe we should head out." Hayden stared back at the door she'd just walked through.

"The sun is up," Drake said. "We could—"

"Stop," Smyth hissed. "You want this to fester away forever? Day and night?"

"Bro," Kinimaka rumbled. "This ain't the time."

"I agree," Hayden said. "We have a big day ahead of us."

Drake watched the interaction between the two. No sign of any change there then. If the years had taught him one thing though—it was that Hayden Jaye wouldn't be able to continue down this path indefinitely. Something had to give.

He hoped Mano was still around when it did.

Then Smyth spoke up in a surprisingly quiet voice. "I'll share if you guys will."

"You mean you're part of the statement?" Alicia blurted out. "Which bit?"

Smyth glared. "Like I said—I'll share if you will."

"But I'm not there, Smyth. None of those things relates to me."

Drake ran the now legendary statement through his mind.

I know one of you is a lesbian. One of you is embarrassed all the time. And one of you is dying. I know that. I know one of you killed their parents in cold blood. One of you who is missing is far from what you believe. One of you will die by my hand in three days' time just to wring those tragic emotions from those who remain. One of you cries themselves to sleep.

Alicia clicked her fingers. "I knew it, Smythy old boy. You're a fuckin' lesbian."

"Do you really wanna make light of everyone's problems?" Mai said softly. "They may not all be desperate or tragic, but they are all very personal."

Alicia glared at Mai, but then bit her lip. "I guess you're right. Imagine that. Hey, I'm sorry."

Drake nodded between the two, finding a moment's relief.

Smyth spoke again. "I am mentioned on that statement."

The next voice was thick, deep, and full of emotion. "As am I."

Drake turned to see Yorgi staring at the floor, feet shuffling gently.

"I never thought . . ." the Yorkshireman began, then clammed up. "Sorry."

"Anyone else?" Hayden surveyed the room to speed things along. "Seriously, Mano's right this time. We gotta go."

Smyth stomped angrily out the door. As he walked he spoke to nobody, but put a weight of meaning in his words. "And I'll tell you who else is on that list. Karin goddamn Blake. And it doesn't take a genius to figure out which part."

Drake headed out after Smyth, reviewing the statement in a different way. With all the events and action of the last few weeks he hadn't really put much thought into figuring out who was who. Just assumed it would all come out in the wash. He wasn't referred to on the statement, nor was Alicia. What worried him most was the stash they hadn't yet found.

Hayden led the party out of Kimbiri. Packs were adjusted and tightened, coats pulled tight and collars turned up against the biting weather. The path ran away before them, twisting across the plateau and into the nearby hills. Brynn made her way to the front, turning with her eyes squinted against the bracing wind.

"I'll lead the way and try to find the short cuts. Any questions, just let me know."

Drake liked the teacher. She was no nonsense, helpful and seemed to care for everyone. The village of Kimbiri fostered thoughtfulness among its inhabitants, taught throughout the village and reinforced by parents. Their community was so small it didn't have room for miscreants. It made for a close-knit group and many friends, which made what was happening to them even harder to take. Drake admired anyone that made a go of it against the odds, and these people certainly didn't deserve to find themselves prey.

Brynn set a brisk pace along the winding path, which soon warmed the team up. Hayden fell in beside her for a while and the two talked of village life and the state of provisions, other weapons and anything else Hayden could imagine might be important to their survival. Drake walked behind, listening.

"So this is the weirdest mission," Alicia said as she strode at his side. "We come out here because a phone signal told us these mountains were the home of an Incan relic smuggler. We came to the village for help, ended up fighting for them against the weirdest set of motherfuckers I've ever seen. Now, we're spending a day trekking to all the nearby villages, getting the lowdown on whether they're affected or not."

Drake unbuttoned his jacket as the sun escaped a cloud that looked like it had been purposely painted. "Aye, love, and even odder. The chateau we found might yet be the home of the relic smuggler. In fact, it has to be."

"Maybe. But what do we really know about the relics? Not a lot. Dahl and Kenzie still ain't here. Karin's AWOL. Nobody here can research like that girl. All we know is the relics are from a trove that's never been found before."

"And the guy's been selling them off for a decade."

"It hardly fits," Alicia said. "Inca relics. Cannibals. Mountain chateau. Spider things. This Dantanion dude has a lot to answer for."

The path began to climb, still meandering through the hills and over the rises, each a little higher than the last. The path was stony; low walls ran occasionally to left and right signaling some kind of territorial boundary. Fields were either barren or fertile, and some held goats and other animals. Alicia eyed each one carefully.

"We're safe, don't worry." Drake watched the advance of a black and white goat.

"Dunno about that, dude. What the hell is that thing?"

He stared. "A llama. Don't you know anything about animals?"

A snort. "Not a great deal, no. I was busy during my school days."

"I daren't even ask."

Brynn then made space for them up front. At first, Drake thought she might be about to start teaching Alicia a little of the local curriculum and settled in for a quiet laugh, but then the teacher pointed out a low dwelling ahead.

"A farmstead. One of three around here. We should check with them."

Twenty minutes later and they had the bad news. The farmsteads, all three, had been terrorized occasionally by monsters, by beings carrying flickering lights.

Drake forced down the anger and pushed on, heading slightly downhill now as they neared Nuno. Of course they already knew Nuno had been targeted, but a quick talk to the village elders told them another attack had been endured two nights ago. One young man had been carried away.

The morning wore on and the team climbed higher. More farmsteads within the area were visited and more incidents uncovered. The picture that started to form was frightening indeed—a nightly reign of terror spanning at least a year. Monsters and lights. The rare plea for help completely ignored. Kimbiri's problems magnified again and again.

They paused for lunch in the lee of a hill, shielded by a stand of trees. Drake found a burbling brook and drank his fill. The team chatted idly. He sat back on a white boulder and rubbed his chest—two bruises where arrows had hit the night before. Bruises were normal and never bothered him, but the toll being taken from these mountain folk did.

Mai crouched and drank from the same stream. "It is worse than we thought."

"Oh aye, I know. The question is—where do we go from here?"

"To know the road ahead, ask those coming back."

"Is that a proverb?" he asked. " 'Cause no one's coming back. Not to these farms and those villages. In fact, I'm thinking we have to do the very opposite."

Mai sat beside him. "You are right, of course."

Drake saw that maybe she'd helped him. "All right. Any other inspiring proverbs?"

"Only my favorite." She smiled into the distance. "Don't open a shop unless you like to smile."

He laughed, content with her. Footsteps sounded behind them then and he winced, expecting a boot to the spine from his girlfriend, but it was Brynn that bent down to drink.

"Of course this area is home to all the Inca legends," she said. "It is Peru and these are the Andes. I know of the one that you speak. The Gold Room of Atahualpa."

It made sense that the teacher would at least have some knowledge of the local legends. Drake berated himself. "Any clues?"

"As to where it is? As to what happened to it?" Brynn laughed. "They say the Incas threw it into a manmade lake. They say it was secreted in a deep cave. They say it was hidden and forgotten after the Spaniards took control; then lost in an earthquake." She spread her hands apart. "Earthquakes hit these mountains frequently."

Drake stared at the ground as if expecting it to shake. "Now bad?"

Brynn rose, tying her hair back. "Most are small," she said. "Some . . . are bad."

He didn't push her. "What else do you know?"

"I know of the Ransom Room." Brynn paused as the others started to listen. "Located now in Cajamarca it is the place where Pizarro held and executed Atahualpa and considered where the Inca Empire came to an end. After the Spanish priest, Valverde, failed to interest the Incas in Catholicism, Pizarro attacked. He captured Atahualpa and imprisoned him in that room, destined for execution. Atahualpa bargained for his liberty, offering to fill the room where he was held, and two similar rooms, with gold and silver. In particular, some of the finest pieces the Incas ever made, including an incredible fountain. Pizarro agreed and waited but, like most conquerors, grew tired of months of waiting and executed Atahualpa anyway. The gold, which was already en route, was then lost forever."

"Do you believe that story?" Hayden asked.

"It's not a matter of belief. It's a matter of record. The Ransom Room was real. The deal was real. Atahualpa and Pizarro were real. The gold was chronicled by both the Spaniards and the Incas." She shrugged. "What is there not to believe?"

"And nobody ever found it?" Kinimaka asked.

"It is said Valverde later found it and went away a rich man. But nobody ever again from that era. Maybe it was lost in an earthquake after all."

The group headed out, climbing again, nearing one of the larger mountains. Along its flanks a farm lay; and more reports of monsters were heard. Over its slopes and bearing down the other side they neared the furthest village still within reach of Kimbiri—a place called Quillabiri. After Brynn talked to the leaders she reported that the story remained the same—not as frequently here but the pattern did not change. Every farm and village within a day's distance of the mountain chateau was under fire, and needed protection.

"There's only one way we're going to be able to protect them all," Hayden said as they finally headed back.

"Full on assault of the chateau?" Alicia said.

"I wish. But it's too remote, isolated and undoubtedly well protected to simply attack. We need a deeper plan."

"We could do it," Drake said. "We've succeeded in harder ops."

"Agreed," Hayden said. "But the odds are way low. And if we fail—who looks out for all these villages?"

Drake bowed his head immediately. It was a damn good job Hayden was thinking everything through. The chateau had been inhabited for over ten years now, the potential source of cannibalism and terror for over twelve months. This Dantanion would have anticipated the obvious.

He walked with the boss. "So what's the plan?"

"Dahl and Kenzie arrive tomorrow. Let's talk to them. And back at Kimbiri, we need to come up with something. I don't know yet."

Drake nodded toward Smyth and Alicia. "Some would say helicopter gunships blasting that house off the mountain."

"Yeah, and others recall what Bruno told us back in Cusco. That people are brainwashed into this cult. There could be innocent men and women in there, Drake."

"Prisoners?" He sighed. "I guess. Well, let's see what Dahl says. The Mad Swede always shows a huge amount of finesse."

Hayden's snort of laughter echoed through the mountains.

CHAPTER TWENTY SIX

They arrived back in Kimbiri way before darkness fell, to a surprise.

Drake led the way up the main street to find a large, hulked figure seated outside a small house, chatting away to villagers, Emilio and Clareta. Drake stopped when he saw the figure, whose back was turned to them.

Blond hair shook as the figure nodded back and forth. To the man's left a woman sat, hair tied back and a sword at her side.

"Shit," Alicia said. "Did we just enter the set of Vikings?"

The man turned steadily. "Oh, it's the chip-buttie boy. We all thought a rogue alpaca had eaten you lot."

Alicia sent a fearful glance to the edge of town. "Haven't come across one yet. Just mountain spiders. Ghosts. Cannibals. Kidnapping. A modern day Dracula. The usual stuff. Are alpacas so bad?"

"I heard about this Dantanion." Dahl nodded.

Drake walked straight up to his friend, unable to keep the smile from his face. "Took your fuckin' time, wazzock."

"So many martinis, so little time. So many yachts, so few hours. So many casinos, so—"

"This is Brynn," Hayden introduced the teacher. "She'll help with the translation."

"Ah, good. The hand gestures were starting to feel like a Yorkshireman ordering a hot dog in France."

Drake knew it had to be an insult, but couldn't figure it out fast enough. Instead he switched to the tried and trusted: "I got a hand gesture for you."

Brynn slapped his shoulder. "There are children present."

"Umm, oh, sorry."

More chairs were brought and the team rested their weary legs. Tables were brought out and quickly filled with meat and vegetables, a tureen full of stew and bottles of wine. Hayden started to protest, but Emilio silenced her with a hand.

"Our thank you to you," he said through Brynn. "Let us show our gratitude as best we can. It is not much."

Drake saw the need in their eyes. To say no at this point would be to cause embarrassment, and there were still three hours before sundown. He shuffled his chair along so that it was next to Dahl's and sat back, letting the villagers do their work, and begin to join in the chatter. Of course, it was hard at first but hand motions and smiles, nods and shrugs were always universal.

"You win at the casino?" Drake asked in an undertone.

"Which casino?"

"Oh, funny. Don't tell me you had time to hit more than one."

"Didn't hit any," Dahl admitted. "SPEAR's European tour had few highlights, I'm sad to say."

"Hardly SPEAR," Drake said. "The Swede and the swordswoman."

Dahl cast a thoughtful eye over at Kenzie. Drake read it without effort. "You think she did well?"

"Yeah. I think she could be a real asset to the team."

"Don't get attached. That's when people start to die." Drake accepted a glass of wine though he had no intention of drinking it. "Sorry, that was thoughtless. And wrong."

Dahl shrugged. "No, my friend. It is true and it is life. Real life. We all have our problems that we must surmount; it is what we do with the good times that counts."

Drake settled back. The round metal tables had been arranged into a cluttered jigsaw. With Alicia to his right and the Swede at his left, he felt content. The smell of cooked meat made his mouth water. Brynn was close enough to listen and talk to. Emilio and Clareta smiled, ate and drank, and invited more and more villagers to join them. At last, Drake saw the happy community at work; the place Kimbiri had once been. He saw children holding hands and listening to their parents. Men fetching the heavy containers and women rushing off to change into their brighter clothing. He saw several marveling at Kenzie's sword and a tiny tinge of embarrassment on the Israeli's face.

Someone brought out a boom box and inserted a CD with an '80s' rock mix. Drake was hoping for Guns N' Roses, Judas Priest and Def Leppard but ended up being treated to Michael Jackson, Cyndi Lauper and "Depeche Fucking Mode."

"It says rock," he moaned. "Look. It clearly says rock on the label." He held the offending plastic case up. "The only rock the makers of this compilation know is the one inside their bloody skulls."

"Remember dino rock?" Mai's eyes lit up in memory. "Dancing to Foreigner in war-torn Chechnya? Listening to Van Halen as we prepared that jump? Speakers blasting away."

Alicia was on it like a viper striking. "He's modernized now, and into prettier more reckless things."

"Oh, clever." Mai didn't smile.

Drake tried to mediate. "I like the new stuff, but I still enjoy a good blast with the old stuff too." He winced a little as Alicia turned a red-hot stare on him. He tried again. "Maybe it would be nice to mix them together."

Alicia growled. Mai blinked. Drake now cringed. "Shit, I didn't mean—"

"Never gonna happen," the Englishwoman said.

"It's the wine talking." Drake held up the full glass.

A party erupted all around them. The villagers had lived in fear for so long they took this one chance to let their guard down, to live. Drake accepted thanks again and again, and started a stilted conversation with a couple that knew enough English to get by. Alicia danced with one young man, then another. Dahl fended off the attention of several twenty-somethings. Even the sun emerged grandly from behind white wisps of cloud, bathing the land with cheer.

"Now that's putting in a great appearance," Drake said to nobody in particular. "Something the English football team should learn about."

Drake tore off a chunk of food and ate, stomach complaining after so many rations during the last few days. It felt good to eat real food. He chewed, drank water and found himself nodding along with Madonna.

Fuck it. The old girl managed more than one decent song in her time.

Brynn returned to her seat after a quick turn around the dance floor—the dusty village square—and then scooted up a few spaces, taking advantage of Alicia's own popularity with the boys.

One time, Drake thought, *she'd have ridiculed the stranger asking her to dance.*

Brynn grinned over at him. "These people are worth your time?"

Drake frowned. "Of course. What kind of a question is that?"

"You are soldiers." Brynn shrugged. "Don't you have nations to protect? Your own citizens?"

"We're not gonna leave you to the wolves. Relatively speaking."

"You are a credit to your profession," Brynn said with heartfelt conviction. "And I offer my most humble thanks."

Drake bowed his head. In all his years as a soldier it was a rare occasion when someone came up and properly thanked him. Face to face, heart to heart. To many he was a man doing a job. To some, a pawn carrying out the maneuverings of others. But he was still a soldier, risking everything for people regardless or not of whether they welcomed or appreciated it. The calling and the conviction was a duty he carried in his heart.

"We're here until it's finished," he said plainly, and then quickly sought to change the subject. "What else do you know of this Inca legend?"

"The Gold Room? This Pizarro, this Spanish conqueror—" Brynn twisted her face in distaste "—was nothing but a power-hungry fame seeker. Killing thousands in the name of Spain for his own infamous ends. Twice driven away easily by the Incas he came to a settlement where the villagers helped him. Gave his men time and food to help heal from their battles. He then sailed back to Spain, distended with knowledge of gold and wealth, and convinced the emperor to finance a return shortly thereafter. Only this time, the deal was he would be made governor of all the lands he conquered. He killed Atahualpa," Brynn said in a tone of disgust, "out of fear. The Spaniards numbered 160, the Incas eighty thousand. The coward falsified charges in Atahualpa's trial and ended up having him garroted. They took Atahualpa so the Incas would have nothing to fight for. General Rumiñahui then hid," she paused, smiling, "seven hundred and fifty tons of gold they say, in the Llanganates mountains. Beyond these mountains."

She nodded over Drake's shoulder.

He gawped. "Seven hundred and fifty tons of gold? Whoa."

"Some say Ecuador. But those mountains are too high. They are soaring volcanic peaks shrouded in mist. The general would not have gone to such lengths with so much treasure, weighing so much, part of a caravan and with a modicum of men. That area boasts the most treacherous terrain and extreme weather conditions. Why struggle to hide it there? Instead, the general came here to a place he already knew. Does that not make more sense?"

Drake nodded. "I guess, but you're second guessing an Inca general."

"Perhaps. But consider this: A treasure made up of life-size figures formed from beaten silver and gold. Thousands of birds, animals, flowers. Pots full of incredible jewelry and vases full of emeralds. And that's not the best of it."

"There's something more valuable?"

"Many things. Not counting the fountain, it is said that thousands of pieces of pre-Inca handicraft and beautiful goldsmith works are among the riches."

"Pre-Inca?" Drake breathed, tearing at a hunk of meat. "Imagine the worth."

"Billions," Brynn said. "But not only that. Imagine the value of such a gift to mankind."

Drake agreed with her in silence. He was only too well aware of the greed of men and the levels to which they would stoop to own that which others could not, to gain even a modicum of wealth and power. It also occurred to him now that Dantanion—if this man was the seller—could never sell the fountain or other principal pieces. The notoriety of such a sale would soon unmask even him. Also, the violence it would attract.

"If it's there," he said, "up there with this Dantanion, we will find it and stop them all."

Brynn nodded vehemently. "These people," she said, indicating the dancers and the conversationalists, all chatting with each other and the guests. She nodded at the servers and the cooks; the men that had chosen to stand watch whilst the soldiers ate. She nodded at new friends. "These people want you to train them."

Drake gave her the widest smile. It was right and it was honorable that a soldier should help people, but when those people expressed a desire to help themselves alongside the soldiers then everything felt right with the world; easing the burdens he carried in his soul.

"Then we will train them," he said.

CHAPTER TWENTY SEVEN

Karin Blake glared hard at the killer desert as if she might be able to force it into submission. They had been waiting hours now, sweating like greasy bacon stuck on a grill, twitching away the insects and forced to use every moment of knowhow they'd gained from their army training to maintain focus on their target.

"I got sweat creeping everywhere," Karin complained to the dirt, which was about three inches from her face. "Literally everywhere."

"Y'know I can help you with that," Palladino said, touching her shoulder to the left. "Shit . . . been trying for months."

"Shut your face, Dino. We're still right in the middle of the shit, trying to help you, remember?"

"Yeah, sorry. Y'know I'm grateful for that."

"Bloody better be. If the Army find us, we're going to prison."

A somber silence fell over the three soldiers. The sun beat down relentlessly as it passed its zenith; the stony brown hills and monoliths stretching to the horizon as if composing the entire world. Dino had likened it to the set of a Mad Max movie. Karin had pointed out it was his family who'd decided to put down roots here.

"No wonder I got the hell out," he'd grumbled.

But Karin knew he loved his family more than anything else. Why else would they be here?

"Do you think we're gonna be in so much trouble?" came a low voice from her right. Wu, the slight Chinese-American from LA, couldn't smooth out the deep, worried crevice that had crinkled his face since they'd set out two days ago.

"AWOL?" Dino snorted softly. "Yeah, they're gonna cream us."

"Maybe you," Karin said. "Not me. My posting to Fort Bragg was a favor. I'm a free agent." But the words were hollow and the other two knew it. Karin hadn't been officially released yet. Couple that with Dino and Wu's absence and she was firmly placed slam bang in the same barrel of camel dung.

"Compassionate grounds," Dino said. "That's what we'll plead."

Karin shifted her weapon—a reliable M16A2 rifle—to ease a cramp in her shoulders. The current dilemma was an interesting one for her—because, despite all her new plans, she really wanted to help Dino out. Take away the bluster, the manly testosterone and immaturity and he was a likable guy, devoted to his family, raised to care for his friends. She could imagine him in another role, as one of those customer service guys that actually wanted to help his customers. Dino had been there for her every time during her stint—when the heart-breaking memories became too vivid or when the anger broke like a deadly tidal wave and threatened to wash the rest of her life away.

"See that?" Wu said, nodding at the horizon. "Dust."

"Tire dust," Dino said. "We're on."

Scrambling up, gear creaking, shedding dust and dirt, they ran low toward the next mound, keeping under cover and only two hundred meters from Dino's old house. They could see the white shutters, the patterned curtains, the low fence. They could see that someone had left the outside lights on. Occasionally, they saw shadows pass the windows.

Dino's mother, father and older brother would be there today.

The dust trail continued to bloom, its source hidden behind another mound of dirt. Karin tracked it, gauging the distance between it and the house.

"Two minutes," she said. "We ready?"

"All good."

"Yeah, damn right."

A short chance to reflect on the consequences of their upcoming actions. On the one hand they were doing the right thing, but on the other much about it was strictly illegal. And in the darkest corner of her mind a nasty voice hissed that it went against her plans.

No. Not exactly.

She would need men like these.

The other life fell away when the new training kicked in. Karin felt like a new person, reborn. At least able to progress, which for the genius, capable woman she'd been shouldn't ever have been difficult. Instead, life kicked her in the chest again and again, constantly forcing her back.

After all these weeks and months of planning, the mind was now ready too.

"Here we go," Dino said.

A dusty Range Rover appeared in the lee of two hills, and followed the half-track all the way to a parking area in front of the house. The dust plume followed it, then billowed around it as the vehicle stopped. A minute passed and then the doors opened.

Figures moved at the house's front window.

Karin glanced across at Dino. "Are we go?"

"Been a go since I heard these clowns were taking a piece of my family."

Five emerged from the car; leather jackets open, jeans hanging loose, faces twisted into hard sneers. One of them pointed a gun at the house and pantomimed a fake shot. Laughter sprang up between the men. One kicked at the fence that bordered the well-tended garden. Another simply jumped over the top.

Karin watched as the door opened and a man emerged, fighting his other son, making him go back inside. A woman's plaintive tones rang out; a threat to call the cops.

Dino's father closed the door behind him and, unarmed, faced all five thugs. "What is it you want this week?"

Satisfied nobody was left inside the car, Dino ran hard and low, using the vehicle as cover. Karin tracked him to the left and Wu to the right. When Dino heard that his family were being intimidated and bullied into unknown deals by a dope gang who'd decided to take over the sparsely inhabited area, he'd flipped. The information was off the record. The police were compassionate but couldn't watch the place twenty four hours a day. If a bunch of guys wanted to move to the near desert and live, then that was their affair. Kept them out of the city.

His father's face was bruised from previous meetings, an eye blackened. Karin knew that Dino's mother's face was also bruised, and his brother's right arm broken.

A swaggering youth kicked at garden ornaments, destroying and scattering them. He put a bullet through the front window, grinning as the glass shattered and the woman screamed. One of his colleagues shot out a top floor window, sheltering and hooting as shards showered all over him.

The tallest man grabbed hold of Dino's father, pulled him close and jammed the barrel of a handgun into his mouth.

"You ready to give this shithole up, pops? Walk away? Only you left now and we can come back every day."

Karin came out from behind the car, walking briskly forward as Dino and Wu copied her progress from the other side. Dino shouted, "Hold it right there, assholes. We got you covered now."

Not an ounce of fear showed as every pair of eyes turned toward them. "Who the fuck are you?"

"Doesn't matter. Let the old man go and get off this property."

"Or what? You gonna shoot us dead?"

The tall leader of the group laughed and waved his small handgun around, still gripping Dino's father's neck. The old man's eyes were alight with recognition, the face twisted with fear.

Karin gave herself room on the right, shifting three times, fully aware of what they could and couldn't do in this situation. It would have been easier to confront the gang in its lair, but they'd not been able to figure out where it was in time. Karin's intellect told her this was the wrong move—but it was the only move they had.

Dino approached the fence. "Let him go."

"How 'bout you turn around an' walk that ass of yours into the mountains?"

Karin breathed out slowly, finger on the trigger. The trouble was—some degenerates just didn't know when Hades was calling.

Wu inched carefully to the other side, ensuring all three soldiers were clear of each other's line of fire. Karin wondered if shooting up the car might help.

"We own these hills," the leader then said, acting as if he was some kind of Wild West gunslinger. "New pad, new deal. We figure we get less heat out here, but can hit the town anytime we like. Old man here, is just in the way."

Dino visibly gritted his teeth. "United States Army, scum suckers. Put down your weapons."

A snort of laughter from the leader was quickly taken up by his followers. "Army? Army? Ha, ha, ha, ha." He made a point of looking closely at their civilian outwear—heavy jackets, dark jeans and boots. "You think three M16s gonna scare us away? Shit, I got ten back at the ranch along with mosta my boys."

Karin knew they had no time. Every moment that passed moved conflict closer. Every minute sent her new plans shrinking further away. And time was ticking there too. Drake and his team might be out of the country, but they would be back before long. Karin simply had to find Webb's special information stash before they did.

Dino risked getting closer, the angles lessening by the step. If Karin had comms she'd order him to stop. Instead, the leader of the dope squad squeezed harder on his father's throat and then threw him back against the door.

"Fuck 'em up."

Blood shot from neck and shoulder and chest, nothing lower. Karin's aim veered less than a few millimeters as she squeezed two shots off and saw two men fall dead. Wu performed equally from the other side. The soldiers did not flinch as two bullets flew in reaction to sudden death. The leader stared and blinked and tried to keep his mouth closed, handgun waving all the time.

"What you done . . . shit . . . my crew, man . . ." The weapon, held at an odd angle, drifted in Dino's direction.

Karin took him down. She had to. Dino was already dropping his M16, shouting out his father's name as the man fell to the floor, shot in the chest by one of the errant bullets and trying to stop the blood flowing out of his mouth. Dino reached him on two knees and cradled the man's head. The front door opened and a woman rushed out, wild, face bruised and puffy, the dying man's name loud upon her lips.

Karin cursed her luck. She let the M16 drop, barrel down toward the ground, as she stood on the spot, looking over at Wu and wondering how they'd let everything go so fast. Life was unpredictable. Outcomes were as volatile as forked lightning. The blazing sun glowered down on an impulsive and chaotic scene.

I just became a fugitive . . .

But even bad outcomes had their beneficial linings: . . . and became thick as thieves with two highly capable soldiers.

Together, they were going to be better.

CHAPTER TWENTY EIGHT

In the end she knew they had no choice. The drug smugglers' ranch would need to be cleansed.

Karin tried to pull Dino away from his father but a stiff arm batted her away. She took the blow across the top of the eye, but didn't flinch. Dino's mother was on her knees in the dirt, head pressed to her husband's chest. Dino's brother was approaching slowly from the house, bewilderment written across his features.

"What happened? What did you do?"

Karin held it all back. Dino himself cradled his father's head in his lap, blood soaking through his trousers and coating the back of his hands. The pale face that looked up at Dino possessed no semblance of life anymore.

"Dad . . ."

Karin recalled hearing when her family died, when Komodo died. An overwhelming grief would have gripped Dino, taking him far away from the present. Karin glanced over at Wu and clicked her fingers hard to get the soldier's attention.

"Look alive, Wu. We ain't done here."

"Shut up, Blake." He shook his head. "What a fuck up."

She concurred. Nevertheless, she could see what had to be done. Clear thinking was one of her fortés. Maybe it was her intellect, or a side-effect of the fortress she'd built up around her past. Maybe it was the training kicking in under fire. But she saw what was needed in the next few hours as clearly as the river bed of a crystal-water stream.

"Keep it together," she said, then turned her attention back to Dino.

"Think, Dino. You know what we have to do."

The old man's face stared up at her from over Dino's shoulders, the accusation written visibly. They weren't going to avenge him; they'd already done that. But . . .

"We need to save the rest of your family."

Dino shuddered. "I can't . . . just leave. Not now."

"You can." She reached down and hauled him up, leaving the widow and her son staring at their father. "You have to leave now and never come back."

The pain wrung his heart out. The understanding aged him as she watched. "The cops won't buy this story."

"They will." Karin saw it all in her mind, thoughts striking as fast as lightning. "Leader already said they use M16s. We leave one near your father. He shot the attackers, they shot him. Cops won't know there's a ranch."

"But . . ."

"Your mother had no idea he'd gotten the rifle. They already reported this hassle to the cops. Look at the bruising. Unless we get friggin' Bosch down here they're not gonna look too closely—it's just another strung-out gang off the streets."

"And when they look for a motive?" Wu asked.

"Dead end," Karin said. "They'll drop it."

"We went AWOL." Wu came closer. "They're gonna put it together."

"Unlikely," Karin told him. "The investigations won't link. They'll be entered into different databases. And nobody can prove we were here, especially when we're deliberately seen in a different state tomorrow . . ." She stared from Dino to Wu. "It's gonna work."

"How the hell did you come up with all that in just a few minutes?" Wu asked.

"In another life I was a writer." She fixed her attention on Dino. "Can you do it?"

The young man rubbed at his forehead, eyes tightly closed. A brisk gust of wind kicked up dirt around them. Dino's brother crouched by his father, head down. Dino's mother sat back on her hunches, a hand reaching out and touching her husband, watching the soldiers.

"My dad just died," Dino said in a broken voice. "How can I do anything?"

"Because your mother and brother's futures depend on it.

Because you want to rid the earth of the rest of these assholes. Because you're a bloody good soldier, that's why."

"In the end," Wu said, "it all comes down to family."

Karin stared at him. Once, she'd had a family. Then another, until she realized all they were doing was leading her from one heartbreak to another. She snapped. She planned. And now she was here.

"Which I always thought you couldn't choose," she said reflectively. "But here, now, I guess we can."

The deeds they'd done together would either destroy or fortify their relationship. Wu looked over at the ticking Range Rover. "Let's finish it."

Karin dropped her M16 into the dust. "You too, Dino."

"Are you sure, Blake? I just can't think straight."

"This is the only way. But get your head on right, Dino, 'cause we're heading right into crack central."

The 'ranch' turned out to be a small, brick-built house with a large garden, stables at the rear, a huge shed, and a double wooden garage. Karin saw that it backed onto the tallest hill in the area, and immediately began running possibilities through her mind. This was more interesting than she'd first thought. The possibilities fed her imagination, widening her outlook, making the cogs turn even faster.

The trio surveyed and waited; took an hour to creep into the grounds and stop with their backs up against the garage wall. The house's doors were all open, the windows too. Rap music blared out, turned up to full volume. Occasionally a shadow passed an open window, stripped at least to the waist. Once, a man came out, slipped out back and returned two minutes later.

"No way of telling how many," Wu said.

"Room by room," Karin said. "None survive."

"You okay with that peashooter?" Dino asked, still trying to get his head straight.

"I'll use it until I find something better. One thing I do know from experience is that a dead enemy never needs his weapons. Besides, the caliber's pretty good."

She peered around the corner, struck by a sudden thought. The discipline, the fieldwork, the routine—it all felt normal to her now. In just a few months she'd managed to change her mindset, her vocabulary and her outlook. Still a long way to go.

Maybe. But eventually she'd see them all in their finest hours.

No movement at the farmhouse. No change in the music. She heard a man's forced laughter. Somewhere, on the second floor, a television competed with the music, canned game-show laughter booming out at regular intervals.

Dino tapped her shoulder. Karin ran low and fast, clothes jangling, until she reached the front door. She pulled up, took a breather, checked the interior and saw all was clear. Another tap told her Dino had checked the rear and all was well. In she went, stopping at the first room and glancing inside. Incredibly, it was empty—a large living room with plush sofa, widescreen TV and decorations. Pictures on the wall showed an older couple—probably the family of one of these crackheads who'd recently passed away.

The explanation made sense. She pushed into the room nevertheless to make sure they left no threat at their backs. Dino stayed by the door, Wu backed her up. All clear. They exited and pushed into the next room.

A topless man sat at a table, drinking milk and dry-feeding himself a handful of cereal. Surprise lit his eyes for all but two seconds. The gun on the table stayed untouched as a bullet took the left side of his face away. He collapsed into his cereal, the noise easily masked by the booming music. Karin again double-checked the room and the closet at the rear. She gave the all-clear. This time, Wu exited first and took point into the last room on the right—a kitchen. It took a moment for Karin to figure it all out, but in an instant she knew—just as the bullets started flying.

The kitchen was the largest room in the house and had been cleared out. The gang were cooking their merchandise here. The smells were sharp, the surfaces clean and reflective. The bodies were dirty, and wore only shorts and masks. Karin took great care—dropping the first and then another. A third got a shot off, the bullet thudding into the door frame. Wu aimed and took him out, sending him stumbling back into a counter. Glass paraphernalia and plastic tubes burst and shattered everywhere. Liquid ran out, mixing with spatters of blood. Karin pushed deeper into the room. A short youth with lank hair was brandishing an M16 in one hand, the barrel shaking at the ceiling. Wu dropped him without a word. Dino stood back at the door.

Crisp, precise and skillful so far. They tidied the bottom floor of the house out; exterminated the vermin with prejudice. The guns piled up. The plastic packets piled higher.

The furthest room on the right held the stereo system and was being played by five more youths. These saw the soldiers coming and ran at them; one with a machete in his hand and the other two with nothing.

Wu managed to get a shot off before the machete descended. He dived forward and rolled as the blade bludgeoned thin air. Karin was behind and suddenly face to face with machete man. She fired. The bullet knocked him back into one of his colleagues. The third then hit her hard, muscled shoulder striking her chest. She flailed away, unable to keep her balance. Wu went further into the room, facing two alone.

Dino kept his head, firing at and hitting the third man, then jumping over his still falling corpse. Karin rose instantly, checking the rear and covering for the front two. They hadn't missed anyone, she was sure, but you never let your guard drop.

She saw legs descending the stairs at pace, and then a head appeared, glaring through the wooden spindles.

"The fuck you doin' here?"

"Garbage disposal," Karin returned, and ran straight at him. The legs twisted, the face vanished. She reached the bottom of the stairs, shouting her intentions back at Wu and Dino. Carefully, she looked up, saw flying feet, and then ran hard two at a time. By the time she reached the top all was clear.

Four doors stretched out along the wide landing—three bedrooms and a bathroom, she guessed.

Perfect.

You're not even close to it yet. Plus—that's not exactly future proof.

Shedding those unstoppable thoughts she waited patiently, heard the TV being turned off and a few snatches of whispered hissing. Through her periphery she saw Wu and Dino approach, both spattered with blood; the former carrying a wrist injury. She nodded at it.

"You okay?"

"Scratch. Go on."

Without another word she rushed the first room, found it empty and double-checked. Closet, cupboard, under the bed. Outside the window. Then she was at the rear as Dino cleaned out the next room, one enemy incredibly fast asleep in the bed and overlooked by his pals. The moment Dino entered, Karin saw their enemy wake and reach for a nearby cache of weapons—bloodied cleaver, battered Glock and serrated knife were all available. Dino put the weapons forever out of his reach.

Without pause, Wu took point, knowing at least one of the remaining two rooms held prepared enemies. It was the next and, as soon, as his bulk appeared near the doorway the gunfire started. The soldiers hit the deck, rolled and fired blindly inside. A man screamed and thudded to the floor. Another continued to fire. Wooden walls and frames splintered above their heads. Karin inched closer until she could see three-quarters of the room. Nothing visible, but then a pair of legs stepped into view. She perforated them, saw the rest of the body fall and finished it with a head shot.

Dino scampered by, a little dangerously. A bullet shot by him. Still at least one active shooter in the room, then. Karin glared at Dino, then both soldiers slipped their guns around the doorframe and fired together. Screams erupted and then a final gurgle. Wu breached the gap, calling the all clear a few seconds later.

He turned around, satisfied. "Ranch cleansed."

Karin nodded with grim determination. "They never stood a chance."

Dino gasped. Karin turned to find him on his knees, head hanging low. At first she thought he'd been shot through the back and checked the hallway for enemies. Finding none she bent low and lifted his chin up.

"I am sorry, Dino. I guess now you can grieve."

The sound of a large door being dragged open ground through the open window, clear now that all the sounds of entertainment had been stopped. Karin rushed over and stared down.

"The garage," she said. "One. I guess he's going for a car."

"On my—" Wu began, but Karin put a hand out.

"No. This one is mine, you watch Dino and start the clear up."

"Clear up?"

"Fuck, man, don't you see? The three of us are already fugitives. We can stay here. Become subsistent. Form a base. Make plans . . ."

"Why would I see that? And what plans?"

"Just get on with it."

Wu acquiesced without question, a good sign. Karin raced out of the room, checking her handgun and finding two bullets left in there. She scooped up a discarded M16, then turned, barreled down the stairs, and headed straight for the front door at breakneck speed. Once there, she came to an abrupt halt and checked the area.

An engine roared in the garage. Karin ran into the garden and then toward the garage, covering the ground in a matter of seconds. M16 raised, she followed the line of its barrel. The garage door juddered as a gust of wind struck it; kicking up a whirl of dust. Karin came boldly into the center of the opening just as the engine revved.

Smiled at the man behind the wheel, then sighted his skull along the top of her gun.

Pulled the trigger and saw the blood explode.

Ranch cleansed.

Time to talk to Dino and Wu and see what the future held.

CHAPTER TWENTY NINE

Drake fell in the dirt, spinning too fast, and caught himself by slamming an arm onto the ground. When he looked up he found a man called Curtis and a woman called Desiree staring at him fixedly, hands on weapons.

Trying not to laugh.

Drake rose, shaking himself down. "Well, folks, that's how not to do it. Lesson learned? Let's continue."

They gave him a wry grin, barely understanding but understanding enough. The few spare guns they had brought had been given to the limited number of villagers who'd used one before—two. Alicia and Mai were imparting basic rules of hand-to-hand fighting to some of the other villagers; Alicia somewhat stumped on the art of using garden tools for weapons. Mai overcame it though, cutting the longer ones down and making the clumsier ones lighter and sharper. All around the village, Hayden oversaw major preparations to fend off an offensive.

They were making traps to stop the mountain creatures before they even reached the streets.

A trench was being dug—not deep—just enough to turn or break a limb, and being loosely covered over. These cannibals loved to use the darkness for an ally—let it be used against them, Hayden had said. Drake had experienced a rush of hope for these people when they responded enthusiastically, eager to get to work. Boulders were being lifted to the top of roofs, ready to be thrown on top of attackers. Four villagers proclaimed a proficiency in archery. One bow was found along with four arrows, causing some despondency, but then the villagers again showed their mettle and their desire to overcome as they set about creating rough weapons of their own.

Torches were planted everywhere—a rudimentary system of lighting they'd agreed upon—so light would bathe the village even in the darkest watches of the night. Drake wondered if the spy was still among them or had fled the area. Those that remained certainly seemed motivated enough.

He paused now, allowing Curtis and Desiree time to take a running, twisting run at a wooden target; teaching them to stay focused and readjust—always readjust. Watch your spaces. Watch your way ahead. Never stop planning.

"Wipe the sweat from your hands before you start," he told Desiree. "Any kind of slip could leave you lying on the ground." He pointed at himself.

She gave him a gap-toothed half-smile. "Then . . . chow . . . time," she said, haltingly.

Well, at least they still had strong spirit inside them. These villagers impressed him more by the hour, stepping up to the plate and fighting for it. The stress they'd been under these past few months would have cowed so many people, but not these. Hardy folk, hardy living—it bred toughness he'd rarely seen.

And humility too. Curtis showed him once more, right then, what he'd been experiencing all over the village.

They watched Desiree run the circuit.

"I . . . thank . . ." The young man paused, thinking. "Thank . . . you . . . for all—" he spread his hands toward the village "—this. For all this."

"No worries," Drake said gruffly. "Nobody could walk away from this."

He knew otherwise, and Curtis's gaze told him the young man knew so too. "You . . . save . . . you save our lives."

Drake watched Desiree complete the circuit, getting better with every run. "We're helping you save your own. Target practice next."

A deep voice came from behind. "Ah, excellent. Why don't you set off running, Yorkie, and we'll all see if we can hit you?"

"Y'know, it was fairly quiet around here without you, Dahl."

"Well, the Vikings always did bring the noise."

"Oh, so you think you're a Viking now? Like Erik the Red? Ivar the Boneless? What are you—Torsten the Twat?"

Curtis and now Desiree were staring at them as if sensing

conflict. Drake laughed it off and slapped the big Swede on the back. "You finished digging your pits?"

"Yeah. I'm thinking of blocking some of the streets off so we can create a kill zone. Bring the creatures right where we want them and then—" He slammed a fist into his hand.

"That might take longer than we have and if not done right could cause chaos."

"I know." Dahl nodded. "But it would end the battle very quickly and deter them from attacking again if they lost dozens at once. Also, they wouldn't be able to retrieve the bodies."

Drake gave him an agreeable shrug. The plan had merit. He asked Curtis and Desiree to take another run as Hayden walked toward them, followed by Kenzie and Smyth.

Hayden held a cellphone up. "I'm waiting to speak to Secretary of Defense Crowe," she said in a worried voice.

"Why the hell did you ring her?" Drake had been dreading such a call since they arrived.

"I didn't, dumbass. Her office rings you, places you on hold and then puts you through."

"Can't you drop it?" Dahl asked. "Flat battery. Gust of wind. Use your imagination."

"I could jam it down your throat."

Kenzie skipped over to Dahl's side. "And you thought they'd missed you, baby."

Drake did a double-take. "That's one ugly looking baby, love."

Dahl gave them both a warning glare. Hayden turned away slightly and began to speak. "Hello, Madam Secretary. Yes, we're there now following some promising leads."

Drake watched her body language, seeing the tension, the worry. If they were called back to DC . . . sent somewhere else in the world . . .

"Now?"

The sudden, snapped word grabbed all of their attention. A few villagers wandered up, perhaps sensing the anxiety.

"Madam Secretary, we're close to ending this. I realize we're operating outside—"

Drake let out a long breath, letting his eyes linger on the

houses and streets of the village only they could defend.

"It's one of the biggest unsolved mysteries of all time," Hayden pressed. "Mostly, I guess, because we know the gold really existed. Dahl and Kenzie just returned from Europe with a solid lead. It will just take a few days."

They were hoping that the creatures would attack again tonight so that they could weaken them significantly; giving a retaliatory attack on the chateau every chance of succeeding. Drake leaned forward as Hayden listened to Crowe's reply.

A minute passed and then she ended the call without another word.

"Shit."

"We're heading out?" Smyth asked without emotion.

Hayden pinched the bridge of her nose. "This thing in Egypt is just too big now. Escalating every day, she says."

"Horsemen?" Dahl asked. "Earth's corners?"

"Yeah, and I thought the bloody planet was round. We've been ordered to report back to DC, hand this off, and make plans for Egypt."

Drake swallowed as eight pairs of villagers' eyes switched between him and Dahl and Hayden. "Bollocks."

The team made eye contact. Kinimaka, Yorgi, Alicia and Mai came up and listened as Hayden repeated herself. Nobody looked impressed. Drake felt an upsurge of sentiment, of empathy. Right from the beginning he'd harbored a feeling that they were in the right place at the right time. The villages of Kimbiri, Nuno and Quillabiri confirmed he was right, along with the farmsteads scattered all around. Right now, it felt like a giant hook was trying to tear him away from where he wanted to be.

"If we skipped heading back to DC," Kinimaka said. "And went straight to Egypt, that would save us a day or so."

"There is no question," Mai said without moving. "That I am staying."

Hayden threw a much troubled expression at them. "I understand. I'm with you. But, as ever, we go where the trouble is worse. Where the threat's deeper. And right now that's not here."

"I will stay," the Japanese woman said again.

"And what if thousands then die in Egypt? Hundreds of thousands?"

The dilemma ate at Drake. In dispassionate terms there was no right answer, but in real, human terms the solution was only too clear. And the other huge conundrum was the person in charge—the team ought to follow her lead.

Hayden eyed the mountains that stood resolute and indifferent all around them. These ancient places had felt the steps of Inca kings, Spanish conquistadors, Asian nomads who crossed the Bering Strait over fifteen thousand years ago. They had been home to one of the oldest civilizations in the known history of the world. They had echoed to the roar of dinosaurs, withstood a hundred thousand earthquakes. In them, she found strength.

"I don't want to hear it," she said softly, her face twisted in anxiety as she waved away the team's protests. "We're going to DC and that's the end of the matter."

Alicia straightened as Mai glared. Drake gritted his teeth to stop an outburst. He felt Dahl bristling alongside him.

Hayden wasn't finished. "As long as I lead the SPEAR team, we follow what Crowe says. Not following orders is incredibly dangerous for all of us. If anything went wrong they'd probably use us as the scapegoats."

Drake hadn't thought of that but he did know governments had no qualms about throwing ultimately loyal and highly successful agents to the wolves when it suited them. Mai clicked her tongue.

"You care about that?"

Hayden forced herself to challenge the stare. "Y'know, Mai, I guess I don't. I guess when I think straight for a minute, there could be a way around this. It's a way I've been considering for a few days now. But whoever leads is gonna be in the worst danger of their lives."

"I don't care," Mai said.

Drake stepped forward. "Let Hayden speak."

Mai whirled. "Why? Do you think we should leave too? Has your new girlfriend beaten your integrity down to her own levels?"

Alicia whistled very softly. "That's a very dangerous thing to say."

Hayden tried again. "I'm your boss," she spoke up. "Like it or not. That's the way it is. Life's beating us all down at the moment, Mai, so quit your whining and your disputes and friggin' listen. There ain't nothing more dangerous than going into the lion's den and since I'm boss—I'll be doing it."

Drake was at a momentary loss. "Not sure I understand, love."

"We don't know how the battle will turn out. We don't even know if they'll come tonight, or tomorrow night. We don't know which village or home they'll hit. We do know attacking the chateau's suicidal. And we do know that Dantanion's recruiting."

Drake measured the words, still not seeing it. Dahl turned, confused, as Kenzie let out a little gasp.

"Hayden Jaye," she said. "Considering what we know, that's one of the boldest plans I ever heard."

Kinimaka thrust out a hand as if to comfort Hayden, then managed to stop himself at the last moment. Still, he appeared distraught.

Dantanion's recruiting. Finally, it hit him. "You're saying you're going into the Cannibal King's lair as a recruit? Fuck that."

"It's a way in. The only way I can see. And Crowe will be forced to capitulate if you say they took me. It'll give us a few days of breathing room."

"But . . . but . . . you know what they do in there, right?"

"Well, I sure know they don't play reindeer games."

"Hayden," Kinimaka could barely contain himself. "You'll be alone. Unarmed. Among more than a hundred enemy soldiers. Monsters. No way of rescue. No communications. No friends. It's . . . suicide. Knowing their ways, it could be worse than suicide, I think."

"Yeah, well, you keep wanting me to change, Mano. Something big, I heard you say, to make me see things a better way. That right? Well, lucky you. Lucky all of you. I am still the boss and this is the plan. Let's make it happen."

For once in his life, Drake didn't know what to say. The team clearly all felt the same—even Mai who might be thinking she'd just bullied Hayden into taking the most incredible risk. It was at that point that a group of men and women strolled up, clad in their colorful robes, with big smiles on their faces.

"Soldiers," one of them said. "We bring you this. We . . . make . . . you this."

They stood aside to show what two of them were carrying—a rich platter of food: meats, breads, fruit.

"We want you . . . stay strong. Thank you . . . for helping us. For training us."

Drake swallowed the lump in his throat, turned away.

"And this too," another said, holding a tiny bottle tied around the top and containing a dark liquid. "It is love aid. Make man focus. Make him stronger and last longer." Her eyes twinkled.

Alicia almost tripped over her own feet she moved so fast. "I'll take that."

Drake found his voice. "Steady on, love. It's not like we need any of that. Is it?"

Kenzie stroked Dahl's shoulder. "Certainly Torst doesn't need it."

"How would you know?" Dahl said quickly, uncomfortably, and then added, "But of course I don't."

Alicia raised an eyebrow at Mai. "Oh, oh. Looks like lil Spritey wants to stamp her wickle foot."

Smyth turned away and Yorgi moved around to Hayden's side. Drake and Dahl accepted the offering and the entire team sat down in the short grass alongside the smiling villagers, their jackets fastened and collars turned up, side by side, to enjoy one last gorgeous meal as a team.

One by one the soldiers all quietly offered to change places with Hayden.

But she only stared hard into the gaps between the mountains as if the next ordeal was going to be one worth facing.

CHAPTER THIRTY

It took only a matter of hours to find Bruno again. A cog in a chain as brutal and controlling as the Cusco Militia could hardly wander far from its assigned position. After all, the machine only ran productively when all of its parts worked and stayed together. Cusco itself was a noisy den of activity, outdoor markets buzzing with life and making a killing on coca and muna leaves—magic leaves that helped alleviate the symptoms of a new tourist's altitude sickness.

The Spanish colloquial feel didn't spread through the entire town—descendants of the Incas still pulled llama trains through the heart of it. The main cathedral attracted many visitors, an impressive baroque structure, but it was the surviving Inca-built walls that fascinated Drake as he strode through the streets— bound together without mortar and incredibly strong, they were an ancient accompaniment to the stone streets.

"It's like the Incas never left," he said aloud as they tracked Bruno down. "Despite the Spanish."

When he clapped eyes on the team, the Cusco Militia's "transporter" was less than happy. Alicia approached first, giving him the eye, and forced him down a narrow alley. Soon, they found a doorway where they could crowd around.

"It wasn't my fault," he blurted out.

"What wasn't?" Hayden held a hand up, no doubt wondering what he might spill.

"The massacre. Landlords weren't earning their keep. I told you—I am transport only. I do not make decisions like this."

Drake decided that they should manipulate more than bully at that point. "All right. We believe you, pal, but now you have to help us."

Bruno's eyes shifted uneasily. "Help? How?"

"Dantanion," Hayden said. "He's been recruiting, yes?"

"Umm, I guess."

"You guess?" Alicia hissed, thrusting her body so close Bruno jumped back and collided with the door, making the frame rattle.

"Yeah, well, okay. He been recruiting. Had a batch yesterday. Another today. He recruiting more now than ever."

"I'm happy to say we had a hand in that," Smyth grunted.

Drake wasn't so sure. He wondered what happened to the fresh recruits that turned them into the flesh-eating, capering servants of an unutterable evil. In the beginning though, they were surely as innocent as anyone.

"Today's batch," Hayden said. "They still here?"

"Yeah. I'm heading over now to prepare them."

"Prepare?"

"They transported in a container, placed inside a truck. Then driven to drop-off where men wait. Then," he shrugged, "taken to mountain house."

"How many?"

"Four today. Three yesterday. It is not often easy to get—" he stopped suddenly, clearly realizing his next few words might risk his life.

"Any ideas what happens to them?" Kinimaka asked.

"I do not ask questions. Most times, it is better not to ask. From what I see they're led into the mountains like a herd of goats. I do not know any more."

"Luckily for you, we don't need to know any more. But today, Bruno, you have five. Not four."

He stared, genuine surprise obvious by his outburst. "Are you mad?"

"Time will tell," Hayden said. "So, you ready?"

"Yes, yes," Bruno said. "I can do that."

No doubt it increased his takings. Drake made a point of catching his attention. "Listen up now," he said. "If you blab a word of this to Dantanion or any of his men, we will all take a piece of you. It will be slow and it will be final. Do you get me?"

"I will say nothing. That is truly what I understand."

They allowed Bruno to lead by half a block, following the man to his warehouse where he said the container was stashed. The walk didn't take long, maybe fifteen minutes, but it felt like the fastest quarter-hour of Drake's life.

"No way do you need to do this," he tried one last time, falling in alongside the boss. "We always find a way. We could hit Dantanion whilst his men are out hunting."

"And risk losing another villager? No."

"We could infiltrate through the mountains."

"Too risky and you know it. They know every inch of those mountains. We know nothing of them. Even the village elders don't venture that far."

"Barrage? A full on assault."

"Maybe. But that risks everyone."

Of course, he'd known all along that Hayden would never back down. Alicia had known too and had prepared some last-minute personalized advice.

"Remember what they do up there, Hay. If they offer you any food with the words 'hung' or 'well' or 'dong' in them, just say no. For me, you're heading in a bit near the knuckle."

Hayden groaned.

"Close to the bone," Drake said.

"A knob of butter," Alicia went on. "Would be far better to choose than a buttered knob. But even then I'd be careful."

The team wasted no goodbyes as Hayden turned a corner to the right and they went left. Drake fought down every instinct, every impulse that raised its heckles in protest. Would a traumatic event help her with her personal woes? He saw the sense of her actions, and he saw the recklessness.

He saw her cravings too.

Hayden heading into the lion's den was the only way they could continue to help the villagers.

CHAPTER THIRTY ONE

Trappings of luxury filled the room, the wardrobes and the walls; they reassured his weary mind that all was as it should be, but he did not need them. Dantanion had built this small community from scratch, in his own image and to exacting standards. It appeared now that the small luxuries he had afforded his followers were the very things that had outdone them all.

Temporarily.

He knew of the fighters in the villages and believed they weren't going away soon. Perhaps the people had clubbed together and bought some protection. Dantanion was starting to believe something would need to be done. His people, his children, deserved nothing less. And speaking of children, the first true child had been born into his care the previous night—one he sired—and one that would be brought up truly and purely within the community he'd built. Celebrations had been intense.

And so to today, when ritual returned. The clock told him he still had eighteen minutes until the next feasting, which presented an opportunity.

Dantanion dialed a number and waited, tapping his finely manicured nails against the highly polished desk.

A rough voice picked up. "Who is this?"

"It is Dantanion. I wish to speak to Toni." Soft spoken as ever, he knew they would jump when they heard his voice. No need for threats when reputation spoke like the mouth of a volcano.

"Mr. D? How are you?" Toni was allowed a few luxuries partly because he was the leader of the Cusco Militia, but mostly because Dantanion didn't care what they named him in their world.

"Yes. I find myself tripping over foreign warriors in the hills, Toni. What do you know?"

"Ah, the Americans. They were sniffing around Cusco too

about the same time as Joshua was murdered. I cannot tell if they did it." A pause. "Though there were many that wanted Joshua sleeping inside a horizontal box."

"You should be wary of the company you keep." Dantanion kept none but his own.

"True enough, Mr. D. They are a Special Forces team out of Washington DC."

Dantanion hadn't expected that. He sank into a chair and reached instinctively for one of the little delicacies his chef had prepared and placed in a round china bowl. The large toe had been stripped of its nail, cleaned, scraped and cooked to perfection. Dantanion bit into the soft flesh and chewed, careful to nibble around the bone.

"Special Forces you say? In Peru? Is there anything we can make our government aware of?"

"I understand what you're saying. And yes, I could probably incite an incident, but not directly and not quickly. It would have to be routed through channels."

"How long?"

"Days."

He tore off another morsel, chewing reflectively. A full, deep flavor filled his mouth. "Go on, Toni."

"Ah," The man spoke for five minutes, mentioning names and tying them to events; villains the team had taken down; bosses and lines of communication. None of it was much use to Dantanion, except to confirm that the threat he faced was the real deal.

"Send me everything you have by email." He reeled off one of the highly protected addresses.

"I will, Mr. D."

"And my fresh recruits? How many today?"

"They just set off. Four, I am told. Yes, four."

"Good. Keep them coming. I must cover my losses." Picking delicately at what was left at the toe he shredded skin from slivers of bone, seeking out a juicy morsel. The meaty flavor only set his appetite blazing in anticipation of tonight's feast.

Quickly, he rounded off the call and dabbed at his cheeks and lips, removing a little drool. That was a good sign, of course, never frowned upon. It showed satisfaction, eagerness, gratification. Time was fleeting and he made his way quickly to the feasting hall, entering unnoticed as was his way and slipping quietly into the seat at the head of the table.

Men and women stood all around, behind chairs and lining the corners of the wide room, chatting, smiling, studying modern artistic masterpieces. They were waiting for the gong to sound. They were his followers, his family, though none sought to catch his eye. Dantanion watched them in silence, testing the room's ambiance, its mood, its underlying layer of feeling. Until now, his family had never lost in battle, never returned home in defeat, never faced anything as powerful as this.

He wanted to see how they coped.

The gong chimed out. The feasters all took their seats, no doubt happy this was their night on the rota. Not only was feasting night their greatest pleasure, it also made a nice change from the caves.

Studying the assembled mass carefully, he waved for the waiters to start serving the meal. Carried on five platters it was the severed arms, legs and body of one of their own; the identity respectfully kept secret by the removal of the head. Of course, the meat had been properly prepared—stripped, cooked and then replaced as best they could—he kept his chefs for their culinary not presentation skills. More waiters appeared with sharp, gleaming knives and started to carve the meat, directed by the feasters who then placed the flesh on gleaming plates and looked to the head of the table, to Dantanion.

"With this feast we gain the strength to overcome our enemies, replenish and renew our knowledge, expand our skills and accept new successes. We give thanks to the offering for giving their essence and all that they were, to nourish and sustain us."

They recited it back and raised their glasses. Servers poured a rich, red liquid until they were half full. Merlot. They drank together.

"It is a fine day for a feast," Dantanion said and tore flesh from bone. With a flick of his wrist he instructed a waiter to pick him a selection of the tastiest looking unmentionables from around the table and a bowl of dipping sauce, its barbecue-flavored contents enriched with a light spray of hot blood.

One more problem preyed on his mind, casting a little pall over proceedings. The buyer for the Inca relics had fallen off the grid. Dantanion couldn't reach him, nor could he reach any of the middlemen. Clearly, something had gone wrong and again, was now a threat to the society.

Dantanion wiped his face with a napkin that came away soaked in red. A waiter appeared, took it away and presented a fresh one.

"Nice sauce," said the man to his right.

Dantanion nodded. "Exquisite."

Unhappiness clung to his aura like a black shroud, ever tighter so that he could barely shrug it off. He managed it though when the most anticipated event of the night began. Every time new followers arrived they spent their first night visiting the feasting hall after the family had eaten their fill. They were seated at the table, watched over by the family, and allowed to show just how grateful they were by severing, cooking and then eating a tiny part of themselves. Dantanion found it helped the initiation immensely and was eagerly awaited by the long-standing members because, until recently, it had been a rare event.

Today there had been three new recruits.

And, happiness, tomorrow there would be four.

CHAPTER THIRTY TWO

Drake took Curtis and Desiree out for some target practice and a little field work. The skills he could teach them were limited to the time he had, but he could at least help them live longer.

Live longer?

That realization came down hard and fast, like a cloudburst. Their situation, for all of them, was pretty dire. Defending a village with a handful of soldiers against a local insane, motivated and organized enemy was the riskiest venture they'd ever undertaken . . . well, maybe. They'd fought through more than one frenzied battle over the last few years, engaged in several do-or-die confrontations.

And here they stood.

Kinimaka and Mai were helping make booby traps around the village. Pits and camouflaged boulder traps; sharpened stakes and rope snares. Smyth was fashioning a hollow in the earth behind the place where the creatures had assembled last time. He would hide here, covered by a ghillie suit of his own fashioning. Made of a strong brown, rough material, originally a bed sheet, he cut it down to cover his body and head, stuck vegetation over it, then covered it in dust, soil and plants. He made sure it blended with the landscape because, soon, it would be his night's resting place.

Villagers helped, and now Drake began to recognize people and remember their names. Basilio and Marco were farmers, helping Alicia get the houses' defenses ready. Anica and Clarabelle were weavers, able to create intricate craftwork, and were helping Dahl, Kenzie and Yorgi to limit access to the village. Fewer routes of entry meant less people deployed randomly.

Drake trained others too; as much as he was able to in the short hours. They sat in the dirt and ate sandwiches at lunchtime. He listened to their stories, spoken in stilted English just for him, often translated by Brynn, who seemed to be everywhere at once. It seemed that every hour a man or woman came up to him offering some kind of good luck charm, or a thank you gesture. He kept focus, working until mid-afternoon when he decided the team needed a small, private, discussion.

Together, they wandered up to the summit of a nearby hill, water bottles in hand, jackets turned up against the wind and the all-encompassing cold. Views commanded every horizon, drawing their gazes. Drake waited a moment and then looked back, downward, at Kimbiri.

"Does anyone else feel responsible as all hell now for those people?"

"Fighting with friends is tough," Alicia spoke up, happy to express herself. "You never know what will happen," A recent loss weighted her words to the dejected side. "But fighting *for* friends?" She sighed.

Mai appeared surprised even as she agreed. "I find it harder because they are all so enthusiastic."

They all laughed a little, more sadness in the sound than cheer. Drake found himself having to say the hard thing now that Hayden was gone.

"And our differences? Can we put them on hold for tonight?"

"At least tonight," Alicia spoke up. "Despite the personal stuff nobody works better as a team than us lot."

Dahl grinned at that. "Even with Kenzie here?"

The relic smuggler clapped him on the back. "Hey!" The movement set her katana shifting from side to side.

"I dunno." Alicia eyed another of her one-time enemies. "I'm taking your word for it, Torsty."

"I'll show my true colors," Kenzie said. "Just make sure you don't miss it by doing your girlie, 'running away from a spider' act when I do."

Alicia cocked her head. "Truly? I can't promise that."

Another round of laughter, another somber silence. Smyth shifted his feet. "I heard from Lauren today."

Kinimaka tapped his pocket where Hayden's phone had been put for safekeeping. "Me too, brah. Through Hayden. Secretary Crowe?"

"Yeah. Crowe's pushing for our return. No Secretary ever pushed us this hard before—I mean to quit a job and go to another. It must be hell in Egypt right now."

Drake nodded. "It's a shitstorm over there. When we hit the ground we're gonna hit it running."

"First, we survive tonight," Yorgi said.

"Yeah. And Lauren finally wants to talk." Smyth hesitated. "Sort our own shitstorm out."

Drake winced. "Great timing, pal. Did you mention . . . Joshua?"

"Crap, of course not! Why the hell would I do that? Anyway, it could be better," Smyth allowed, infected by the odd, mixed mood of cheer and melancholy. "But it's better than what we had . . ." He paused again and Drake looked away, sensing the gruff soldier might have more to say.

"When I said I was mentioned in Webb's statement," Smyth said. "I wasn't fooling around. I am embarrassed all the time. That's me."

Alicia clicked her fingers. "So that's why you're a temperamental wanker twenty hours a day."

Drake made a face and took Alicia's hand in his own. "Still a long way to go, love."

The Englishwoman turned her face up. "What? He is!"

"I'm embarrassed because of my family. Because of my past, and because of my name."

Alicia was on it like a starving piranha. "What name? Smyth ain't so bad."

"My first name."

Alicia considered it. "Always wondered about that. Well, so long as it's not Biff or Cliff you should be okay."

Mai made a small noise with her throat. "You know, my friend, you don't have to share this with us."

Drake wondered if she too might be in the statement, though he couldn't decide which part might apply to her. He backed her up though. "Yeah, mate. No need to force yourself."

Alicia nipped his arm. "Shhh!"

Smyth growled at the whole team. "Whatever. My name's

Lance. There you have it. It's out there, and I'm clean. Well, apart from the family shit."

"Lance?" Dahl repeated. "That's a good American name."

"Ya think, do ya? Well, it's short for Lancelot."

Alicia's eyes widened to saucers. "Fuck right off."

Kenzie started to bow, but Dahl caught her. Drake somehow managed to hold back a witty comment, though a dozen suddenly floated through his head. Smyth studied the group.

"Get 'em all out, guys. Might as well."

But even Alicia knew now was not the right time. "Tomorrow, maybe. Or next week. Because today—we're all business."

Kinimaka pointed at the distant mountains, capturing their attention. "And Hayden's out there. I hate to think what she's enduring right now."

Drake decided not to voice his own misgivings. As Alicia attested, now was not the time. The team agreed positions, signals, made sure their comms system was working. They discussed the traps and the villagers' positions. They considered where the night creatures might attack and then run off to. It might be good, this time, to give chase—maybe putting a sense of fear into them. Smyth mentioned making traps all along their escape route—a sound plan—but the plateau and the hills were so wide open a direction could not be decided upon.

Drake sniffed the cold air, watched the scudding gray clouds above. "Night's on its way," he said. "Best be getting ready to fight."

CHAPTER THIRTY THREE

Hayden watched Bruno carefully as the militia transporter walked around to the front of the truck. Two other men waited there, dressed in warm clothing. Bruno had whispered hurriedly that they were the men that would take the new recruits to the chateau. They were Dantanion's men.

She flicked her attention to the back of the truck. It was small, no larger than a Transit, with white rusted paintwork and dented doors. The body was in disrepair; one of the plastic light covers shattered. One of the rear doors stood slightly ajar, and through the gap she made out seated figures. It occurred to her then that she could save these people—get them out of here—but then their one chance of gaining entry to the chateau would be gone.

Greater good, and all that.

She'd been working for and choosing the greater good most of her life. Where had it gotten her? No personal life to mention. Not even the sniff of a social life. A love life in tatters. The only thing she was good at, it seemed, was tracking down and engaging with bad guys.

Footsteps caught her attention and then all three men appeared around the side of the truck. "Get in," one told her, and Bruno gestured at the open rear door.

"Wait," the other man said. "We have to check her, brother."

"Ah, thank you, brother. I almost forgot."

Bruno rolled his eyes as the men stepped forward. One said, "You or I this time, Diaz?"

"You, Benedict. I will again check the truck."

Both men bowed slightly to each other. Hayden stood without moving, trying to affect a beaten, weary stance which was as far from her character as possible. She dared not let Diaz see her eyes. In these men she saw a fluid grace, a well-contained power, and also a deference that could only have been forced upon them. The manner in which they engaged was the product of some kind of system, some other person's ideal, for good or bad.

Diaz patted her down, pressed here and there, but did nothing to aggravate her. After a minute he nodded at the truck.

"Get in."

She didn't look at Bruno as she climbed into the back and took a seat on a dusty wooden bench. The seat was incredibly hard, and the backrest only the side of the van, making her hope they didn't have far to go. Four people sat across from her. Three sat next to her. Two were men in their thirties, she guessed, the third a younger woman maybe early twenties. It was the younger woman that somehow managed a smile.

"Hey," Hayden said.

"You don't talk," Benedict said, thick jacket rustling as he walked. "You don't smile. You don't stand. This is the law until you reach the chateau. Am I understood?"

Hayden wanted to challenge him with a stare, to stand and force the issue, but sat as meekly as the others, staring at the dirty floorboards that lined the base of the truck. Benedict grunted as if satisfied before jumping out of the back door and locking it. Moments later the engine started and the truck rolled out.

Hayden wondered if some kind of listening device might be planted somewhere around them. She didn't want to risk the mistreatment of her fellow passengers so stayed mute. The journey gave her time to think anyway.

Snap decisions had brought her here. Was it time to change everything? They couldn't run around like this forever. Mano annoyed her because he hadn't made the right call—but who was she to judge that? And could she even trust her own judgment?

The truck jounced, rattling her spine. The smooth roads turned into ragged ruts, slopes and inclines. Hayden held onto the wooden bench seat as tightly as she could, catching the girl beside her when once she fell.

"Thanks." A whisper.

"You're welcome."

The two men glared.

Hayden breathed more easily when the truck stopped and the back door opened. Outside, they lined up. Benedict and Diaz checked the area before signaling for Bruno to get on his way. The afternoon sun was bright, but offered no warmth, and the four of them shivered in silence.

Diaz waited for the noise of the truck to abate before speaking "We have quite a trek so prepare yourselves. You will not speak. You will not smile. You will follow in the exact place in which we put you. Do you understand?"

Hayden knew why she offered no objections to these slight, imperious oafs, but wondered why the others stood in submissive silence. She took their lead though, and fell in at the back, with Diaz bringing up the rear. The path they chose was tough, with the two chateau-men showing no signs of tiredness. The constant ups and downs, the ruts in the path and the rocks that sometimes appeared to try to trip you, took a toll on the four recruits though; even Hayden nursed a pull in her calf muscle and fought a tightening in her legs. Three times she helped the girl over tough spots, seen by Diaz but not commented on.

They did not stop for food, but Benedict passed a bottle of water back from which they all drank. Up here, Hayden found the air becoming thinner and thinner and was glad she'd gotten used to the altitude. Still, the lack of air sometimes made her gasp.

Topping another rise they saw a deep valley below and, across the delve between high lands, the chateau built into the side of the far mountain.

"Our destination," Benedict said. "Hurry, or we will be late."

Hastening the pace, the man set off. Diaz backed him up from behind. Hayden helped out where she could, again catching the girl an instant before she fell. The two men panted and walked with loose shoulders, almost exhausted. The slope leveled out, became flat land, and then started to climb again.

The chateau hung over them like the world's biggest arachnid.

Hayden shuddered inside as she thought of the description. Shadows lengthening across the land helped fuel the illusion. The sunlight was lowering by the minute.

Up they went, straining every muscle. The slight girl paused for a rest at the halfway point but received such a glowering look from Diaz that she whimpered and forced herself to go on. Hayden followed close, physically helping her over two piles of boulders and a thick, bristly patch of brush. The thistles were so strong they forced themselves up Hayden's trouser leg and raked her flesh, but she said nothing.

At last, Benedict stopped. The bottom edge of the house overhung them by several feet, jutting out over nothing at all. Beneath it, Hayden now saw a door had been fashioned into the rock, a black keypad with glowing blue numerals the only adornment. When Benedict entered a number—she saw three, five, six, but missed the other two—the door clicked ajar. He moved inside and, at Diaz's urging, so did the recruits.

A rocky passageway led upward, hewed out of stone, rough and standing in pitch black. Benedict used a flashlight to light the way. Still Hayden's calf muscles tugged at her and she felt for what the others must be experiencing. At the far end stood another door, giving the impression that the tunnel was a kind of defense system, that could be defended with ease. Maybe there were some infra-red cameras around too. Hayden saw none but since this was part of her mission, kept her eyes open every inch of the way, remembering, questing, cataloguing. The information would be invaluable for the team's assault.

Beyond the second door they were led along a wood-paneled corridor, now angling downhill, through a couple of nicely furnished rooms and down a wide spiral staircase.

"Keep going," Diaz muttered irritably as the slight girl pulled up again.

"Please," she said.

"One minute can't hurt," Hayden appealed.

"It can if you're flying off the cliffs," Diaz said. "Now keep moving and shut up."

When Hayden turned her face to him he was smiling sickly-sweet, like icing covering a cockroach. She guessed Big Brother might be watching.

"We're all friends here," Benedict said from the front. "Just one big, happy community, fed and strengthened by a family attachment."

Yeah, Hayden thought. *What else you fed by?*

A few more corridors; the sound of a large kitchen at work; brief glimpses of apparently normal people, normally dressed, involved in their chores; and she began to feel a draft. Nothing like a chill or a tiny, errant flow of air, but a deep chill that flowed inexorably at her face.

She shivered.

Diaz grunted. "Get used to it. The caves will be your home until full initiation."

She dreaded even to imagine what that might mean.

CHAPTER THIRTY FOUR

Left alone for a while, Hayden saw a chance and took full opportunity.

An extensive cave system seemed to exist beneath the house, stretching all the way into the mountain. Efforts had been made to close off all but the smallest tunnels with wooden doors, but nothing could prevent the deep chill of underground chambers from penetrating. Individual cubicles had been fashioned, mere places to sleep or rest, using metal framing and plasterboard to a height of eight feet. Above all those, suspended from the cave's high ceiling by more metal latticework, hung an array of CCTV cameras.

"Great," Hayden muttered. "Not only are we friggin' freezing our asses off they're on camera too."

The slight girl had stuck with her and now giggled. "You're funny. Thanks for your help back there."

"Anytime." Hayden stuck a hand out. "Call me Hayden."

"Hayden? Hi, I'm Fay."

Wondering which way to proceed, Hayden decided upon a more self-deprecating point of view. "How the hell did I end up here?"

Fay seated herself on a hard rock, since no chairs were in evidence. She was slim of build, around five-foot-four, and with a narrow, pretty face. Her hair was long, sleek, hanging forward over her shoulders. Her eyes, deep and round, now studied the ground as, it appeared, was normal for her.

"Bad choices, I guess," she said.

"You're American, right? That accent . . . California?"

"Started off there."

"Ah, I'm terrible too. Can't remember where I slept yesterday."

Fay tugged at the sleeves covering her arms, ensuring they were fully concealed. Hayden knew the girl was betraying herself, telegraphing the problem without proper knowledge, and smiled.

"I'm in no position to judge. Done some bad shit in my time."

"But you seem . . . all together."

Hayden looked away, genuinely evaluating herself. "Dude, I'm more of a mess than late night TV. I stand up for myself, that's all."

"My dream." Fay didn't look up.

"Late night TV?"

Her new friend laughed and kicked her feet in the air as she jumped off the rock. "Let's explore."

So they did, having had no orders stating otherwise. The cave structure led down three different tunnels, all ending at wooden doors locked and bolted. To banish any further doubt red signs had been glued to each door.

"Keep out," Fay said. "Maybe that's where they conduct the experiments."

Hayden came to a standstill, frowning hard. "What experiments?"

"Isn't that why you're here? Two weeks for two thousand dollars. I passed the checks and I was in. Didn't really listen to the lingo. Something about crossing barriers, they said. Overcoming taboos." She shrugged. "They said it could be uncomfortable, but hey, I've been uncomfortable since I was nine."

Hayden thought hard. "Do you have any family?"

"Not since I was nine."

"Oh, I'm sorry."

"It is what it is." Fay nestled in a fatalistic shroud. "People like us ain't gonna change it."

"But we don't have to accept it."

"There you go again. Strong bitch, ain't ya? If you didn't sign up for the greenbacks why are you here?"

"Oh, I did," Hayden said hastily. "Just threw me when you said experiments. They didn't say that to me."

"Oh. Well, what the hell, right? Two weeks for two grand ain't bad. They can stick me on camera all they want for that."

Hayden turned away, sorry and at the same time extremely

angry for the girl. Defeated by life, this is where she'd ended up. Exploited. Used. Essentially taken from the face of the world. How many men and women, boys and girls, disappeared daily this way? How many desperate souls lost just because they hadn't found their place in life?

Others watched them as they passed by. Hayden studied their faces. None looked particularly unhappy, but then none were grinning either. Most got about their business of sleeping, reading, chatting quietly or just staring up beyond the bank of cameras at the roof. Toward the far side of the cave a row of shower stalls and toilets were set up, none of them private, nothing but functional.

"Guess I'll skip the shower tonight," Hayden whispered, hoping to make Fay laugh, as an older man stepped out, hairy and bare from head to toe.

The young girl stared at her. "Who are you?"

"I told you."

"No. Like I said, I've been basically alone since I was nine. My kind of people—we know each other. We're the same. You see that guy . . ." She pointed at a youth sat staring into space. "I can share shit with him. I never met him but I can see. That woman . . ." A platinum blonde with old scars running down her face. "Her—I can sit next to. Pass a day. Talk shit. Never see her again. That's a good day, you see, 'cause we ain't being owned by some bastard who thinks he's in charge. Big man always tells you what to do."

"And you tell him to go to hell."

"No, bitch. Not if you wanna walk away you don't."

Fay stared at Hayden now, and for the first time a hardness tougher than raw diamond shone out of her eyes. A lifetime of misery, of regret, of hardship and long-lost chances had turned to stone. Once, even up to the age of eight, Fay had been like every other girl her age—a living firecracker of emotion, fun and spirit, as mighty as a God in her own world, doted over by parents and looking forward to the rest of her life. But how quickly, how insanely fast, everything could change. You lose that security too young, Hayden thought. You lose.

"You don't know me." Hayden knew the only way through this

was to return the challenge. "You don't know my choices. So what if I grew up different to you? So what if think and talk different to you? Don't mean I ain't got problems."

Fay dropped her gaze toward her own feet. "I guess."

A flurry of chatter rushed through the room, bringing heads up and emptying the shower stalls faster than an arctic blast. Hayden watched as the people she'd come to think of as recruits rose to stand beside their makeshift beds along rough, rocky walls, or just froze where they stood. She sent an enquiring look toward the nearest figure.

"Dantanion." Fear crackled through the word like lightning within a storm cloud.

Hayden followed Fay's lead this time, and studied the ground. She expected the man would check over the new recruits, and wasn't disappointed. Within five minutes he was swishing up to her side. She saw the surprisingly boot-shod feet, a pair of shoes worth ten grand if ever she'd seen them, and the bottom half of a black robe. Unsure, she waited. Presently, she felt a finger under her chin, raising her face to his.

"We give thanks to the offering," he said cryptically. "All the offerings. You are welcome in our community. All of you."

Hayden allowed a slight smile, fighting hard to remain pliant. Dantanion was a tall individual, and thin, wiry, built like a rake. His black hair was lustrous, his eyes pools of mystery, his skin swarthy, giving him an enigmatic air she was immediately drawn to. When he stared hard at her like he was doing now she felt like he might be able to see right into her soul.

And she felt a little weak.

Crap, what are you doing?

Hayden hardened her face before it gave her away. Dantanion moved on to Fay and then the other new recruits, welcoming them all. It was a moment before he then turned to address the entire room.

"Maybe you know by now, but we call each step of your journey an initiation." He smiled, a tanned and inexplicable figure wearing a stretched white T-shirt under the half-open robe, showing muscles worthy of a top athlete. Hayden dragged her eyes back up to his face.

"And you will all be glad to know," he continued, "that the first initiations start right now."

All of a sudden, his physical appearance vanished completely from her mind.

CHAPTER THIRTY FIVE

Drake saw the first of the half-dozen flickering torches descending from the mountains and knew their inexorable destiny approached. The villagers were prepared, the team well-placed. The shadow of inevitability approached, driven by some twisted desire, a ravenous, unstoppable fate.

Alicia crouched at his side; the two alone for the briefest of moments in the steady passage of time. "It's good to be together again," Drake said. "I miss you when you bog off, gold hunting."

"Aw, you're such a silver tongued old bastard."

"Old? Thanks. Now I'm wondering why I missed you."

Alicia snuggled in for just one second. "Because I'm the love of your life?"

He felt her pull away, then looked askance. She studied the hills, the flippant comment now a concrete moment in an unsteady past. If they meant so much to each other why were they still fighting for others, with others? Shouldn't they be off somewhere together, living life?

In the greatest way, the change in Alicia Myles was what brought them together again. Perhaps life and circumstance helped, but Alicia herself was the catalyst.

"How do you rate our chances, Drakey?" She didn't turn her head, just waited, as if weighing a lot on his words.

Over on the other side of the roof, he saw one of the village youths starting to get antsy and knew they didn't have time for this discussion right now. "All depends on how you brush up on your car knowledge, love. There'll be tests next week."

"Really? Want me to join you in petrolhead heaven? I forget, is the Sprite a car geek too?"

Drake saw the danger in any reply and let it drop, which was probably what Alicia intended. The youth stared straight at him as he approached.

"It'll be okay, mate," Drake said. "You'll do great."

"Should I be scared?"

"Only of me," Alicia said as she approached. "If you don't buck up, I'll kick your ass harder than any of 'em."

She ruffled the lad's hair and took a casual look over the side of the roof. Signals were passing between several knots of villagers. Drake looked to the spot where Smyth lay and then to the others' positions. He sought out Curtis and Desiree, Anica and Marco, but could not be certain he saw them among the shadows. His heart went out to them, defending their home.

"Once more to the arena," he said. "Once more, we risk tomorrow."

"Where'd you hear that?" Alicia asked.

"I just made it up."

"Fuck off." She chortled. "Thick bastard like you couldn't make up a bed."

At least it made the youth laugh.

Drake finally saw the shadows moving as the creatures made their final approach to the village. He saw the oncoming wave, still chilling, the joint movements enough to set his skin to crawling.

"This time," Dahl said over the comms, "we're gonna catch one alive."

"Don't think we haven't tried," Drake said.

"But this is me speaking now," Dahl came back. "Maybe I've been away too long and you forgot my voice."

"Nope. I'd recognize the Swedish chef almost anywhere."

"You want a little wager, Pork Pie Boy?"

Drake took offense, not at the inferred insult but at the fact that the best pork pies weren't made in Yorkshire. "I'll take that."

"Me too," Kenzie said.

"And me," Alicia agreed.

Drake made ready, knowing the friendly bluster would only make them sharper. The first screams began as the creatures triggered several traps. Drake found it hard to tell with the shadows but thought he saw two ditches already uncovered and a man swinging by his leg. Another rope looked to have misfired and caught someone about the waist, but they'd take every fluke they could get.

"Do it," he said through the comms.

Someone lit the touch-paper and columns of fire went up around the town—stakes covered in tar, rudimentary but enough to illuminate most of the town. With nowhere to run, nowhere to hide and sneak and slither, the creatures abandoned their pretensions and rose up on two legs, ripped off masks and took out bows and arrows. Drake took it all in before moving.

The comms crackled again. "Heads are up, guys," Yorgi said. "I see two handguns out there."

Drake moved, knowing the rest of the team would be fully invested now. He fired several shots from the rooftop, gesturing for the villagers to kneel up and use whatever projectiles they'd managed to gather together. The streets below were crawling with enemies. Drake saw one fall flat, shot through the leg; another ran for a house door, took a rock the size of a wing mirror to the temple, and collapsed without a sound. Arrows whizzed through the air, shooting up over the roof, most landing harmlessly behind them. A villager screamed as a bolt lodged through his bicep, then went down clutching the muscle. Their designated nurse rushed over, trying to help. Drake knew the older man would do all he could—they'd only had chance to train a handful in the basics of first aid, but natives living out in the wilds always had their own ways.

The villagers stayed atop the roof whilst Drake and Alicia rushed through a hatch and headed for the street below. They came out the back of the house, straight into a wandering attacker. Drake grabbed him by the waist and threw him to Alicia.

"One to help you along, old girl."

Alicia took it, knocked him unconscious and tied his hand to a black railing. A gasp of horror escaped her when she saw the two-fingered hand before her.

"The downside of being a cannibal," Drake said, "is when your boss fancies a snack."

The man pulled hard at his bonds, making blood spill across

his wrist. Drake saw sharpened teeth and a feral snarl. "What does it take to get from human to that?"

"Must be tricky for a stoner," Alicia said. "I mean, if one night you just say: 'let's share a joint, dude.'" She weighed both hands. "What happens?"

The man showed no sign of understanding, no humanity at all. Drake intercepted another attack, doubled the man over and threw him up against the same railing. Snarling, the attacker came right back, blood flying from his skull and hand hanging at a ridiculous angle. Drake winced, but was forced to disable the man again. Even with a broken foot, arm, and blood blinding his eyes he attempted to rise and pounce again.

"They have to be on some kind of drug," he said. "Hallucinatory? Listen," he tapped the man on the knee, "if I promise to rustle you up a set of Swedish meatballs will you answer a few questions?"

The face shot forward, the jaws snapping an inch from his fingers. Drake cringed. "Guess not."

They left both men tied up and moved into the street. Figures stood at every doorway, trying to gain entry. Frustration showed on all the faces they could see. Drake saw many hobbling and bleeding, and assumed the traps they'd fashioned were working just fine. He didn't shoot anyone except when attacked, but every creature they saw turned and attempted to pounce.

They saw Kinimaka in the middle of the street, throwing smaller beings left and right. His victims struck walls and cracked doors and even went halfway through windows. The Hawaiian was beset with worry for Hayden and just wanted this attack to be over; wanted the morning to come so that they might get word. Drake was worried too, not over their boss's prowess but over her recent behavior. The thing she was looking for might never show up—what then?

Out in the street and with all the torches still blazing he took in a good view of the village. Knots of villagers accompanied by Mai, Yorgi and Kenzie kept the attackers at bay. Curtis stood at the top of a narrow junction, shooting all who emerged. Desiree stood at his back, facing the other way. Together, the pair scared off more creatures than they shot. Drake grinned and gave them a thumbs up.

"That's reet good!" he cried. "Watch out for that tosspot!"

Luckily, Curtis didn't need a translation and noticed the attacker creeping up on them. Drake finally found Dahl, waving a lit torch in the face of three attackers. As he approached, a pair of goats clattered across the dirt road between them, adding more of an unreal sense to the scene. Dahl was standing his ground, but the creatures were on two feet, snarling, lunging at the fire, and pulling back at the last moment. Their faces were savage and barely human in the flames, eyes blazing and mouths drawn back in a hateful rictus.

"Which one of you is first?" The Swede sounded remarkably calm. "Because I assure you, I'm taking all of you down."

Alicia yelled a warning as a fourth black-clad man leapt from the shadows. Dahl lunged aside, but not fast enough. The cannibal fastened on to Dahl's leg . . . with his teeth.

Dahl yelled, striking down with the torch. That gave the three he'd been holding at bay chance to attack. Drake was already in motion, racing to his friend's aid with Alicia a step ahead, but neither of them were truly fast enough.

Kenzie shot from the darkness like a ghostly avenger, face set as hard and grim as old stone. The katana flashed straight down and to the side, flames dancing down its silver blade, glinting along its edges. A creature fell, gurgling his last into the ground. Another flurry of fire, another body fell. Kenzie twisted and turned with grace, evading a clumsy lunge, ending up behind her enemy and running him through. He fell, still with the katana in his chest, wrenching it out of her hand.

"Poor form," Alicia growled. "There goes your super samurai badge."

Dahl lifted the fourth attacker, whom he now had gripped around the neck. "Bloody hell! I wanted them all alive."

Kenzie reached down, stuck her foot on the dead man's back and yanked her sword free. "Sometimes," she said. "We don't always get what we want. But we keep on living."

Drake wondered about the double-meaning, if indeed there

was one. Kenzie always played it close to the chest and Dahl knew her better than anyone. The Swede watched as Kenzie wiped her blade off.

"Thanks for the help."

Drake surveyed the town. The creatures still came at the citizens in any way they could. From experience he now knew that when he left the area creatures would sneak in and try to steal the bodies of their slain. Not this time. The team rounded up the dead and tied them to nearby stakes or railings, anything they could, with bonds they'd fashioned earlier. If this brought the enemy out of their comfort zone, then the mistakes they made would be all the bigger.

Moving down Main Street, the four made more than a powerful image, they were a force of nature. Kenzie took lead, swinging her katana in epic fashion to left and right, cutting down a swathe of foes. Drake and Alicia came next, to the sides, using handguns to stop charging creatures in their tracks. Arrows whistled between them, passing dangerously close but parting nothing but air. The Mad Swede brought up the rear, tackling foes with a low shoulder, hefting them in the air and bringing them down hard on their spines or necks. Drake grew accustomed to the sight of bodies tumbling through the air and sprawling headlong close to his feet. He broke away quickly to deal with a black-clad individual that appeared to be getting the better of a villager, helped the local pierce the attacker with his own knife, then motioned for the villagers to join them.

And proceeded once more up the street.

More melees were stopped, more knots of aggressors taken out. Villagers crowded around the original four, stalking the streets alongside them. Machetes were raised and used, kitchen knives thrust into flesh. Kenzie stayed that little bit ahead of the wedge, unnerving Drake intensely when a severed head flew off the edge of her sword right past his face. Another inch and they'd have been nose to nose.

Kinimaka joined them from the right and Yorgi from the left, the Russian confirming that the two shooters had long since been taken care of. Curtis and Desiree and a dozen others joined them. The slow-marching phalanx was unstoppable, buzzing with energy and comradeship, each person watching the other person's back, every pair of eyes searching out danger not just for themselves, but for everyone. Drake felt the mood of the villagers change right then, the instillation of belief and confidence a tangible feeling. Those that were scared stood strong. Those that were strong led the way. And the SPEAR team walked with them, proud to be a part of it, happy that they had helped make a difference.

Ahead, Mai waited, an exhausted enemy in each hand, letting them hang so their knees scraped the ground. Her flawless white face was serene as she singled Alicia out among the pack.

"How many, bitch?"

"Three, probably. I don't think it matters now though, Sprite, do you?"

Drake felt happy for his girlfriend. Inspired enough to suspend her war of words with the Japanese ninja. The ground was littered with dead and groaning bodies, the creatures trying to spirit some away, fleeing between buildings and screaming as they ran, most likely tripping snares on their way back. Smyth reported that he was carefully dispatching a handful, but didn't want to reveal his position in case he was needed again. Drake stopped as the march staggered to a halt, the villagers looking at each other, around at the village and then to the skies.

They had successfully defended their homes against a superior force. Many fell to their knees, some in gratitude, some in exhaustion. Many cheered and began to hug their friends. Drake found himself at the center of a group celebration amid the dirt and the blood and the biting winds. He clasped shoulders, grinned stupid grins with the villagers and let the tension go for just a few minutes. He danced around with one woman, high-fived a man, and saw people he knew by name holding bloody daggers and half-broken cleavers. He saw Brynn directing people to round up the captives and make them secure. *Brynn is a teacher! Well, she makes a bloody damn good general as well.* They moved to the village square, happy to be alive, and the SPEAR team managed to come together.

"Kimbiri lives on," Drake said.

"But a long way to go," Mai said. "There are other villages and we can't be there for all of them."

"I say we chop the head off the snake." Smyth trotted up to them, covered in dirt and vegetation. "And I say we do it now."

"Don't worry, Lancelot." Alicia winked. "Your queen will still be there when we get home."

"Those assholes are running and they're scared. In turmoil. We won't get a better chance," he huffed. "Take my advice or leave it."

Drake studied Smyth thoughtfully and then said with some worry in his voice. "We do have to decide what's the main priority."

"Hayden," Kinimaka said.

"Hit 'em while they're down," Dahl said. "Before they can make plans."

"It does sound appealing," Alicia said.

"And tonight we got a little lucky," Mai added. "What if they'd attacked Nuno or a farm instead? We won't get so lucky again."

Drake nodded, gaze drawn over to the excited huddle of villagers. Curtis was beckoning him to join in. Brynn was waving them all over. It was good to celebrate victory tonight, Drake thought. But tomorrow would be a different day. Tomorrow Dantanion and his horde of cannibals could just reset and start again. A man with his means might even have an arms cache on the way. Secretary Crowe would not be held back.

"We achieved so much tonight," he said. "But I don't feel it's enough. I think . . ." He gazed up at the mountains. "I think we have to finish this. Right now."

"Hayden will be pissed," Kinimaka said. "She pretty much just got there."

"And the chateau's still inaccessible," Kenzie pointed out. "Nothing has changed there."

"Not to me." Yorgi kicked mud from his boots. "I could climb up the walls and find a way to let you all in."

"Right into cannibal central?" Alicia drank water. "They'd just think you were the appetizer."

"Is there another way?" Yorgi challenged.

Dahl nodded around a mouthful of food. Brynn had gotten fed up with waiting for them to join the impromptu celebration and had dashed across with a few bowls. She now listened to their conversation with interest.

"I know of a way," the Swede said, and proceeded to explain.

Alicia rolled her eyes. "For fuck's sake, Torsty, can't you ever just use the front door?"

Kenzie came to his rescue. "I like it," she said. "It breeds stamina."

"It breeds bruises. That's all it breeds."

Drake eyed the Swede. "You think it can be done? I mean it's not like we can come over the top of the mountain. The peaks are way too high."

"Look over there. See how they shine under the full moon. What do you see?"

Drake did his best to discern anything other than shadows and lofty heights. "Shit, what did you put in that food, Brynn? The Swede's finally lost it."

"The passes." Dahl waved indignantly. "Can't you make them out against the mountain?"

"Mountain passes," Mai said quietly. "There will be a way around the side of the mountain and thus above the chateau. It is the distance down we can't control."

"And how do you propose to find the right path?" Smyth asked.

Dahl nodded at Brynn, still chewing. The teacher nodded back immediately. "I do know several who could take you into those mountains. But it is up to them to decide if they want to go. Perhaps we will find one."

Mai smiled agreeably. "Of course."

Drake stared around at the group. "So we're really going for the Mad Swede's plan?"

Dahl looked offended. "I haven't done anything mad in days."

"Hold on, Hayden," Kinimaka said so softly he probably thought nobody could hear him. "We're on our way."

Smyth shook the vegetation from his jacket. "We all going then?"

Drake smiled. "Yeah, and Lancelot can lead the charge."

"Oh, don't start with all that. Just don't. I came clean, I fessed up. Don't see anyone else doing the same."

Silence as deep as the depthless caverns inside the mountains fell over the group, making everyone feel a little uncomfortable. In the end it was Brynn who broke it.

"Shall we ask around?"

"Yeah." Drake eyed the path of their future. "And then finish this thing."

CHAPTER THIRTY SIX

"Your first step. Your first initiation," Dantanion purred, his voice soft and liquid, like honey poured over a spoon. "Anything new may be abhorrent. To open the eyes, we need persuasive stimulation. To open the heart, we need compelling emotion. But to open the mind, do you know what we need?"

He paused, but continued quickly, not expecting to be interrupted.

"A weighty shock," he said. "Something sharp that cuts deep. Something that changes our outlook on what we see and know. So here, this is for all of you."

Hayden watched as two men came forward and offered the four new recruits a paper cup. Half filled with a clear liquid it was clearly yet another rite of passage. Hayden saw no choice, trapped and surrounded as she was. Fay took the cup and tipped it back without blinking. One of the men asked what was in it.

"A cushion," Dantanion said.

Hayden thought, *what the hell,* and threw it back. Experience was everything, right? Especially in a life that had largely been led hopping from one major case to another. A warmth drifted through her system, dulling her senses and taking the edge off.

A cushion.

But a cushion for what?

She saw at least half the people leave the caves then, and wondered if Dantanion might be conducting a raid on one of the villages tonight. Fear for her friends broke the rising inner miasma for a few seconds, but then the blurriness returned. The stuff was better than three quick shots of neat rum, and was that a fox's tail now growing out of Dantanion's head?

Crap. This is not good.

Feeling vulnerable, she folded her arms and leaned back. Dantanion waited for another minute. "Tonight, you will first witness a small feasting. Then, later, in the darker watches, you will offer a part of yourself—to yourself. The fundamental ritual. And it must be completed on the first day. If this shocks you, ladies and gentlemen, just remember—you signed up for it."

Hayden had signed nothing. Or had she? Truly, she couldn't remember much past just now and the edges were all blurry. Probably best to just nod and get on with it. She watched dispassionately as Dantanion and two of his followers squatted down to show them how to move differently, how to bend their limbs for some kind of game. She had a feeling she'd seen it before, but couldn't place the memory. The teaching stuck in her head though. A robed man was then brought forward, his hand placed on a square of stone like an altar sticking up through the floor, and a scalpel introduced to the hand.

Hayden felt a rush of fear, a hot panic, but shrugged indifferently. It was only a sliver of flesh, only a blade, and only a trickle of blood. The portable stove helped cook the flesh and then the man offered it up to Dantanion. In ritual mode, the leader smiled inscrutably, warming the whole room before generously taking the flesh and offering it to another. This man popped it into his mouth and chewed happily, swallowing it down after a minute.

Dantanion addressed the recruits. "When the cushion is removed you will find that your mind has changed," he said. "The initiations have begun. Be ready for later tonight."

Hayden allowed herself to sink onto a bed, watching Dantanion walk away and enjoying the experience. Should it worry her that if he grinned at her right now she'd chase after him like a faithful hound? Probably. But she couldn't seem to care. The deceptive, illusory aspect that now constituted reality didn't seem half bad.

It took some time, she didn't know how much, but the effects of the drug started to wear off. Fay ended up beside her, sniffing and staring at the ceiling, mesmerized by the endlessly adjusting cameras.

"You okay?" Hayden asked.

"I've been better, and that's saying something. My head hurts and my throat's dry but I guess I'll be okay."

Minutes passed and then Hayden said, "Did I understand it right? They just ate some guy's skin?"

Fay pulled a face. "And will make us do it too."

Hayden laughed. "Yeah, they can try."

A woman with short-cropped hair was passing, stopped and leaned down to fix Hayden with a worried stare. "I was forced to pass the fundamental ritual last night." She hugged herself. "It's bad, very bad, but easier than the alternative. Those that refused . . . they threw them from the cliffs."

"Is that a bad joke? Are you kidding?" Fay blurted.

"No, no. They keep saying we signed up for it. Do you remember signing up? The whole thing's a blur for me. And I sure don't remember any flesh eating rituals in the friggin' contract. Nor any cliff divin'."

"Crossing barriers," Fay said. "Overcoming taboos. I read the damn form three times and that's what it said."

"Well, they weren't friggin jokin'. After two weeks of this shit my brain's goin' to be a jelly."

Hayden listened, wondering if the woman hadn't hit the proverbial nail on the head. Dantanion's process had to be a concoction of drugs, brainwashing and enforcement. Vulnerable people were more susceptible. Those without homes craved families. Any family. In any case, the immediate future was incredibly clear.

She had just a few short hours to find out what she needed to know and get the hell out of there.

CHAPTER THIRTY SEVEN

Kinimaka made the call very quickly. The rest of the team, apart from Mai and Dahl, stood around for moral support.

"Of course I'm being straight up with you, Secretary Crowe," the Hawaiian grimaced, "and we're close to deciding on a plan of action."

He listened for twenty seconds.

"I realize we're angling for more time, and this sounds like the perfect way to gain a few days, but—"

He stopped as she interrupted.

Drake leaned over toward Alicia and stage-whispered, "She's not daft."

Kinimaka held out a hand as if to say, "why would you?" Drake realized his whisper might have been a little loud.

"Nobody, ma'am, just a passing villager. I speak for all of us when I say . . ."

Now Alicia whispered back. "She's got ears like a bat."

Kinimaka looked like he wanted to throw the phone at her. Again he apologized. Again he brushed the truth with away with a thick, bristly veneer. "They came as we were readying to leave. Hayden was—"

Another interruption. This time, Kinimaka listened and frowned over a much longer period.

"Understood. We're totally on board with the Egypt situation, ma'am, and anxious to get involved. As soon as we rescue . . . yeah, I'd better stop talking and get a move on. Bye, then . . . bye." He was left staring at a dead phone.

"That went well," Smyth jested.

"She's not stupid. She knows something's not quite right."

"Next time try to sound more whiny," Alicia said. "Like when Smyth's talking to Lauren."

"Shit," Smyth growled.

"Or when Taz sees a Reece Carrera movie," Mai said, having just returned. "Please Reece. Ah, Reece, ah, ah."

"Hey, I watch those in private."

Drake was counting bullets. "I'd forgotten your old nickname."

"Yeah, the bikers gave me it. Seems . . . out of place . . . now."

"There's something else," Kinimaka said quietly. "Crowe said, 'we'll sort out the consequences later.'"

"Fuck that," Drake said. "We've time for all that. Right now, are we ready to bring this storm down on Dantanion's head?"

"The cannibals are going to be pissed." Dahl grinned.

Kenzie finished cleaning her blade. "And Peru made a little safer."

"We sure the plan's in place? CIA prepped?" Kinimaka played devil's advocate.

"Took some doing," Drake said. "But yeah. They're ready, and will be along whenever the hell they feel like it." He took a moment to breathe and then nodded toward Dahl and Mai. "How did you guys get on?"

Mai managed to look a little uncomfortable but Dahl blustered right on in. "Brynn got it very wrong," he said. "Three she said. Three villagers might know the mountains and only one might be willing to help us." He sighed. "More like the whole bloody village is gearing up to come along."

Drake felt gratitude and affection rise inside and attempted to keep it hidden. "The entire village?"

"Dahl may be exaggerating somewhat," Mai said. "But they all want to help in some way. These people possess such a sense of integrity it reminds me of my old home."

"We settled on eight," Dahl said. "Eight of them. Eight of us."

"But how will we get them down—"

"Matt." Mai held up a hand to stop him. "We will find a way."

The night deepened. Animal screams or worse flowed down out of the mountains. Drake fancied he could see torches wavering up there, distant as the stars, showing something the way home. A sense of urgency fired his soul and then a sense of loyalty as the eight chosen villagers walked up. They carried extra jackets for the soldiers.

"The cold cuts deep up there," Brynn said. "We will all need the extra protection."

With quiet and heartfelt goodbyes the soldiers, along with Curtis and Desiree, Anica and Marco, Brynn and others, took their leave of Kimbiri and lit their torches, following a landscape of flame and shadow, treading the final path that would either finally rid them of a terrible, clinging evil or send them plunging into a pit fashioned in the more desperate chambers of Hell.

A torchlit procession wound up the mountain, guns and ammo strapped around their waists and chests and thighs and anywhere else they could physically attach it. Utter darkness crouched just beyond the flames, a tangible force. Distant, bleak, stars glittered high above and half of a barren moon lit the edges of scudding clouds with silver. Drake and Dahl walked ahead.

"Seems like we're always heading out on some do or die mission, mate," Drake said.

"Not like this," Dahl replied. "I've never done anything like this."

Drake took in the surroundings, the team and their compliment of villagers. "Shocking that nobody would help them."

"But look how they've thrived with just a little help." Dahl took the lead through a narrow gap as they started to ascend a mountain. "Sometimes, that's all a person needs."

"I do feel responsible for them."

"You and me both, pal. You and me both."

Onward and upward, circuiting first one mountain and then another, following narrow trails cut or worn into the bare rock, by turns inching along a rocky outcrop with a deadly fall to the left and then hugging pitched stone faces as they climbed a random rockfall. In one way they followed a trail left by the cannibals, in another a route recommended by some of the men. One by one they helped each other along, pulling, prodding, encouraging. Sixteen chasing many and with retribution on their minds.

And finally the great house that clung to the mountain came

into view, lights ablaze warding away the night, walls thick and lofty and strong and seemingly insurmountable. Drake flinched as a terrifying, vicious howl echoed through the night.

"What the hell was that?" Alicia was suddenly an awful lot closer. "Alpaca?"

"Worse," Dahl said. "Sounded remarkably like—"

"We've heard these stories," Brynn said, shuddering, face cast into fiery shadows by the torches. "Killer wolves. They're guarded by killer wolves. I didn't think they were all true."

Fearful, the villagers regarded the moving shadows.

Drake listened as more mournful voices took up the call, as the baying grew louder and hungrier. He watched the track ahead.

"We're about to find out," he said.

CHAPTER THIRTY EIGHT

Hayden soon found that the few short hours she thought she had vanished faster than the last embers of a dying fire. Fay questioned her some more and then last night's victims spoke up about their ordeal. It wasn't as if Hayden didn't know what was going to happen. The question was—were all the situations she saw unfolding around her worth going through it all?

She saw frightened youths—male and female—who'd signed up to participate in a test and wanted out. She saw others on the road to an unsteady acceptance—either because they liked the idea of belonging or were too scared to protest. She saw others who appeared intoxicated with the drug Dantanion had introduced and were desperate for more. Within the group wandered older initiates, spreading more poisonous persuasion and honey-coated lies. Each one was fair of face, lithe of body, and displaying a fixed smile that looked like it had been carved in place. Hayden had seen it before on ballet dancers and pageant queens, and thought it about as hideous a subversion of true happiness as was possible.

She wandered to the bolted doors, but saw no way through them except by key. The locks were gleaming and large. She imagined a guard carrying it around his neck. When two initiates came over and gently guided her away she knew they were all subject to a vigilant eye. She did take a few moments to examine them though, and saw gloves on their hands, under which the impression of bandages could be seen. Did they walk awkwardly too? Did one of them wince every time he touched his own chest? She didn't want to delve too deeply—the monstrous imaginings that slithered through her mind would last forever.

A gong sounded, deep and ominous. The initiates all clapped, grabbing attention but grinning now with just a little more venom. It was time for the real party to begin.

I'm a prisoner. They wanna take my body and leave my mind intact to remember every last minute of it.

"We will make our way to the feasting hall," one of the women said.

Hayden saw Fay blanch, saw the indecision, and held out a hand to the girl. "Stick together," she said. "We can get through this."

If Fay was eighteen she was lucky, but she looked on Hayden with eyes that had suffered too much. "I'm scared."

Hayden wanted to say, me too, but held it back. They joined the line and waited. Dantanion's underlings walked up and down the line, ensuring all stayed together and answering questions with nothing but knowing smirks. Presently, they moved and Hayden shuffled forward. The line filed through the door and then up a narrow corridor, lit by artificial sconces. The going was slow, hesitant, but seemed to suit the assistants. As Hayden neared the end of the corridor she saw those ahead turn to their left and disappear. Soon, the loud noise of chatting, laughing and quiet conversation filled her ears.

Roll of the dice.

What to do?

No actual guards were in evidence, but Hayden was totally alone and she knew what the spider creatures were capable of. She saw them now as she entered the feasting hall, capering around the outsides to the beat of an unknown song. Clad in black, they cavorted like jesters, some partially climbing walls, others flitting between the crowd and encouraging shrieks. Hayden took a long look at all the recruits.

Young and pretty. All alone. And this was the work of the Devil.

Torches flickered all along the walls. An enormous table dominated the center of the room, already laid with cloths, cutlery, napkins and warming dishes. Servants flitted here and there, barely noticed. Bottles of wine stood open, breathing, everywhere. Plates of nibbles were distributed through the gathering which, to Hayden's relief, looked to be bread in all its forms.

The throng quietened on seeing the recruits, staring with

mixed gazes dripping with appraisal, judgment and expectation. Hayden saw a man standing on a dais—clad in a sheer black bodysuit—and striking a pose on one leg with one arm around his back. How he stood so still for so long she didn't know, but was forced to wonder about the symbolism.

She saw banners unfurled along a far wall, floor to ceiling, black with a red logo that she had to assume was Dantanion's personal crest. In a far corner musicians strummed quietly, faces red probably from liquor or drugs. Pedestals rose among the people, surfaces taken up by silver plates full of plastic cups that held a clear liquid. Dozens were ingested every minute, invoking some darker pall that fell over the crowd. The table itself was so brightly illuminated it caused after-images to blur Hayden's vision.

"I . . . I don't want to do this," Fay echoed her own thoughts.

An underling heard her and leaned in. "You signed up for it." He hooted. "You're being paid for it. So it's eat, or take the long fall."

"The what?"

The underling mimed taking a dive. "From the cliffs." He shrugged. "Whatever. It's fun either way. The boss—he knows. He knows when you're faking it. When you're pretending to be part of the family. But once he roots them out," he rubbed his belly, "they make a fine feast."

Hayden pulled Fay away as the line started to move. One by one the recruits were seated around the table, filling one half of it. Hayden sat staring at an empty plate, a heated dish and some shiny cutlery. Hundreds of hungry, half-rabid eyes stared at her, gauging her response. At that moment a flash of black caught her eye and Dantanion appeared, without ceremony, from behind one of the banners. Quickly, the man walked to the head of the table.

He eyed the recruits.

"It is a good day for a feast," he said.

Cheers erupted around the room, startling Hayden. Cups were raised. Servants appeared from a door, each one carrying something that made Fay—and Hayden, truth be told—cringe.

Skulls. Empty skulls. *Oh fuck, they're not replicas.*

Dantanion spoke again: "With this feast we gain the strength to overcome our enemies, replenish and renew our knowledge, expand our skills and accept new successes. We give thanks to the offering for giving their essence and all that they were, to nourish and sustain us."

Hayden felt her cheeks flush red and fought down the sudden fear. In this room, among so many enemies, she was about to die.

"Tonight you give a piece of yourself," Dantanion said. "And then you will enter our family. This is our sacred ritual. This is our proof to you. And the proof . . . is in the tasting."

He took his seat now, the black robe about his body drawn tight. Hayden studied his face, his eyes, wondering how such a striking figure might perpetuate such a mysterious and macabre past. The slight smile he afforded her sent butterflies through her stomach. *Whatever it is I don't want to do it but still, I'd like to make him proud of me.*

Empty skulls clunked down on the table before them as a select few took seats opposite. Hundreds of others crowded around, some leaning on the back of the new recruits' seats. Soon, even the whispering stopped.

"Take up the knife," Dantanion said.

Hungry eyes fixed on Hayden, on Fay, on all the newcomers.

"See its edge? Feel it. Test its weight. Grip the handle. Study the fine blade. Are you ready?"

Hayden picked up the knife with reluctance, seeing no way out for any of them. The hall was full, the table surrounded; Dantanion's family expectant and fueled with a cocktail of drugs. Someone then quietly slipped a plastic cup in front of every new recruit. Hayden looked ahead and saw eyes gleaming at her, shining at the prospect of what was to come. She knew immediately that if she took that sip she wouldn't be able to stop any of it.

And what are your chances if you don't?

Worse than zilch.

Already, some eager recruits had slammed down the shot as if it was golden tequila. Hayden turned to Fay, ignoring the glistening eyes and mouths that watched.

"Together?"

The tear-filled stare wrenched at her soul. "I can't do it."

Fay pushed at the table, sending her chair away and into those that were gathered behind. They pushed back, trapping her. Hayden reached out quickly, trying to calm the girl with a gesture.

"It's the lesser of two evils."

"No it isn't. I'd rather die."

She was right. It wasn't. Hayden didn't feel exactly the same, but understood. "If you die, everything ends. No more chances. No future."

"As if my life has been a carnival so far."

But there is always a chance, no matter how small. "Keep trying. Stay alive. Never lose sight of your dream. Be doubtless. Be tough. Be fierce. You will win."

Fay hung back, reluctant. Hayden saw half a dozen men and women licking their lips only four feet away. Incisors, sharpened, slid free. An insatiable hunger burned in those faces—hotter than furnace fire.

A recruit further down the table tried to bolt. The pack fell on him, tearing, shrieking, enjoying every minute. Hayden saw him dragged off cut and bleeding, flesh hanging in strips, stomach bleeding.

She turned the knife in her hands. "Live," she told Fay and positioned the blade at the tip of her little finger, above the nail.

Dantanion's voice was soft, impersonal. "Fill their skulls."

Hayden swigged the clear liquid as a servant filled the empty skull with red wine. She repeated herself one more time.

"Live," she said.

A fever started in her brain, infecting every nerve receptor and cell. It traveled quickly down the length of her body. It calmed her fears, making her wonder what Fay was being so frigging fussy about.

Fay hesitated with the cup to her lips. Hayden reached out and tipped it, sending the liquid into the girl's throat.

Dantanion raised his own wine-filled skull. "Eat," he said.

Hayden pressed down on the knife. The pain was short, the fire that shot through her finger brief. The slither of flesh came away, and rolled onto the table. Blood followed it and she reached out with the napkin, mopping it up. A bandage was swiftly offered by a servant who appeared from nowhere. Hayden applied it to the tip of her finger, wincing at the raw pain even through the rapture. Then, with a pristine set of tweezers she took hold of the snippet of flesh and placed it upon the hot dish. Every other recruit did the same, even Fay, who somehow managed to look sick and ecstatic at the same time.

"Eat," Dantanion intoned. He bent slightly as an aide appeared to whisper into his ear. Hayden was good at reading lips, but this message made so little sense she wondered if she'd misread. *The wolves are loose.*

Hayden turned the flesh over with the tweezers, trying to give it an even roasting on both sides, then brought the piece of herself up to her own lips.

Hesitated.

Every base instinct, every human impulse, fought hard to resist. The vilest of sins lay before her, sizzling, and whatever vile feelings rose inside had to be quashed. To live, she must first be abominable.

Fay chewed first, head down. Hayden then ingested the morsel of her own flesh and chewed until she could swallow. They could not take wine with it, but when the piece was gone they were allowed to wash it down.

"Now," Dantanion said. "You have become family. Go below and rejoice. You are free in your new home." To the servants he said, "Bring out tonight's offering."

CHAPTER THIRTY NINE

Drake bent as the first slavering beast came into sight, running hard around a bend ahead. It was large and lean, jaws bared, fur matted to its body. Within seconds its brethren could be seen rushing behind it, the pack incensed by something their handlers had done and clearly set on the intruders.

Gun up, he dropped the first, scattering it in front of its fellow runners, upsetting their balance. Dahl was at his side, also crouched because on this narrow path nobody else could come alongside. Behind and above them stood Alicia and Smyth, also firing.

Bullets ripped into the pack. The wolves screamed and howled, their cries echoing between canyon walls and surging across the mountain. Other, far away, plaintive cries took up the call. Drake doubled down—two shots for each wolf. He had more compassion for these creatures than any mercenary, but they were still trying to kill him. The speed of the beasts rapidly closed the gap between them.

A wolf slowed and then leaped, sleek and graceful, legs straight, jaws endlessly snapping. It landed to the right of Dahl, rebounding off the mountain wall. Smyth managed to wing it as its paws hit the ground and then again as it recovered and snapped at Dahl. The Swede never lost concentration on the oncoming pack, ignoring the wolf and trusting Smyth to have his back.

Drake whistled softly at Dahl's trust. "Not even a twitch?"

"Balls," Dahl replied, "of steel."

"More like brains of mush."

"Seeing is believing," Alicia piped up from behind.

"Hey." Kenzie was crouching frustrated to the side, fingers nervously flexing mostly because they were empty and feet inching forward at every snarl and howl and animal grunt. "I got first dibs on those."

Alicia grinned, dropping a wolf. "All right, I'll ride shotgun."

"How would that work?"

"Y'know, top and bottom. One—"

"Hey!" Dahl cried. "I'm right here, for fuck's sake."

"And me," Drake added.

He counted eight wolves left alive with eight more dead or dying. The ones at the rear of the pack struggled to make ground, hampered by bodies, but the more creative of them—or the hungriest—soon began to use their fellows' bodies to leap from. A wolf landed at Drake's feet, snapping, dropped by Smyth. Its fangs brushed his sleeves, leaving a string of drool.

"See. I got dem balls too."

"That's just stupidity." Dahl eyed the drool. "Stop trying to be me. Never gonna work."

Drake rose fast then as a wolf leaped desperately high and cleared its fallen. The gun was useless. Its body slammed down, heavy as a man, smashing hard against his shoulders. He caught it, wrestled with the balance of weight, then dashed it onto its back hard against the rock floor. It squirmed hard, jaws snapping around. Alicia leaned around and shot it. Dahl stepped forward to meet the last three oncoming wolves.

Drake stared. "Really?"

One used its incredible speed to partially mount the right wall of the canyon, claws tapping, and came at Dahl at an angle. He caught its leap, grabbed its haunches and threw it straight into the next running wolf. The two collided hard, tumbling together in a mass of legs. The third would have latched onto his shoulder, again using forward momentum to perform an incredible leap, but Kenzie rushed forward with perfect timing, drew down with her katana and ended its assault with one smooth stroke.

Dahl winced, splashed by blood. "Jesus, Kenzie. Have a care. They're wolves, not bloody mercenaries."

"Yeah, just mindless animals," Drake said.

Mai crouched watching. "A good description of every mercenary I've met."

Kenzie wiped her sword. "Who ended their poor suffering quicker? You with your bullets or me with my blade?"

Drake knew several animals were wounded and moved quickly to end their pain. Mai joined him and then Kinimaka. The villagers congregated further down the canyon, keeping an eye out for any further ambush. Drake walked beyond the dead wolves and peeked around the furthest corner, Dahl at his side.

"You think that goes all the way above the house?"

The pass twisted to the left and ran upward at a sharp angle, still traversable but only just. Drake could just make out twists and turns as it progressed, and thought he saw the briefest sign of it continuing beyond the house, edges picked out by silvery skies.

Brynn was at their backs. "Nobody from Kimbiri has been even this far," she said. "There could be other traps."

Drake broke out the pencil flashlights, their beams tiny but powerful, and waited until everyone switched to theirs. The procession began to pick their way upward, exposed to the elements, scoured by winds and cold, shocked at turns by the sudden drops that almost seemed to jump out to left and right. It was at these hazards that the team moved closer to each other, holding onto jackets at times to make sure their closest neighbors didn't stray to their deaths.

The path wound hard, up and up, and they lost sight of the house to their right. Drake saw it only twice, the high, brick walls rising like pillars of darkness toward some distant, high altar where blood sacrifice was performed.

They climbed together, but fought separate battles. Drake worried for the team—how Smyth might overcome his fears for Lauren, how Mai and Alicia might end up, how Dahl struggled with his wife and she with him, how Kenzie might turn out, how Kinimaka and Hayden would end. Unable and unwilling to affect any of it, he nevertheless was good-hearted enough to worry. The team was in flux—but wasn't change a good thing? With Webb's statement still largely unaddressed what did that bode for the future?

And where the hell is Karin Blake?

They fought the slope, a step at a time. They used rocky handholds to pull themselves up. They rested on outcroppings as the trail wound to both sides. Once again they saw the chateau, this time unexpectedly and abruptly. A sheer brick wall greeted them at the end of another passage. Drake stopped and looked up, now able to see the top of the roof and the continuing mountain above.

"Almost there," he breathed. "Pass it along."

Mai, Smyth and Kinimaka dropped back to help the villagers, though all were fit and hardy and wouldn't accept assistance to walk up a mountain. Nevertheless, they let the soldiers walk with them, primarily as guards. They paused momentarily at the edge of a mountain plateau, the deep valley running away from the chateau spread out before them. Drake caught his breath for a few minutes.

"I've rarely seen anything more stunning," he said. "Remember Iceland? During the Odin thing? That was pretty good."

Dahl was so close Drake could hear him breathe. "Been a long road, matey. So many adventures. I wonder where it'll all end."

"Our finest hours," Drake said with certainty. "That's where it always ends."

The group looked ahead, and moved out. Drake hated being fatalistic, but adventure couldn't go on forever. The pass continued at a sharp angle for two more minutes, views open and deadly to their left, away from the house, until the route leveled off and an opening appeared up ahead and to the right. Dahl arrived first, nodding into the darkness. Drake came up alongside him.

"Risky," he said.

"Strap on your big panties." Dahl nodded in agreement.

Alicia made a sound of protest. "Don't tell me I have to climb all the way back down to go get them."

Smyth walked along the chest-high promontory, looking out over the edge. "We can attach the hooks here," he said. "It's pretty solid."

"Yeah, Lancelot," Alicia said. "That's why it's called rock."

Kinimaka came up. "Make it a firm fix, guys. I don't wanna end up crashing through that roof and ending up on a dinner table."

"Might be a better plan." Kenzie glanced over the edge at the hundred-foot drop. "You would keep them occupied for hours, Hawaiian."

"Well, thanks," Kinimaka said grumpily. "Maybe you could join me and help 'em slice me up with that sword."

"Happy to."

Drake ignored the bickering, and helped find the pack with the pitons, hooks and rappel lines. Between them, Smyth, Dahl and he fixed four lines to the side of the mountain and tested them for strength.

"Mano proof?" Alicia asked.

Dahl puffed. "We're about to find out."

The Hawaiian laughed. "I doubt there's anything truly Mano-proof. Even this mountain. ."

"We ready?" Smyth pushed. "Hayden ain't gonna last forever."

Alicia glanced over. "Is that a cannibal joke, dude? 'Cause it's not funny."

Smyth hissed at her, the annoyance rising red in his face. Without further comment he climbed out over the mountain and waited until Kinimaka and Dahl worked together to strap Brynn to his sturdy back. This way, making two trips each, the soldiers planned to get everyone down to the roof relatively quickly. Smyth set off and then Drake climbed over, followed by Dahl.

Anica and Curtis climbed on. Alicia took Desiree, and then the whole group were either rappelling down the mountain or huddled on the bleak roof of the house, totally exposed to the elements. Smyth moved over to an air vent, unscrewed the fastenings and took a look inside. Drake crawled over, the group now operating only by the light of the moon. Silver turned his face stark and serious as he addressed the soldier.

"We good?"

"Yeah, but it's tight."

Drake leaned inside. "Looks doable."

"I didn't mean for me."

Smyth climbed inside, feet first and started to let himself down slowly, tethered by another rope. The group followed slowly, taking their time. Drake found himself surrounded by a darkness blacker than pitch black, but praised the fact that they were finally out of the wind and the cold. Now, he started to drip with sweat.

"Bollocks. Can't bloody win."

They inched down through the ventilation duct, which to Drake's burgeoning and ghastly imagination had been built essentially to remove fumes generated inside the kitchen. The interesting realization that the cannibals' lifestyle choices provided their enemies a way into their castle did not improve his horrifying theory.

The shaft was made of mildly flexible steel and ran smoothly save for the joints. The team continued down until Smyth passed a quiet "stop" command up the line. Drake found himself swinging, heels brushing Dahl's skull and being scraped on his own by Mai's toe. The Japanese woman's angry whisper echoed along the shaft.

"Alicia, if you don't stop tapping that tune out on my head I will tattoo it on your forehead."

"I'm good. I'm finished now. Never heard a drum solo sound so hollow."

Smyth took his time bending almost double to investigate the access cover below. "Crap," he said. "Should have guessed, of course. The screws are on the other side."

Fifteen faces stared down at him, all grimacing guiltily.

"Can it be dragged up into the shaft?" Dahl asked. "I mean are the flanges on the outside or the inside?"

"Inside."

"Then tie your end of the rope around it and we'll pull."

Two sweaty minutes later, they had yanked and twisted and buckled the vent cover until it pulled free of its moorings. Smyth used it as the new floor and quickly leapt out of the shaft, followed by Dahl and then Drake. They came once more to level ground—a narrow corridor, barely lit and cold, unfurnished. He waited patiently for the rest of the group to arrive as Smyth and Dahl proceeded carefully toward both ends. Dahl soon returned.

"Nothing," he said. "Dead end."

Smyth used the comms. "Walk this way."

The door he found possessed a viewing pane, through which

Drake saw a much wider, plusher corridor running away toward a distant set of double doors. The area was deserted. They pushed through quietly and carefully, aware that silent alarms might be set on the access doors but seeing none. Moving as swiftly as possible they made the far set of doors—a plush, oak-paneled, self-important affair with golden pull handles.

Smyth tested one. It moved easily. Checking weapons and positions, and guarding the rear with Yorgi, Curtis and Desiree, they breached the door hard, spreading out as they entered the room. Drake saw instantly that it was an office and empty.

"Quick check," he said. "See if there's anything that can help us."

Smyth and Kinimaka moved over to the desk, the latter switching on a desktop PC. Alicia headed for the picture window and the view across the dark mountains.

"Big knob's office," she said. "Probably this Dantanion."

Mano used a flash drive to copy data from the computer. Smyth rifled the drawers. Mai shifted paper and pens, trays and bowls around on the polished surface of the table. She beckoned Drake over, pointed into a white porcelain bowl.

Drake wondered at her secrecy, then saw what was in the bowl. Gorge filled his throat as he saw three full-length fingers, complete with blue-painted nails, cooked to a brownish shade and nibbled around the edges.

The things you see, you can never unsee, he thought. A basic fact around the protective net parents threw over their children. He closed his eyes and turned away.

"Let's finish these bastards off once and for all."

It took five more minutes to walk the corridor, descend a staircase and then traverse another hallway. By now they were hearing a great, swelling roar, a gathering of people in one cavernous space. The closer they came the noisier it got. Smyth stopped when he reached the end of a hallway and peered out over the railing.

"How's it look?" Kinimaka's voice came over the comms. It was easier and safer than crowding forward.

"Massive set of doors leading into a huge room. Probably

hundreds of folks. No obvious guards. Can only see floor and legs. A few heads. Looks like they're all partying down there."

"Move out," Kinimaka said with haste and venom.

"Wait." Brynn must have been listening through Yorgi's earpiece and now spoke up. "How do we know who is prisoner and who is true enemy?"

"Same way we always figure it out," Alicia replied. "If it attacks you, fuck it up. Now let's gatecrash this mother."

CHAPTER FORTY

Dantanion's scream: "Kill the newcomers! Kill them all!" ripped the air to shreds. Hayden saw the man see the SPEAR team almost instantaneously; saw the recognition and the incredibly swift intellect assess the situation; saw the certainty that this was about to become the bloodiest of all fights to the death.

She was part of a group lining up to leave the hall, the effects of the drug already wearing off. When Smyth stepped through the door she saw him and ran the possibilities, but not as fast as Dantanion, it seemed. Within seconds though, a plan came to her. A plan centered around the survival of the innocents, because there was no way her saviors could know all the bad from the good.

"Stick with me." She grabbed Fay's hand and beckoned to the others. "Now!"

They ran; most complaining that their fingers were really starting to hurt. Hayden ignored the gunfire and pushed bodies aside, rushing at her friends. Already they were fanning out, taking aim and waiting for the attack. Hayden ran in first, dragging Fay along.

"Three with me!" she cried. "We have to secure the caves and protect some of these kids."

Kinimaka, Smyth and Yorgi peeled away, joining her group. Running away from the hall was easy; it was the team she worried about and what she now saw were quite a few of the villagers. She struggled with elation and fear, trying to maintain focus. Kinimaka handed her, her comms back, and she smiled, relieved to see the concern on all their faces, but especially his.

"I'm fine," she said over the comms. "Just a scratch."

"So long as you didn't give 'em a helping hand," Alicia quipped darkly, "or end up in hot water."

"Good to hear they weren't nasty bastards then," Kenzie said surprisingly, then added, "Did they butter you up instead?"

Hayden grunted angrily. "Stay alert, fools. There's a hundred sets of teeth in there with your fucking names on 'em. Chew on that."

Down they went, reaching the caves and bracing against the cold. Hayden met a guard blow for blow, then took a punch to the face as Smyth squeezed by to engage a second. Her head jerked back, just giving Mano enough room to plant his enormous fist into the guard's nose. Not even a whimper escaped him as he slithered into jelly. Smyth shot the next point blank.

"No fucking around," he said. "No more."

Hayden pulled him back. "I found the cave entrance," she said, "but couldn't get inside. We have to get down there. It's below the house, not a part of it. If the others fail, we can defend it."

Kinimaka looked shocked. "Fail?"

"Worst case scenario," Hayden said. "But I have to entertain it. Oh, and the Inca treasure is down there too."

"Ah."

She engaged the next guard, and took him down in a headlock. He struggled wildly until she increased the pressure on his jugular. "Where's the key?" she whispered. "The key to the caves?"

"Fu . . . fu . . . fu—"

"No, no, no. Do you wanna die, or run?"

Straight into the SPEAR team.

"Run," he choked. "Please run."

"Just tell me."

He balked. Kinimaka dragged over another, more pliant individual. The scrawny guard looked like a toothpick in the Hawaiian's grip.

"Over there." He waved. "Office. Safe code is seven-oh-nine."

Hayden hadn't noticed an office on her previous reccy, but put it down to anxiety and lack of time. Smyth bounded away and soon returned, the gleaming key grasped firmly in one hand.

"C'mon, guys. Let's see what's down there."

"You really think treasure still lies down in cave system?" Yorgi asked. "And not above somewhere?"

"Nah, he kept it extremely hard to find," Hayden said. "The man's a loner. Trusts nobody. I bet he went down there alone and brought each piece back separately. One of the reasons he took so long about it. Wouldn't want his family torn apart by greed. I bet it's a warren."

"Traps?" Smyth asked worriedly.

"Only if Dantanion made them," Hayden said. "I hope."

Smyth approached the arched wooden door that barred the entrance to the caves. Hayden heard cries all around and turned swiftly as Fay began to shout and point. Behind them, filling the corridor and the entrance to the caves, came a surge of attackers, mostly guards but with some of the human-spider creatures among them.

She took a Glock offered by Kinimaka. "Thanks."

"If what appears to have happened to you did happen, I have to say—that took some bravery, Hay."

"I don't want to talk about it. They're coming."

"Neither would I," Kinimaka said. "But I know damn well you didn't do it for yourself."

Hayden pushed Fay behind her. "Just shut the hell up and start shooting."

Kinimaka smiled. Hayden couldn't figure out why, and then the attackers were rushing down upon them, brandishing sharp weapons and clubs, axes and hammers, their cries making her blood curdle.

The attack on the chateau had come early, too early. Many would live or die today depending on the skills of the team and the villagers they'd brought along. Innocents were at risk, but wasn't that always the case?

She stepped forward to defend them with all she had.

CHAPTER FORTY ONE

Drake let loose the fury of war as a hundred snarling enemies charged.

One shot per man, one downed and another tripped over and then another with each shot. The mags emptied fast but the attackers kept coming. Dahl ranged to the right, Alicia to the left. Mai chose hand-to-hand combat for the first wave, sending each to the ground, and then used intricate holds to twist them against the next. People fell around her, but if they weren't dead or unconscious they were still extremely dangerous. No reaching for lost weapons here; the cannibals came at her with their teeth.

Kenzie used her Glock; part of the weapons cache they'd liberated from members of the Cusco Militia. A man jumped at her, shot through the chest, but on landing bore her to the ground, bleeding all over her and snapping with his teeth, trying to take the end of her nose off. She held him away with one hand, and brought her gun around with the other.

She pulled the trigger, then moved on to the next.

Drake aimed and fired two bullets, then looked down in horror as something jerked at his arm. Jaws were fastened around his wrist, the teeth gnashing hard at the leather and cloth that protected the flesh. He could feel the points through his clothes, cutting deeper. He smashed the cannibal on the top of the skull, then again, and finally a third time as hard as he could. The figure slumped away; the teeth marks forever impressed in the leather around his sleeve, torn through and almost reaching the skin. He saw a woman leap for Dahl's throat to be brushed aside by the Swede's arm.

Not just a battle. This is raw, visceral bedlam.

A bite on his thigh made him scream. Shock and disbelief tore the sound from him. Kenzie came down hard on the offender, unleashing her katana and severing the offending body part.

"Do you like me now?" she asked.

"Fuck yeah." Drake waded into a group of cannibals. Kicking, smashing with hands, knees and feet, he forced them apart, shooting his weapon until it ran dry.

"Should have kept some, ya knob." Dahl was close by. "Look up there."

Drake raised his eyes above fang level. Along the upper reaches of the hall were arrayed a row of interior balconies, mostly for show, but some of Dantanion's men had climbed up to them and were aiming their bows from above, sighting in on the team. Dahl shot one down, but two more loosed arrows. Bolts slammed into the crowd, parting Curtis and Desiree but hitting neither. Brynn struggled with an aggressor but Mai was soon at her side, flinging the woman away. The villagers still kept hold of their own guns, though did not advance on the crowd, overwhelmed and alarmed.

Drake flinched as another arrow flew down. This one glanced off the polished floor at his feet. A body took him about the waist, but not in the usual sense. This one contained a set of teeth that instantly started worrying at his stomach, biting and tearing and trying to find a way inside. An elbow to the neck sent the aggressor to the floor; a boot to the same area finished him. The next onslaught came and he deflected the leap, allowing the body to fly past. Dahl picked off another archer. Two remained though, and now sent down bolts that struck Mai and Kenzie.

"No!"

Kenzie fell to one knee, gasping. The black bolt had pierced her clothing, but only an inch of skin, flashing through at pace and drawing a long furrow. The wound bled, but she ignored it, stabbing at an oncoming victim. Mai saw the arrow coming and dodged faster than the eye could follow, but even then it would have struck her forehead if a foe hadn't deflected it with his own. Still it came though, tumbling though the air, striking her with the bulk of the shaft and leaving a mark. She fought on without stumbling, blinking furiously.

Alicia saw her struggling and moved toward her back.

"Thanks," Mai gasped.

"Wouldn't want you to miss our showdown, darlin'."
"Of course."

Spider creatures now jumped away from the walls and came swarming across the floor. Many hopped up onto the colossal table, and sent pots, pans and plates spinning as they surged across it, bodies cavorting and limbs pivoting at practically impossible angles.

Kenzie, alone, jumped up onto the table and stood tall, immobile, her sword pointed at its surface, resting. "You will not get past me," she said to them all.

They capered straight for her. With grace of movement, she lifted and swung the katana, a deadly arc of artistry, blade flashing, glinting, and then washed with blood. The downward swing became a sideways sweep and then an upward curve, painting the air with trails of crimson. Three were at her feet, twitching. A dozen more came.

Kenzie stepped forward with economy of movement, a shuffle of her feet at a time, using the table's width and dancing from left to right. The katana swished and curved and diced the air, chopping through a creeping body or catching one in mid-air.

Alicia ran down the side of the table to help, picking off a few stragglers at the back with the last of her bullets. Kenzie painted new and skillful shapes of blood in the air, stepping among the showers, dripping red, and starting to attract the attention of more than just the spider creatures.

Drake saw nostrils flaring and jaws widening as they aimed toward her. Taking stock, he quickly evaluated their position. The villagers were knotted in one corner of the room, Mai before them, taking their fair share of attackers away from the main battle. Drake saw to his dismay that two had already fallen. Dahl was in front, softening the onslaught. Up ahead, he watched as Dantanion studied the fight, the enigmatic leader saying nothing and moving little, but seeing everything. A shrug of a shoulder sent the last of his spider creatures into the fray, all bounding creepily toward Dahl and Alicia. And still he watched, both hands holding a ghastly chain of finger bones that hung around his neck.

From behind Dantanion came the feast that had been prepared, only now it was being propelled by two huge men dressed in chef's uniforms. The strangeness and creepiness of it all staggered Drake, but he rushed forward anyway, barging two cannibals aside and punching a third in the head. The huge lead chef confronted him, cleaver in hand.

"You ruin it alllll!"

Drake staggered back as the chef upended the huge platter onto him. The prepared dead body looked whole, but had been quartered, so the arms and legs fell separately to the main cadaver. Drake warded off an arm but was struck by a falling leg, the bone hitting his forehead like a fist. It was only by luck that he then saw the descending cleaver—its blade flashing and catching his eye.

Thrusting both hands up, he caught the wrist as it came down, halting the blade a hair's breadth from his face. The chef jumped upon him, weight bearing down, face a snarl and teeth bared. Coming around him now, Drake saw the legs of the second chef.

No way was he going to be able to move the big bastard atop him. The edge of the cleaver was already parting the tiniest hairs on his face. Every ounce of muscle, of concentration, was being poured into stopping that cleaver.

Chef number two dropped down to one knee beside his left ear. This man held a steak knife in one hand and proceeded to slowly level it up with Drake's ear. He then placed a hand behind the shaft.

"Say when you're ready," he said to the first chef.

"Skewer its brain," came the grunt of a reply.

Drake tried to twist away but there was nowhere to go. The second chef pushed the steak knife hard into his ear, but then the momentum stopped. The hand holding the knife fell to the floor and the bloody stump that was left flew up, spraying as its owner screamed.

"Let's see how you like it." Kenzie had swept the table clear and jumped to his aid. Her sword sliced and diced the second chef and then impaled the first. The man kept pushing despite the pain, seeing the end but trying to take Drake with him. The ex-

SAS man pushed back with everything he had, holding the weapon at bay just long enough.

Kenzie pushed harder and all the strength fled from the chef. His face creased, his will all but sapped. Drake rolled him off and took the hand Kenzie proffered.

"Cheers, love," he said.

"Just proving a point." She waved the katana in his face to emphasize the wit.

"Always fancied the chef's special," Drake said. "Never thought I'd become it."

"You will never take us alive!" Dantanion screamed above it all. "It will all come crashing down before we die!" He ripped the finger bone necklace from around his neck and threw it into the air—the chain broken and the digits dropping down all around him.

Ah, the quiet man finds his voice and his anger. At last.

"Sounds desperate," Kenzie said.

"My job is almost done," Drake said grimly. "Let's push the bastard over the edge."

Only three men separated them from Dantanion. To their right Dahl slipped in blood, fell to one knee and saw a knife thrust at his shoulder. Unable to twist to evade the attack he kicked the assailant's legs away, felling him, and then stared right into the man's eyes.

"Stab me whilst I'm down would you?"

The blade slashed at him. Dahl caught it, turned it, and planted it in his attacker. Another spider creature landed on his back, striking with elbows and knees, face mask lifted so the teeth could come into play. Dahl put a heavy boot into them and watched the black-clad man shrink away. Above, there were no more archers and the hall was becoming much less crowded. Mai managed to close the gap between them and the villagers, bringing the entire group closer together.

Dantanion screamed something about his family, his vision. The world he had built. As he finished, his self-imposed fangs glinted, a savage promise.

Standing alone, he did not run away.

Drake and Kenzie cleared the path before him.

CHAPTER FORTY TWO

Hayden fought her way to the cave door as the living quarters rapidly filled up. The crush worked against them; made up of attackers, defenders and those that wanted no part of it. They had nowhere to go. Some were being stabbed or crushed just to make space for more. Dantanion's guards surged into and around the place, hunting out the insurgents.

Struggling, she tried to get the key into the lock. An arm swiped at her, making her lurch. She pushed the attacker in the chest, forcing him back. Aimed the key again and forced it into the lock. Yorgi kicked out at her side, forcing another away, doubling up a woman. When she looked up again her eyes were glowing, her face rabid. Hayden knew she'd ingested a ton of cannibal juice.

Cannibal juice?

Well, what the hell else would you call it? She twisted the lock, heard a click, and flung open the doors. Just in time. Another surge forced her down the narrow passage that was revealed and into a blast of cold air. Yorgi stumbled after her, then Fay. She'd already lost Smyth and Kinimaka, but assumed they were just trying to cope with the crush. She'd already checked and knew the Glock had six bullets remaining. Now, she pressed on, seeking out a niche or a junction where she might be able to stop and help her friends.

Above, she could only see rock and knew they were below the foundations of the house, its lower edge probably jutting out into space over them. Built as it had been against the mountain she knew it had to be anchored further up, and the concealed caves delved below. Two guards caught her first, and she beat them hard, rendering both unconscious in less than a minute. Fay stared in amazement.

"Why didn't you do that before? At the feast?"

"Because I didn't have backup then. And I thought I could find the keys alone. And—"

"All right, I get it. Jeez."

Yorgi used the rock wall to gain forward momentum, running a few steps up at full speed and coming down hard onto another guard. Hayden backed further away. The cave entrance began to fill and then the passage. All manner of people followed her.

And attacked without conscience. Anything went in the caves. Men came low and she beat them down. Another slashed with a sharpened stick and she perforated his lungs with it. A spider creature crawled along the side of the tunnel where the wall met the ground, black and chilling. Hayden decided it was worth a bullet and saw it bleed red blood.

Thank God.

Still, they forced her backward. The tunnel opened out. Behind her came the sounds of a flowing stream. It crossed their path and continued underground. More attackers thrust forward. Hayden smashed one on the temple and then another. She fell atop them, forcing them under the water and kneeling on their heads. She fended a third off, catching punches and blows on her wrists and biceps, gaining bruises and not losing any ground.

Fay knelt beside her, crying.

"If you want to live," Hayden panted between punches, "fight!"

A guard slipped in the stream, smashed his head against jutting rock. His weapon had been a baseball bat, so Hayden scooped it up and used it on the next. Yet another she smashed around the knees, three blows, until finally she felt the fight give in those she had drowned, and rose up.

Backing further away.

She took Fay by the jacket, pulled her back. The tunnel angled downward now, its walls moving further and further away. Hayden ignored her soaked feet, her soaked legs, and jabbed at another oncoming opponent. Beyond him now she saw the huge bulk that had to be Kinimaka, the shape of Smyth who grumbled even as he fought. The latter engaged a spider creature, pummeling it until it dropped, but failed to stop two guards sneaking around his back.

Kinimaka ended them with two shots.

Smyth jumped away. Hayden saw recruits coming now, the ones she'd arrived with and a dozen more, filing past Smyth and chasing after her; their eyes wild and petrified, their faces bruised and bloody.

"Nobody signed us up for this," one yelled.

"I don't remember signing up for anything!" another replied.

"Is it all part of the initiation?" Still another.

"Listen up!" Hayden cried out. "You're now running for your goddamn lives. So believe that. And fucking fight!"

Fay stared up and down, left and right, eyes wide with horror. Hayden saw more than just fear of battle in that stare. "What's wrong?" she asked, then gently patted the girl's face. "What's wrong? Fay!"

"Stories I heard earlier," she whispered. "About flesh eaters that never leave the caves. Fed old meat through a hole. They're just left down here to roam and . . . and . . ."

"And what?"

"To watch out for strays," she murmured. "True monsters."

Hayden looked down the darker tunnel that stretched ahead, knowing it led toward the long lost Inca treasure. "We must go deeper. We're under attack. We have no choice."

Smyth came up. "Get a fucking move on!"

"There's more," Fay breathed. "A story of two brothers gone mad and wild who live down here together, worse than the flesh eaters and far hungrier."

"Sounds like shit to me," Smyth said. "Move your ass."

Hayden used another bullet on a spider creature and Kinimaka fired two into guards. With the bulk of the people out of the way now they could puck off their assailants with ease, forcing most of them back up the tunnel and toward the house. Hayden stared into the dark passageway once more.

"Stick together," she said. "We go down."

"Not me," Fay challenged. "I'm staying right here."

"Where you're just as vulnerable," Hayden protested. "From above and below."

"I am not moving. You see, I'm starting to stand up for myself."

At the perfectly wrong moment, Hayden thought. *Like so many kids.* "All right, then I can't help you. Any of you who stay. I want to . . ." She faltered. "Come with us. Please."

Fay refused; others sat beside her. In the end all of the recruits chose to stay, especially when all sounds of footsteps along the tunnel back to the chateau died away.

Hayden eyed her team. "Looks like it's just us, guys."

Yorgi inclined his head. "I will stay with them. I have a full weapon and I can protect these boys and girls."

Hayden saw vulnerability in his eyes then, and guessed he saw much of his old self in the gathering of lost souls. He wanted to go with the team, but needed to protect the kids.

"Good luck," she said. "We'll see you soon."

Smyth and Kinimaka followed her into blackness, trying not to hear the whisperings and slitherings that suddenly started up around them.

CHAPTER FORTY THREE

Drake stopped before Dantanion, expecting the usual barrage of bodyguards to launch a last-ditch assault. After ten seconds he began to feel exposed, after twenty a little silly. Finally, after more than half a minute Alicia tapped him on the shoulder.

"Hey, you gonna say something. Drakey? You scared of the mighty cannibal king?"

"No, I'm not bloody scared," Drake spluttered. "I was waiting for something to happen."

"Seriously? Because you looked scared." Dahl peered at him.

"The only thing that scares me, mate, is when the sausage is done before the bacon. 'Cause that way you're not gonna get your fatty edges nice and crispy."

"Then I guess this dude and you might sometimes have the same problem," Kenzie said, placing the point of her sword against Dantanion's throat. "Do you have any bodyguards lying in wait? A ninja or two?"

The inscrutable leader sniffed but made no movement. "It took ten years of hard toil to build this movement. The shattered bones of many men. It takes ritual devotion and sacrifice to provide and care for this family, something you would never understand. You have come here, invaded us, and destroyed it all in ten minutes."

"Fifteen." Alicia tapped her watch. "Maybe even twenty. But then we are dragging weight." She winked over at Kenzie who flashed a wicked grin.

"We made the world a safer place," Drake said. "Or this part of Peru at least."

"The warmongers will never assuage their greed. The hungry politicians will always believe they can kill, maim and take whatever they want by force. And the worst part is—they think they have the right to do it. That they were born to rule and lead and make war, regardless of the innocent people they displace and murder."

Drake shrugged. "Crazy as you are, pal, you just made sense."

"Can whacko go full circle?" Alicia asked. "I mean, y'know, all the way around and back to sane?"

"Of course there will always be war," Dahl said. "But knowing that our current and potential world leaders might be power-hungry dictators, and that others want to live in a post-apocalyptic world doesn't exactly earn you a medal these days. Turn around, asshole, and put your hands behind your back."

Drake still waited, still expected an attack. But it never came. For once this maniac, this Dantanion, was all he appeared to be—a calm, intelligent maniac with a long-term plan and the wealth to back it up.

"Maybe he's a ninja," Alicia said, turning once more from a quiet surveillance of the room. "Watch him, Torsty."

"It's all about the spectacle," Dantanion said with utter coolness and then threw his hands in the air.

They erupted from behind black banners that ran floor to ceiling—half a dozen spider creatures with blades attached to their elbows and their knees, all capering in mad, haphazard fashion and striking out straight for the soldiers.

With the spiders came a man dressed like a skeleton, bones on the outside, a spear clasped in one hand. Alongside him strode two more seven-foot-tall giants, both with skulls tattooed over their real faces. They were naked and they were eunuchs and they carried maces. Drake was in shock, mouth hanging. Dahl cleared his throat and even Alicia remained speechless.

It wasn't over—not by a long shot. A hunchback shambled free, face as wizened as ancient bark and, cackling, he raised a crossbow. Finally came the worst of all—a broad, fit individual who once might have caught a lady's eye. That was before the surgery.

They had taken his lips away, and part of his jaw. The teeth were exposed all the way from ear to ear, and every single one had been impossibly sharpened. Drake suddenly wished for all the world that he had saved a mag of bullets for this terrible circus of horrors.

Dantanion shrieked for an attack, then joined his horrendous sideshow. Drake dodged a mace, bent low and, ignoring his attacker's nakedness, drove a fist into the muscled abdomen. The mace swung around, missing his body. The second mace-swinger converged on him. Drake skipped back, then dived in, giving them little room. Well-placed punches sent them staggering. Alicia fought the man dressed as a skeleton, took his spear away and fell backward, allowing him to jump after her and impale himself. She then scrambled free, and leapt at Dantanion himself.

Dahl assessed the worst horror of them all, wondering where a weakness might lie, then turned to ward off two of the spider creatures. The four found themselves suddenly beset, surrounded, and unable to defend against every blow and thrust and sharpened edge. Mai then descended, kicking and killing two spider creatures and maiming a third in one leap; and with her she brought the villagers.

Curtis and Desiree still had bullets. Anica and Marco used guns as clubs and scrapped for their very lives. Brynn wielded a knife, stabbing and evading, cutting and nipping aside, the school teacher was fighting for her friends, her village, their very existence. Others came too, mourning their dead, but seeing their killers, their terrorizers, found courage in unity.

Drake caught a mace just below the ball, yanked its wielder off his feet, then slammed the ball itself into the skull of the other man, having to leap upward in the process. Both giants fell hard, bleeding. Mai took out the final spider and then launched a flurry against the hunchback. Dahl engaged the man whose exposed teeth inspired terror, slamming stiff arms and fists into the fleshy part of his body. A strike at the face produced blood only on Dahl's knuckles.

Alicia pushed Dantanion back and back, toward the rear wall. The man appeared to have no fighting prowess at all, and she pursued him only to put him out of action, giving him no chance of escape. His face grew bloody, his left arm hung limply. Still he stood and still he glared with purpose. In the end, the wall halted his retreat; he stood laughing.

"The end is upon us."

Alicia flexed her bruised fists. "Stand still and take it. We're in a hurry."

"Did you not hear me?"

"Something about the end is upon us." She walked closer.

"No. before that. I said I would bring it all crashing down upon us. And I meant it. Literally."

Alicia put it all together in a split instant; the fastest her mind had ever worked. Suddenly it was all forgotten—Dantanion, the horror show, the surviving cannibals.

Suddenly it no longer mattered.

"Drake!" she screamed. "Run! Just fucking run!"

Dantanion reached behind him to the wall, pressed a button and watched a compartment slide open. Inside, a red button glowed. With pleasure, reverence and a sad prayer he pressed it.

The house that was built on the side of a mountain exploded.

CHAPTER FORTY FOUR

Stunning bravery elevated the next few minutes, and stunning, sickening evil marred them. Drake grabbed an embattled Dahl by the shoulders, tore him away from the sideshow freak, and pushed him toward the rear of the house. Alicia spun and ran, catching hold of Mai and dragging the shocked woman along with her as Dantanion ran screaming toward the windows. Kenzie leaped over fallen foes, screaming like she never had at all of the villagers, urging them to run as if flesh-eating demons were at their heels.

And all this before a single explosion.

Then it happened. Dantanion sank to his knees beside the windows and the valley view, smiling in contentment, the robe settling around him. A blast like thunder shattered the air apart, rocked the house. A second and then a third followed and then came the most terrible groaning sound. More timed explosions, two below and two above, and then the great three-story chateau began to pull free of its moorings. Pure terror laced the air like hellfire. Dantanion had lured them into this trap knowing full well that he could never lose. Drake found Alicia and Mai, still pushing Dahl, and raced as one unit, running nowhere but never giving up.

A part of the ceiling fell in, rubble collapsing to Drake's side. Dantanion's horrors came after them, still battling. A spear flashed past Dahl's head and struck a villager, taking him down and making him tumble away, already dead. The Swede slowed, turned and met his aggressor's assault. The man with exposed teeth struck him full on, but Dahl didn't wilt. He head-butted and kicked out and still ran with Drake, wrestling as he moved. Drake slowed and traded punches with another as Mai found two fleeing guards and fought to best them. Alicia helped, snapping teeth from one's mouth with her boot, sending him flying.

As they fought, as they fled, the chateau shuddered deep in its foundations. Moorings set deep in stone began to pull free. The floor tilted, and so did the view from the windows. Debris slid into Drake's feet, pushing him back. He fought it. The house juddered again, slid a little more. Glass smashed in every window and the frames buckled. Huge shards and planks of wood tumbled down the mountain. A screaming gush of icy wind blasted inside.

Drake leapt over the debris and let it slide into the far wall. Another sickening, fundamental lurch and they felt the entire structure pulling away from the mountain, growing more unstable with each judder. Dahl sent elbow after elbow into his attacker's face, targeting the exposed teeth and ignoring when his arm began to bleed and then his flesh began to tear off in tatters. Blood flowed, but teeth broke too, and one came away in the Swede's arm. He ignored it as they came up against the far wall.

"It's not the mountain wall!" Brynn cried. "C'mon!"

What she was thinking Drake didn't know, but understood that a corridor ran behind this wall and probably alongside the face of the mountain. They ran for the door, lurching once more as the floor swayed and then grew rapidly skew-whiff. A villager fell over and began to slide. Mai caught him and dragged him up. Alicia caught her and pulled her along. Brynn reached the open door and hung on to the frame.

More structural shrieks. Drake saw the empty windows tilting, the view down now terrifying, the bottom of the valley almost visible as sunrise flashed over the mountains. He saw the madman, Dantanion, sliding straight toward the new drop and smiling, robe billowing. He grabbed the shoulder of the man who fought Dahl, a part of the human chain. Below him two more people held on—Curtis and Anica.

Brynn struggled through the door and then more villagers. Arms reached back inside to help pull the weaker folk through. Mai and Alicia helped the chain along. A chunk of masonry fell from above, followed by a bank of wiring, sparks flying from the exposed ends. A waft of flame traveled the length of the cabling.

Drake punched Dahl's opponent in the neck and felt the strength fall away from him.

Oh, shit. Why'd you have to do that?

He staggered to one knee. Drake used the right thigh to jump over, dragging Curtis and Anica along too. Dahl reached out and took hold of Drake's arm. A scream sounded, hollow and terrifying, and another villager lost their grip of the door frame just as the house seemed to bounce. Bolts fought their anchorage, as the weight pulling against them began to prove too much.

"Drake." Alicia reached out for Dahl and him, her expression hopeless. "There's nowhere to go."

And no way to stop it . . .

CHAPTER FORTY FIVE

Hayden led Kinimaka and Smyth deeper below the mountain. If Dantanion had spread the rumors of mad brothers and wandering flesh-eaters to deter the curious then he had done a decent job. Despite their caution and constant vigilance, they saw and heard nothing. They followed a trail marked by wall torches down and down, largely ignoring them when Smyth broke out some excellent flashlights that shone as far as the eye could see. Maybe the blinding lights kept the cave-dwellers away. A wide cavern with enormous stalactites was traversed and two skeletons found, clothes rotting off the bodies. Hayden marked their spot, but knew it was impossible to tell who they were right now. They pressed deeper. A sprinkling of cave dust occasionally revealed footprints, mostly shoes but also some rather unnervingly showing bare feet.

The passage rarely branched off and when it did the adjoining passages were narrow and impassable. When they found the entrance, it appeared entirely unremarkable. Just another rock wall with a narrow, ragged archway and then a right turn into a larger cave. Without the intense flashlights they might even have missed it. Hayden saw the gold glittering as the light picked out its keen edges, pure golden liquid pouring across the floor.

"Oh, wait," she said. "I think . . . I think we found something."

They crowded around the cave entrance, dumbstruck. The hollow stretched a long way into the rock, ran high and widened. The cave was crammed full with treasure, enough to take the breath away. Hayden struggled to take it all in, simply staring at the reflected glow.

Vases full of golden flowers, engraved masks studded with rubies and emeralds, bracelets and necklaces and sparkling anklets; daggers, short swords and headdresses; animals fashioned out of pure gold and silver; plates and bowls adorned with rubies—all comprised just a portion of what was the most incredible vision she'd ever laid eyes on. If she stared at the shimmering wealth any longer she feared it would blind or corrupt her forever.

And the centerpiece crowned it all.

A four-tiered fountain, formed from pure gold, shining like burnished sunlight on the brightest day the world had ever known, stood at the center of the cave, the lesser treasures arrayed around it. Gleaming with it, and its myriad reflections, they complimented it but stood back in awe, stunned and reverent. It took Hayden over a minute just to take it in.

"All this to ransom one man?" Kinimaka found his voice. "Gold and silver mined from the Andes mountains and then returned to them."

Hayden looked speculative. "And I remember reading that this wasn't the best of it. Something about the Royal Fifth." Seeing Mano's blank look she went on. "Twenty percent of all loot taken was reserved for the King of Spain. The 'Quinto Real' or Royal Fifth. Pizarro trusted only his brother, Hernando, to take the treasures they'd already stolen straight to Spain. Most were melted down, but just a few of the most exquisite pieces were left intact and displayed for a while before they too, were melted down. Such a terrible cultural loss for the world."

Kinimaka still hadn't turned away from the incredible golden vista. "The Incas must really have loved their king."

Hayden nursed her finger. "And how much would you ransom for Drake? For Dahl? For me?"

The Hawaiian smiled. "I dunno. All of El Dorado?"

"Ha. Would you believe that the myth of El Dorado was inspired by this very Inca treasure that stands before us now? Europeans heard of the riches and came running, hoping to join expeditions and get rich. Tales of a king who covered himself in gold and a city whose walls were built of gold quickly spread, but many died in the steamy, disease-ridden jungles, sun-blistered plains and ice-covered mountains without seeing a single nugget. El Dorado was a shiny illusion, driven by factual stories of a genuinely glorious Inca treasure. So how much would you give?"

An insipid sensation wormed through her mind, almost as if the darkness were reaching out, trying to touch her. She ignored it, concentrating on the gold and remembering how the deeper shadows always seemed to hide the worst demons.

Kinimaka was looking at her. "How much would I give? Everything, I guess."

"The Spanish captain, Pizarro, lost all this because he couldn't keep it in its sheath. An old lesson, never learned."

Something touched her hair as gently as mist. The wind? She reached back to brush it off, imagining a spider, and her fingers touched rough, bare knuckles.

"Ahh!"

It launched from off the wall, where it had been crouching in an alcove; raw, twisted arms worming a way around her neck, teeth already drooling into her face and gnashing, spraying less than an inch away from her skin. She fell back, hit the floor hard, and cracked her skull. Smyth was skipping away as if a rat pack were slipping between his legs. Mano was trying to catch up. Hayden brought her hands up fast, repulsed as she touched bare skin and dirt and sticky sweat. Her flashlight bounced to the right, aiming back down the tunnel. The teeth closed in and she pushed her head back as far as she could, straining her neck into a bow, using every ounce of strength just to keep the teeth at bay.

No way did she possess the power to throw this being off.

And now, behind them in the flare of the flashlight, she saw something else detaching itself from the ceiling above their heads, sliding down a dank piece of rope like an arachnid might slide down a web, arms and legs splayed.

"Jesus!" cried Smyth, seeing it too. "Flesh-eaters! Look lively."

Hayden planted her elbows into the ground, barely managing to keep the hissing, plunging creature away. By the waving, strobing light of three battery-powered flashlights she watched Smyth and Kinimaka engage the second attacker, meeting a lunge head on and batting the head aside. A snarl crawled up the tunnel and up her spine. The thing atop her kicked at her shins and thighs with bony legs. It gritted its teeth so hard its gums began to bleed, dripping right onto her face. She wrenched her head aside, felt fangs on her cheek, thrust back with all her might. The body bore down. Her muscles shook.

Kinimaka whirled in the darkness, missing his attacker completely. Teeth latched on to his shoulder, a blow to the ribs made him scream. Smyth was right there, tearing the body away and dashing it against the wall. A crunch didn't stop it or slow it down one bit. Kinimaka turned, breathing hard and it was back upon him, forcing him down; taut, scrawny sinew pulsing with power. Whatever Dantanion had made and cast out down here used their limbs every day—perhaps he fed them still.

Hayden tried to roll, but her assailant just thrust down again and again with savage strength and she knew her time was almost up.

"Help!"

Kinimaka jerked up at the cry, just in time to unknowingly smash his head right up under his own attacker's jaw. Shocked and surprised, the creature fell away. Smyth launched himself atop it. Kinimaka also looked amazed, then lunged toward Hayden, scrambling in the dirt and the dust and the filth, crossing flashlight beams, his face clearly aware of nothing else but Hayden's peril—terrified, driven, suffering.

Hayden let it all go and stopped holding the man off. His own force sent him face first into her shoulder, momentarily surprising him. Then Hayden felt teeth tearing at her jacket, skeletal fingers digging into the spaces between her ribs as if ready to pull her insides out. Maybe they were, but Kinimaka bowled into it then like a wrecking ball striking a wooden hut. The impact was huge, the outcome devastating. Bones shattered and the figure stilled; whatever it had been was now a lifeless shell, a mockery of humanity. Hayden looked up to see Smyth climbing off the other flesh-eater, bleeding but nodding grimly.

"And there it is," Smyth panted, nodding again at the treasure cave. "Everything, right there. Job done. We should head back now that we found it. Give the guys the good news and get reinforcements down here. No telling how many of these things are creeping around."

"And help the team," Hayden said. "The kids are all fine so let's go. C'mon."

They retraced their route, found Yorgi and Fay, and continued on toward the house. It was when Hayden walked into the cave's living quarters that the explosions began. Smyth stopped beside her and Kinimaka took ragged breaths.

"What the hell is that?"

Above, the entire roof began to break away. It was only when Hayden saw it wrench upwards and rubble began to rain down that she realized it was the bottom foundations of the house.

And they were ripping from their moorings.

As the ceiling canted over, the caves became open to the skies and Hayden was witness to the entire chateau breaking free.

Shocked to the core, shaking uncontrollably, she fell to her knees.

CHAPTER FORTY SIX

Drake heard screams as the house no longer paused in its descent, but pulled away from the wall and started to slide down the mountain. Wreckage smashed everywhere, exploding through walls and the floor, collapsing from above. The great table slid straight through the picture window, tumbling end over end into the vast void. The only option was to run, and run they did.

Racing uphill, fighting momentum, they attacked the sloping floor like it was an enemy they sought to conquer. The far right-hand wall of the house began to crumble away. Drake saw cracks spreading everywhere, even underneath his own feet. Brynn and the villagers were already out in the corridor and, as he reached the doorway, he saw why.

Wooden panels had been ripped from the wall, hands were bleeding profusely. In other places the structure had sheered away, exposing the places where the house had been moored to the jagged rock face. These moorings were large and craggy, full of metal, rock and deep niches; torn joints and couplings. Already, several villagers had climbed inside and were pressing hard into the rock to make room for more.

Drake jumped up again and again, gaining a few feet with every leap. Dahl dragged him and the others dragged the Swede. Alicia and Mai made it through the door, then Kenzie. Curtis somehow managed to hold tight at the end of the line, barely able to walk. Then, a deep groan and the entire floor sank a bit, smashing down just a few centimeters but jarring everything that continued to hold it together. Drake lost balance, but swiftly regained it. Dahl fell to his knees, grip broken with those who pulled him up, and suddenly, terrifyingly, it was just Dahl now at the top of the line, holding out a huge hand that gripped nothing.

Nothing at all.

Dahl's face turned from determined to stunned and destitute in the span of a heartbeat. Those below depended on him. The Swede's muscles bulged; cords standing out along his arms, neck and forehead. His knees slipped downward in the dust and rubble. He labored even harder. Drake somehow tried to grip those below tighter whilst putting less strain on Dahl, but wasn't entirely sure it worked. Dahl let out a tortured bellow and heaved. His knees held, his body bent upward—an inch was gained. He yelled again, scrabbled for purchase here and there—anywhere. Just a few centimeters from the wall and he took a deep breath for one enormous effort, lunged, heaved the entire line along with him and grabbed hold of the door frame, four fingers gripping the wood.

A moment's respite, then pulling again. Drake planted his feet and heaved upward; Anica and then Curtis too. The man at the end of the line faltered, body swaying to and fro more than the others. Dahl made sure his grip was strong and hoisted the line mightily one more time.

The wooden door frame cracked around his fingers, destroyed by his grip and the pressure it was exerting. Dahl was left holding splinters.

"No! No! Bollocks!"

Only sheer, perfect balance kept them from sliding down, but even that would only last a few more seconds. As Dahl wavered and reached desperately for a solid surface that just wasn't there, the line began to slide down the tilted floor of the house toward the broken windows and the great drop beyond. With one last superhuman effort Dahl stalled the momentum.

And saw Alicia, held by Mai, struggling through the shattered door. Holding hands, the two managed to reach out to Dahl, grab his arm and pull. Mai was joined by Kenzie in the doorway, adding her incredible strength. As Kenzie pulled, her katana fell away unnoticed, clattering down to the floor. Together, the three women pulled Dahl up through the doorway and then took responsibility for Drake, Anica and Curtis.

Drake put his back against the corridor wall that separated it from the great hall and heaved until the two villagers came through, then hugged them close.

The chateau screamed in its final death throes.

"Drake!" Alicia cried. "Run! Jump! For God's sake, jump!"

The floor was breaking away from the mountain wall, the entire area crumbling square meter by square meter. A groaning, thunderous crash told them the other wall had torn free. Drake and the others were now standing on a ruined floor of just a few feet in width and length, exposed to both sides. The enormity of the valley beckoned below.

"The moorings!" he cried.

They leapt through empty air, hands outstretched. They caught hold of steel stanchions and bent pilings, of torn framework and half-destroyed scaffold that jutted from the mountain. The steel was still sound where it went into the rock; nothing could change that. Drake grabbed hold of a jutting piece of pipe, wrapping his hands around it. To his right Curtis managed to skip into a niche where some of the foundations had once been. The roaring of a dying beast accompanied the final destruction of the chateau. Bricks and mortar, slabs of concrete, incredible metal support skeletons twisted free and fell away. A huge sliding skin of debris slipped part way down the mountain, crashing like a wave, rebounding again and again and smashing upon rock after rock, a great tidal wave of rubble until it swept right off a precipice and became a tumbling waterfall all the way to the valley floor.

Drake watched the slithering ruins. "That's why it didn't fall right away," he said. "The ground underneath wasn't sheer. It was flat and then just a slope."

Several grunts and groans of agreement and appreciation were sounded out. As Drake looked beneath his feet, looking for a safe place to jump down where the rock was flat and not littered with debris, he saw a familiar face staring up at him.

" 'Kinell," he muttered in broad Yorkshire. "Now that's a welcome sight if ever I saw one."

Dahl swung from one jutting bar to another, the drop and the near-miss not fazing him. "What on earth are you . . . oh, Hayden. Well, yeah, that's odd."

"Can you make your way down?" Hayden shouted up.

"Ropes would be better," Drake shouted back. "Give us a

minute to think it through, 'cause I guess one of has to take a risk and jump down, then clear the way for the others to land safely and—"

He stopped, because Dahl had already jumped to the nearest bed of rock and was sweeping the rubble away with his hand.

The Swede looked up. "You thought it all through yet?"

"Oh yeah, mate. I think you're the biggest dickhead I ever met."

He let go of the pipe, landed safely on two feet, and pretended not to notice the Swede's big hands close by, prepared to steady or catch him.

"Over there," Dahl said.

Drake glanced to the left and saw a ridge of smooth rock leading most of the way to the very pass they had used to climb beyond the chateau earlier. "Our way out," Drake said.

"Our way home. All we have to do is rig a rope across the drop and swing over."

"Oh, is that all?"

"Yeah. Don't worry, I'll fashion you a harness like they have in baby seats."

Drake caught Curtis as he swung down. Alicia came over next and took a long moment to hug him, the embrace only broken when Mai landed lightly beside them. "Can I join in?"

Drake looked hopeful. Alicia turned and gave the Ninja a flat stare. "I saved your life up there, Sprite. Now back away."

"Ah, did you save my life or did I save yours?"

Alicia shrugged and held out a hand. "A little of both, I think. But Mai, let's talk. As soon as we get away from here, let's friggin' talk."

Drake's mouth fell open in confusion, in happiness, in admiration. Alicia Myles had thrown away all the bonds of her life and opened up, offered to resolve an impossible situation, spoken first to help an old foe out of an intolerable corner.

Mai found her voice after several seconds. "I would like that. Truly I would."

The ledge soon became crowded as more and more people jumped down. Dahl and Kenzie swept off another ledge and then another, keeping busy, hearing Hayden's story and trying to decide how to help the people in the caves leave securely.

"It'll be a slow process, and hard," Dahl told them all. "But we use ropes. The same ropes we have tethered up there." He pointed to the rappel lines that now hung against the mountain and dangled about ten feet above. "We untie them, get people cross to the mountain pass, and then get more people up from below. Are we ready?"

Sunshine blazed down, a sign of good hope for all.

Drake started to climb for the first rope.

CHAPTER FORTY SEVEN

Tonight, the sun diminished in the west, the shadows lengthened, and darkness began to broaden its reach across the lands. Tonight, there was little light shed by the moon as clouds warped all around it and fought to quench its brightness. Tonight, the mountains rose pitch black and eternal, barely outlined, uncompromising and uncaring sentinels standing resolute against every elemental challenge that was thrown at them.

Tonight, Kimbiri stood without chains—free, liberated, secure for the first time in many months. The villages of Nuno and Quillabiri and homesteads that spread for miles were similarly released and had all made their way to Kimbiri for the celebration. An enormous fire, laid out atop a nearby hill, marked the center of the merriment, and around it many sat cross-legged on the grass or leaned against low walls. Conversation vied with the crackling embers for the most decibels, but the sound of happy laughter always came out on top. The SPEAR team had been busy for days, but now the recruits were safe in Cusco, the militia was on the run and even the CIA were comparatively happy. One last night, Hayden had said, and the others capitulated with ease. The villagers needed this—and had played their part right from stepping up to help protect their village, to putting their lives on the line to fight alongside the soldiers.

Hundreds now filled Kimbiri. Food was prepared and eaten, and the homemade brews were starting to flow.

Alicia, full of good food and of contentment for tonight stood staring at a warmly dressed farmer and his son, who'd brought along some of their livestock. All furry, wrapped around with the thickest of clothes, and viewed through eyes that were only slightly hazy, she found herself squinting hard.

Inca Kings

"I don't get it," she whispered into Drake's ear.

The Yorkshireman coughed delicately. "What's the problem?"

"Which one's the alpaca?"

"The animal, dear."

Alicia stepped closer. "Huh. All look the same to me. But if I'm being honest, I'd leg it if I saw any of 'em coming over the hill."

Together at last, the team reveled in a night off. Painkillers helped with the scrapes and bruises, but nothing would ever rid them of lasting images. By mutual agreement they'd all decided that if it didn't need to be covered then it would never be spoken of again. Their encounter with Dantanion and his followers was the most bizarre op they'd ever undertaken, but also one of the most rewarding. As Drake said, when you save New York from a nuclear event, nobody knows and you fly straight off to the next mission, but when you save a small village and fight alongside its people—you make friends and receive embarrassing thank yous that soldiers never asked for. Still, this once, it humbled even the most jaded members of the team.

Kenzie sat alongside Dahl, as quiet as Alicia had ever seen her. The ex-Mossad agent couldn't hide the happy awkwardness in her eyes and hadn't been able to crack a nasty jibe all night.

Could Dahl be right? Could Kenzie be reprieved?

No mind. Truth be told, she found it hard to trust anyone anymore. Anyone, that is, beyond her most trusted circle of friends. Drake, Dahl and, oddly, Mai. The slow change in her had been welcomed by most, if not all. Of course, nobody could change if they didn't want to or if the new person was a phony. Alicia was becoming the person she'd always wanted to be, always should have been.

The alpacas approached and she shied away, still seeing treble. One snorted as it passed, she couldn't tell if it was human or animal, making her reach for her gun; but of course it wasn't there and Drake stood laughing. Alicia punched his arm. They wandered back among the villagers, shaking hands and smiling, hugging those who'd fought with them and thanking those who'd let them go. Kimbiri would survive all this because of the spirit of its people; and the same went for all the others in the area.

Nobody could keep a good person down forever.

Alicia forced her way into a circle formed by the SPEAR team with Drake at her side. "Boy," she whispered. "Am I fucking glad all that's over."

Dahl nodded in agreement. "Give it a week and some normality and we'll start to forget how bizarre it all was."

"Hope so," Alicia said. "I really do."

"That man had so many so cruelly trained." Mai stared into the dark heart of their circle, where the flickering flames didn't cast light. "And they accepted it. I saw it in my childhood and I see it still. Will the world ever change?"

Drake shook his head. "Nope. But there will always be people like us."

"Not enough," Mai replied.

"I agree."

Dahl coughed, staring over at the fire. "And now on to Egypt," he said. "A world event, they say. And then the other corners of the earth. Just to make it clear—we draw the line at bloody Yorkshire. We ain't risking our lives to save fish and chips, Meadowhall and the York Minster."

Drake allowed the Swede a serene smile, letting him have the joke. "Can't say Harvard and Eton are high up the list either."

"Matt Damon? Natalie Portman?" Dahl asked.

Alicia growled softly. "Yeah, I'd save both. For a special reward."

"Both Harvard alumni," Dahl said, then turned away as if wondering why the hell he was defending a place he'd dropped out of. Alicia listened as tomorrow's travel plans were clearly stated and watched the surreal vision of a pair of goats picking their way through the villagers.

"Never ceases to amaze, or make me smile," she said. "Or I drank more of the potato punch than I recall."

She found herself seated beside Hayden, the boss sporting a new bandage that covered the end of her finger. Of all of them, Hayden had suffered in the most personal way and had, so far, been the quietest. Alicia took a moment to think of how she could help.

"Sorry you had to go through that, Hay. Even I seem to be at a loss for words."

"It sure sucked balls." Hayden waggled her digit and then sighed. "But it bought us time. All of us."

"Saved lives."

"Sure. I'd do it again." Hayden studied her hands. "But only nine more times. After that, I'm struggling."

They smiled. The fire crackled, black smoke billowing straight up at the skies. Alicia basked in its warmth after being exposed to the elements for so many days. It was a good way to end and celebrate their victory, so good she could almost drift away to sleep.

Guard down. Content. Feeling fortunate. Who was she?

She squeezed Drake's hand and then saw Mai across the circle, still studying the center and looking a little lost. Alicia was about to rise when Kenzie beat her to it. The swordswoman pushed herself quickly to her feet, so fast Dahl almost scrambled up with her, sensing trouble.

But Kenzie held out a hand, smoothed her hair and took a deep breath. "Since I've never felt more accepted," she said quietly; and hearing the words made Alicia even sadder, "I wanted to share something with you."

They quieted around the circle, looking up at the woman. Kenzie gave everyone a personal, surprisingly shy look before opening her mouth once again.

"I too am a part of Tyler Webb's statement. It is shameful, but it is a part of me and I . . . I want to come clean right now."

Alicia held Drake's hand all the tighter, felt him tense up. Nobody spoke, and the entire team concentrated on Kenzie, letting her find the right words.

"Most nights," she said. "I . . . I cry myself to sleep. I do. It's a fact. And I shudder to think that man invaded my privacy so deeply, so terribly, and would use the knowledge to humiliate me."

"It's okay," Dahl reached up, touching her fingers. "We will never judge you."

"I cry myself to sleep because I lost my family. Because

powerful figures in my government let it happen. Because I could not avenge them." Tears stood proud in her eyes now, and she sat down, crossed her legs, and smiled.

"There," she said. "Now you know the worst of me."

Drake and Dahl made comments that expressed Alicia's own feelings—that if Kenzie thought such things were the worst of her, then she was welcome to watch their backs anytime. Alicia voiced it too, in her own way, and Kenzie thanked them all without words—just a grin.

"You all know that only leaves three," Smyth spoke up gruffly. "From the original statement? One who is a lesbian, one who is dying and one who killed their parents in cold blood."

Kinimaka shuffled around. "Way to go with the mood quencher, Lancelot."

"Yeah," Alicia said. "Bog off on some quest or other. Give us some peace."

"He's missing our Lauren," Drake said. "Give him a break."

Smyth regarded them all wearily. "Maybe she could meet us in Egypt."

"Lancelot needs reinforcements," Kenzie laughed. "Sound the horn."

Alicia waited a moment and then caught Mai's eye. With a jerk of her head she indicated that the two of them should leave the group. Quietly, she disengaged from Drake's hand and smiled at the question in his eyes.

"Don't worry."

She met Mai close to the fire. In the burning heart, surrounded by sparks, cinders and flares, they finally came eye to eye.

"You finished it. You didn't know if you were coming back," Alicia said equably. "You told him as much."

Mai watched fire leap and flicker. "I guess I was surprised at how quick it all happened."

"A man like Drake? You shouldn't be. And you know we've loved each other since we were kids."

"Kids?"

"Army kids. New to the regiment."

"He loved you before he loved me," Mai agreed. "And then you went dark. And then you changed. Looks like you came full circle, Taz."

Alicia tensed, aware Mai's body language had grown subtly dangerous. "If I hadn't changed we'd be wrestling on the ground right now."

Mai raised an eyebrow. "I doubt that."

"Oh, c'mon, just 'cause you're a bad-ass, scar-faced, doe-eyed ninja, doesn't mean you'd beat me in a proper fight, Sprite."

Mai stepped back. "So Pat Benatar me, bitch."

"Take my best shot?"

"You got it."

"Shit." Alicia saw now, and in her heart always had seen, that this confrontation was going to come down to a fight. They were both warriors, both strong women, and both utterly determined. In truth, she'd always know what kind of a fight it would end up being too.

"First to hit the floor?"

Mai struck without warning, catching Alicia along the eyebrow, just a glancing blow but one that caused a jet of pain. Alicia danced away, keeping the fire at her back, making Mai look at the bright flames. The Japanese woman struck again, three times; blows which Alicia fended away. Her forearms burned with the impacts.

But it wouldn't do just to take the punishment. Mai wanted and deserved a real fight. Nothing else was right. Alicia dove in, took a blow to the cheek, and delivered three of her own, the last making Mai stagger. The Japanese woman only spun though, catching Alicia with a spinning elbow and making her cry out. Alicia pulled away, and watched Mai rub her ribs.

"Had enough?"

"Barely awake."

"Ohhh."

They came together, both leaping at the same time and trading blows quicker than the eye. Alicia's elbow strike turned into a punch, then a pivot of the hips that Mai swiveled around. Alicia was momentarily open, took a kick to the thigh that almost killed the muscle and a shot to the back of the neck that sent her to her knees.

Mai pressed the advantage, coming down hard. Firm strikes and punches came at Alicia's face, two out of three blocked but the last bringing up an immediate bruise. Alicia twisted, struggled to stand, but Ma's onslaught was unstoppable. For every blow she blocked, another sneaked through, but still Alicia refused to go down. Her mouth bled, her nose bled. Her body ached.

Mai backed off, looked down at the Englishwoman, raised her hands, and started another attack, showing no mercy.

Alicia swiveled. Punched hard straight into the oncoming stomach. Mai doubled over and fell to her knees alongside Alicia, the two grappling, elbows, shoulders, arms and hands.

In the end, Mai held Alicia's head in both her hands. A hard twist and her opponent would have no choice but to fold down to the ground. Either that or her neck would break. Mai stared hard into Alicia's eyes, grip unbreakable. Alicia held it together, panting, gasping, staring back with nothing but compassion in her eyes.

"I won't go down willingly," she breathed. "Never. Do your worst."

Mai mercilessly wrenched her neck to the side.

CHAPTER FORTY EIGHT

Even before Mai completed the killing move, Alicia had known she would do it. Had she fought well? Had she fought as hard as she could? The doubt was there. The doubt that, against comrades, she could never fight without concern ever again.

Mai pulled her down, and let go at the crucial instant. Alicia collapsed to the ground, now weary of it, staring up at the Japanese ninja who knelt above her.

"I'm done," she said. "Are you?"

Mai grudgingly held out a hand. "I can't promise to be perfect," she said. "But I'll always be there to watch your back."

"Same goes to you."

"And Alicia . . ."

Time stopped. "Yeah?"

"If you ever let him go I'll be right there, picking up the pieces," Mai whispered. "You know that don't you?"

"Oh yeah, I'm perfectly aware."

"Great."

Mai helped her up and dusted her down. Alicia tried to pick a few branches out of Mai's hair but it didn't feel right. An awkward moment passed and, pretty soon, the women parted and returned to the group.

Kenzie grinned. "Not bad, not bad. If you wanna win next time, Myles, come to me. I'll give you a few pointers."

"There won't be a next time," Alicia said, but made a mental note to speak to Kenzie later. Just in case. She also noticed Mai narrowing her eyes wonderingly at the ex-Mossad agent. As long as she'd known Mai, Alicia had never known anyone her equal in combat. But somebody, somewhere, was better. They had to be.

Drake winced up at her, sighting the bruises, but said nothing. Dahl patted her knee consolingly, which intentionally made her heckles rise, and then Hayden rose with a glass in her hand.

"To good friends and good soldiers," she said. "Who—no matter their differences—always have our backs."

Her gaze went first to Mano Kinimaka, who raised his own in acknowledgement of saving her life back at the chateau. "Good friends and good soldiers," he echoed.

"I can't imagine never having your backs," Drake said. "Cheers."

Alicia toasted and so did Mai. The flames crackled and spat at the pitch-black skies. Dahl rose with cup in hand to make his own little speech.

"Never forget," he said. "When you open your eyes in the morning always imagine the Devil dreads hearing your feet hit the floorboards. That he's thinking, 'Oh, fuck, what's that bastard gonna do today?'"

"Amen," Drake said.

And finally the quietest of them all, Yorgi, rose in the night and made a show of filling his own glass to the brim. Holding it high he declared: "And I'm the one who killed my parents in cold blood."

THE END

For more information on the future of the Matt Drake world and David Leadbeater's novels please read on:

Inca Kings

With *Inca Kings* I tried to create something different, an action/adventure novel steeped in archaeological mystery but with an in-your-face twist of horror. Not supernatural; I have gone to great pains to ensure the words and writing do not err to the magical side of things (and always have). I hope you agree.

I am currently looking hard at developing another story along the same lines of the Drake series, with brand new, very different but likeable characters. The Drake series is still wildly popular, but I thought another series, in the same vein but with very different perspectives, would help keep both fresh and preserve their longevity. If it goes ahead this series would start after the next Drake. If you have any thoughts on this idea, please get involved and drop me a line. It does help. Several passages, story threads and events in my novels have been suggested by readers in the past.

So, next up will be Drake 16— already underway and to be released early March 2017. I have an idea that Alicia 4 will also be released in 2017. No more Disavowed yet, but I am still hoping to finish the Chosen trilogy next year.

Other Books by David Leadbeater:

The Matt Drake Series
The Bones of Odin (Matt Drake #1)
The Blood King Conspiracy (Matt Drake #2)
The Gates of hell (Matt Drake 3)
The Tomb of the Gods (Matt Drake #4)
Brothers in Arms (Matt Drake #5)
The Swords of Babylon (Matt Drake #6)
Blood Vengeance (Matt Drake #7)
Last Man Standing (Matt Drake #8)
The Plagues of Pandora (Matt Drake #9)
The Lost Kingdom (Matt Drake #10)
The Ghost Ships of Arizona (Matt Drake #11)
The Last Bazaar (Matt Drake #12)
The Edge of Armageddon (Matt Drake #13)
The Treasures of Saint Germain (Matt Drake #14)

The Alicia Myles Series
Aztec Gold (Alicia Myles #1)
Crusader's Gold (Alicia Myles #2)
Caribbean Gold (Alicia Myles #3)

The Torsten Dahl Thriller Series
Stand Your Ground (Dahl Thriller #1)

Inca Kings

The Disavowed Series:
The Razor's Edge (Disavowed #1)
In Harm's Way (Disavowed #2)
Threat Level: Red (Disavowed #3)

The Chosen Few Series
Chosen (The Chosen Trilogy #1)
Guardians (The Chosen Tribology #2)

Short Stories
Walking with Ghosts (A short story)
A Whispering of Ghosts (A short story)

Connect with the author on Twitter: @dleadbeater2011
Visit the author's website: www.davidleadbeater.com

All helpful, genuine comments are welcome. I would love to hear from you.
davidleadbeater2011@hotmail.co.uk

Printed in Poland
by Amazon Fulfillment
Poland Sp. z o.o., Wrocław